CLOUD 9

ALEX CAMPBELL

HOT
KEY
BOOKS

First published in Great Britain in 2015 by Hot Key Books
Northburgh House, 10 Northburgh Street, London EC1V 0AT

Text copyright © Alex Campbell 2015
Cover illustration copyright © Levente Szabó 2015

Extract from Dylan Thomas's 'In My Craft or Sullen Art' is taken from
The Collected Poems of Dylan Thomas: the New Centenary Edition (Orion)
and used with the kind permission of David Higham Associates Ltd.

A CIP catalogue record for this book is available from the British Library.

ISBN: 978-1-4714-0354-5

1

This book is typeset in 10.5 Berling LT Std using Atomik ePublisher
Printed and bound by Clays Ltd, St Ives Plc

www.hotkeybooks.com

Hot Key Books is part of the Bonnier Publishing Group
www.bonnierpublishing.com

To Lucy, the truth-seeker,
and Duncs, my best mate

LIES

Above all, don't lie to yourself. The man who lies to himself and listens to his own lie comes to a point that he cannot distinguish the truth within him, or around him, and so loses all respect for himself and for others. And having no respect he ceases to love.

Fyodor Dostoyevsky, The Brothers Karamazov

1

Sadness is a scourge
Leata

Her
Live life with hope . . .

. . . I get the usual burst of pleasure tapping out my catchphrase, seeing those familiar words, black on white. Proudly, I lift my fingers from the keyboard, drumming them on my lips. *What next . . .?*

It's imperative I keep every post fresh, see, and more importantly, *uplifting*. I mean, people actually live their lives by what I say! What I say matters.

I switch from my blog's dashboard to its proper site, checking out today's pop-up. *Leata*'s promos often inspire what I write . . . There, see! Artistic as ever, and oh-so pretty! All sepia print with swathes of colour painted in. Like always, the advert holds a moral story: a confident, cool-looking boy strolling relaxed and happy through a field, while blue and yellow hot-air balloons rise up behind him. There's a girl with him he's making laugh – who, hey, if I'm honest, doesn't look that unlike me! Right?

Dark brown hair, olive skin, even the dimple in her chin. Which reminds me of that nice comment from *EvieR* last night:

You make the perfect Leata poster girl, Hope!

Wow, thanks, Evie! Believe it or not, you're not the first to say that. ☺

Cue a stream of believers. My followers are all adorable. There's so much love on my blog and my channel!

So what do my followers want to hear today? I can't just write anything. There are millions of other blogs and vlogs and random posts competing for a piece of *Leata* sponsorship. Not that I'm in it for the money. No, for me – it's enough that I'm helpful to others. That I bring positivity into millions of lives.

Okay: click back and curl my hands above the keyboard – like I'm about to play piano. No – I'm simply making music with my words – ha! But seriously though, it's what I'm known for: 'Yeah, like Hope, the *Live Life* blogger? You know: *Livelifewithhope?*'

I am known therefore I am. Isn't that what some ancient philosopher said? At the end of the day though, it's not about me, I understand that. It's about making others my age feel connected and good about themselves – that'll be my 1,998,042 total subscribers (and counting) – ahem, need I say more? I am incredibly blessed.

Except still, my fingers remain poised mid-air.

I can sense it, something blocking my words. The something curling snake-like at the far corners of my mind. *The funeral.* Is it today?

I dance my shoulders about a bit, take a deep breath. *Don't even go there.* Squash. It. A smile, there you go, that's it: *a big beam of a smile.*

Okay! Countdown Back to Happiness!

Ten: 'Bad thoughts lead to bad lives.'
Nine: I have an incredible family.
Eight: Fantastic friends.
Seven: 'Life's short. Enjoy it!'
*Six: Nearly TWO MILLION SUBSCRIBERS! And let's
not get started on Twitter and Instagram!*
Five: My followers LOVE me . . .
*Four: . . . They're forever telling me I'm beautiful! That I
bring positivity into their lives!*
Three: 'When darkness comes, turn the light on brighter.'
Two: I have a BRIGHT future.
One: I can become whatever I want to be.

It always works. Every time. I really must tweet again how the
Ten Second Countdown is the best tip from LeataLiving.com.
And I love the app for it. It counts down with you, then leaves
you with a mirror at the end, *Smile for a Leata selfie!*

I copy out that last quote onto my draft post (officially, one
of my favourite *Leata* messages to date!) as Mum calls up the
stairs, 'Girls! Hurry! You're going to be late!' At the same time
the bathroom door opens – *fin-a-lly, Rose!* I hear her padding
barefoot to her room. I swing off the bed, darting onto the landing.

Knock slam into Dad.

'How many times?' he snaps. His hands are up like he doesn't
want to catch something. 'Do *not* run around the house in
only a towel, Hope!' Smartly suited, his harried face is the
only creased part of him.

I beam a big 'sorry' at him as Rose pokes a wet head out of her door. Dad continues along towards her, his voice softening. 'Honey . . . that Egyptian project you're working on, I was thinking about a trip to the British Museum . . .'

Wow, Dad can be so sweet, despite being seriously stressed. What with being a senior partner in his law firm, and PharmaCare his main client (so, so, sooo proud). And of course Mum doesn't work; it's Dad alone who pays for all *this*. Massive house; our education; clothes allowance; skiing holiday; summer holiday; occasional in-between holiday! I watch Dad tuck a wet strand of hair behind Rose's ear. We're privileged to have a father who's such a family man.

I *am* incredibly lucky.

Him

He rubs a hole in the condensation on the cabinet mirror. Stares blankly at himself. A younger version of his dad stares back. His insides churn. Tom darts back to the toilet. He's been about ten times already, even though he's not eaten since god knows when.

He's drunk though. Yeah – his tongue skates over the morning-after fur in his mouth – he's drunk all right.

Tom flushes again. One hand circling his battle-strewn stomach, he returns to the sink.

'I don't want to go,' he murmurs at his reflection. Somehow it makes it seem more final. He doesn't know why. It's not like his dad's not already dead. His mum went and saw him DEAD two months ago. Accompanied by his godfather, Ralph – Dad, lying in a morgue, life leaked out of him; a parcel label probably hanging off his toe: MATT RILEY: DEFINITELY NOT IN HERE ANY MORE.

Yet somehow, putting his dad into some cushioned box into a worm-hole in the ground . . . means it's really over. *Dad isn't coming back.*

How can Dad not be coming back?

How can that even be possible?

Tom picks up his black-rimmed glasses from the side of the sink, pushing them on. His features grow magically defined: a junior version of Dad's widow's peak hairline, same shade of mud brown. A thin crooked line of a mouth beneath a straight nose partial to flaring. Not a great legacy, but then his dad was all about the inside. His dad had life sussed.

Pity he didn't inherit that too.

What would Dad say for right now? *No one knows when the light's going to get switched off, Tommo.*

Tom bangs a fist against the cabinet, rattling its contents. *But couldn't you have bloody warned me you were going to switch yours off?*

The dread that's ever-brewing in his stomach boils more furiously. *Shit. Shit. Crap. Shit. Just. Want. You back. Dad. Here. Home.* Each thump on the mirror accelerates the pumping rhythm in his head. It's becoming second nature, to have a permanent hangover, pulsing under his skull like some crap Ibiza dance tune.

Physical pain, it might alleviate the other kind, but it still hurts. Flipping open the mirror, he roots through the cabinet for pain relief. Constipation, diarrhoea, anti-histamines, old pills, new pills.

New pills. His breath slows. A whole box of them. The prescription label, made out to his mum. He lifts out the blue

7

and yellow branded box. *After PharmaCare ruined Dad? How can she?* Tom slides out one of the foil trays. There, the messages he's only ever heard about, printed over every *Leata* pill, a tiny flowery font, stamped in blue and yellow. *'Turn your face to the sun'*, the first one says. *'Sadness is a scourge'*, the next. The stuff of Chinese fortune cookies. Except his dad said a good few million pounds a year goes into paying people to think up these. *PharmaCare expect a return on their investment: for other people to suck them up* – that was the by-line his dad used on his final national story, five years ago. The story where he accused PharmaCare of paying GPs to prescribe *Leata*. The story that did nothing to stop the nation taking the small blue and yellow pill. But lost Dad his job when PharmaCare brought criminal charges against him.

Tom roughly shoves the box back in the cabinet; grabs the ibuprofen and pops out two pills. He swallows them with cold water cupped in his palm. Bowing his head down low, he grips the edge of the sink, fingers tightening against the pain as a message of his own copies out detention-style inside his head: *Why did you kill yourself, Dad? Why did you?*

WHY DID YOU?

Her

'At *last*, Hope,' Mum says to me, as I wander into the kitchen. 'Do you *want* to be late for your first day of a new school year?' She's sat in her satin purple dressing gown, making mice-nibbles at her toast (her latest diet is to take small bites of everything).

'Morning, Mum,' I smile at her, ignoring her question. 'Sleep well?' Mum's not a morning person, so she needs my help

8

to stay cheerful. It's not like she means to be critical. I read a really good piece by a journalist recently whose column is sponsored by *Leata*. She was saying how confrontation only confronts your own anger, and that if we meet any kind of negativity with positivity eventually positivity will win out.

I go and kiss Mum on her cheek. She's talking to Lily – 'you're going to be the prettiest little girl in your drama show' – but staring ahead. Her hair's not yet brushed and her face looks flushed and bloated. Courtesy of the number of empty Pinot Grigios by the recycling bin? I wonder if I should write another post about the dangers of drink and leave my tablet lying around for her to see.

I take a seat at the new table, banquet-long and shabby chic wood, the chairs, all colours of the rainbow. New things make Mum happy. So every now and again she points to a style magazine and says '*that*'. And everything changes in our house again. I liked the last table, *but*, having a house that's forever on-trend is a big plus. Your environment has a major effect on you, right?

Rose, along from me, has her Saxon-blonde head buried in a book – as per, she's very serious. Lily, kneeling up on my other side, is chattering away like a little chirpy bird. Mum always encourages it. 'My beautiful baby girl.' So I try to as well.

'Good luck on your first day back, poppets.' Dad rushes in, midway through stuffing folders into his briefcase. He bends over Rose's head, kissing the top of it, then moves past me and does the same atop Lily's. I lift my eyes to catch his glance like I notice Mum does, but Dad's propping his briefcase up on the other end of the table, wearing a frown beneath his thick sandy hair as he flicks through inside. Poor Dad, he's got so much on.

I start buttering some toast.

'Easy on the spread, Hope, you don't want hips like Grandma Lizzie.'

I scrape some off onto the side of my plate and Mum nods approvingly. She has two fingers pressed to her mouth as if she's smoking. It's a habit of hers since she quit a few years ago at a PharmaCare Health Farm. Because you really mustn't smoke on *Leata*. It cancels out some of the benefits.

I can hear Rose and Dad continuing their chat about the British Museum. I glance over, waiting for a polite gap so I can speak. Take away the fact he's a forty-five year old man with lines framing his eyes and mouth, he's a doppelganger for my fourteen-year-old sister. I watch his gaze take her in, like he's *really* listening. Despite all he's got on. My stomach lurches with love for him. For all he does for us.

Rose goes quiet; I clear my throat, start bouncing around on my seat, like I'm an engine revving up. 'Dad, can you believe it: I'm just a thousand off *two* million total followers and subscribers. That means soon my *Leata* advertising income will increase!' I let out a squeal.

'Good, you can buy your own car when you pass your test then,' he replies distractedly, his eyes back in his briefcase.

'Daddy, I want a red Ferrari when it's my turn,' Lily pipes up.

Dad clicks his briefcase shut and goes over to Lily, pressing her pale blonde head against him. 'That's because you're one of life's racers, princess.'

I smile at Lily. She's only nine. Young enough for cuddles and kisses still. Whereas me: 'You act so capable these days,' Mum always says. I'm proud of that fact.

I join in laughing with Dad and Lily as Dad starts raspberry-kissing Lily's neck and Lily giggles and Dad tickles Lily and Lily giggles. I try to recall the times when he did stuff like that to me, when I was Lily's age and – my memory's so bad these days! Early Alzheimer's or what? Too much thinking in the present. As it should be! The past is a bleak place. No one lives there.

I look down at the toast in my hand; drop it back onto the plate. You know, I'm not really that hungry.

And heck – No. Thank. You – I do not want hips like Grandma Lizzie.

'Get a move on, Bryony,' Dad's saying to Mum. He's looking a tad peeved. I feel for him. I wish Mum could get dressed before she comes down in the morning. Put her face on for Dad at least. Millie says she'll wear overnight make-up when she starts sleeping over with her boyfriend, Ryan. She has a vlog tutorial all planned out for it.

'Give me half an hour, Jack.' Mum pushes her bed-hair back from her face, getting up slowly. 'Girls, remember, Mrs Chichon is taking you to school.'

'Why, where are you going, Mummy?' Lily looks over, baby-face worried.

'Your dad and I are attending Matt Riley's funeral,' Mum says brightly, as if for funeral she means wedding, for Lily's benefit I'm sure.

Meanwhile, I'm trying to ignore the fist that seems to have appeared from nowhere, grinding my stomach. Really! It won't do to go thinking about Matt Riley . . . and how he died . . . and Tom. I mean I've hardly seen Tom come out of his house since it happened. I have looked for him of course. Not that Tom's known for being that pleasant to me. But if I can catch him, I want to share the positivity I'm known for. Tell him the best cure for grief is to be with other people. Happy people. You can't help but smile when you're around smiles.

'And you're sure I shouldn't come?' I stare at Dad, frowning uncertainly – *say no* – then Mum when he doesn't look over. 'I mean, I did used to play with Tom lots.' My frown deepens at the statement; something sharp now is prodding me from inside. Why? . . . I mean, it's been years since we were friends. *'It pays to forget. It hurts to remember.'* Thank. You. *Leata*.

'A funeral might make you sad,' Mum cuts in, her face expressionless, '. . . you're better off at school.' Those two ex-smoker fingers are back tapping at her mouth, as if she's blowing me an awkward kiss.

I nod vigorously. Right answer. Death. It doesn't pay to be reminded of it. Life is for the living.

And Tom? All I am to Tom now is the girl who lives next door. He probably never thinks of when we were tight. Best friends. And the treehouse.

I know I don't. *Really*, I don't.

Him
Tom resumes horizontal on the guest bed, re-connecting with the damp patch on the ceiling. His favoured view this past month. There's a new spiral-bound notepad, the kind his dad liked to use, lying next to him. His dad always said pen and paper helped him find answers. Trouble is Tom has no other questions except the same one that won't stop circling his head. *Why, Dad?*

Matt Riley must have been depressed, the coroner said when he finally made it official, 'suicide', and released Dad's body for burial. *Dissatisfied with his job*, he also hinted. *Not on Leata*, the local newspaper noted. Tom's insides clench, cramping as if he needs the loo again. He claws at his shirt collar, the whole suit's suffocating him. A size too big – his brother Nathaniel's – it might as well be straitjacket tight. He pats the bed for Dad's silver hipflask. The blackness grows like spilt tar through his mind the minute he's sober again. It's best to keep drinking. His hand finds it, lifts it up, his thumb stroking the engraving, from when Dad left the *Daily Herald*: *The truth is never told during working hours*. Hair of the dog. Tom knocks it back, the whisky burning his throat, as if it's ripping away a layer of his insides. He reckons if he keeps on ripping soon there will be nothing left. And then he won't feel so bad. Will he?

Another slug, longer this time, wiping at his mouth where the liquid dribbles out. Breathing out dragon-heat, he props himself up on his elbows, staring round the guest room that also acted as Dad's study. Nothing's changed. Preserved in aspic, like a museum piece: even his dad's favourite old cardigan is still lying over the back of his chair, like his dad's just left the room for a piss or to sneak a smoke.

His head jerks at a familiar soft wailing noise from the next room, like a subdued siren.

Soon there's another sound. Nathaniel! To the rescue! Pounding down the landing; Nathaniel knocking on his mum's bedroom door . . . Tom's skin stings as if it's burning under a hot sun – just *Mum's* bedroom.

'What's wrong, Mum?' Nathaniel's asking in that responsible-adult voice he's adopted. *He's the man now.* Tom can't hear her reply, it's muffled by snuffling, choking noises. She will be trying to stop crying now she's been caught out. She's never been one to bawl in front of them. Not like his dad. Dad would blub at anything and everything. *Wall-E*, when trains left platforms, the life of a mayfly. *You've got to let it out, Tom!*

'Tom!' Superson Nathaniel's calling for him.

He pushes himself off the bed, shuffling across the patchwork floor of papers and files. The detective left them in the exact same mess after he came checking for a suicide note eight weeks ago. DS 'Call-me-Ethan' Miles, like he was family or something.

Bloody hell, Dad. Tom's mouth releases a jagged noise. *Why couldn't you have just left a note? A text even? A Facebook status: I'm about to kill myself because . . .?* He reaches a hand out for the chair, digging his fingers into the scratchy wool of his dad's cardigan, as he looks out the window, onto the back garden. It always seems too large now that he and Nathaniel are no longer kids. The treehouse in the distance – it hasn't been used for years, but he can see his dad building it as if it were yesterday, knocking together flat pieces of varnished oak, cursing when the hammer caught bone not wood. 'A place for you and Nat to hide,' Dad said, smiling through a mouthful of nails. Though it soon became Tom's and Hope's. Nathaniel never was into hiding.

Tom lifts the hipflask again, tipping it back. Pushing it in his pocket, he stumbles out onto the landing to face them.

Nathaniel's worked-out arm is tightly hugging his mum's thin shoulder. Her face is pink and scrunched up. Eyes rabbit-red. She widens them as if to show Tom she's fine.

'You all right, Mum?' he asks. He wants to say something better. But he knows now there aren't any words for what's happening. He needs a whole new dictionary for describing how everything hurts. Now Dad's not here.

'Don't worry about me, Tom,' she sniffs, trying hard to smile. 'You look smart.' She makes that face, like she's in pain. She blames herself. Tom can see it ever-present in her eyes. He tries hard not to blame her too. That his dad might still be alive if she hadn't told him to go. Muffled words flying out, front door banging – just a week before he killed himself. Some stupid row, probably over money. That was Mum's usual beef with Dad.

Back soon, when things cool down, his dad's text to Tom had said.

But he never came back.

He never came back.

'You ready? The car'll be here soon,' Nathaniel is saying, in his throat-clearing best 'father' voice. He's suited like Tom, except his fits. Like Tom, he has his dad's blue eyes, minus the myopia. Nathaniel always was the blessed child.

'Yeah, I'm aware of that.' Tom returns, more acidly than he means. The ibuprofen's not kicked in yet, blood's pumping hard behind his eyes.

'It'll all be okay, Tom.' His mum reaches a hand out into the space between them, pale and frail like the rest of her. Nothing like she used to be.

'Sure,' Tom says, grazing her fingers with his own. He takes a breath, trying to find some nice words to give her, to battle with what she's telling herself. But he still can't find any.

'Have you been drinking, Tom?' Nathaniel is sniffing the air in front of him.

His mum moans, 'Oh, Tom, have you?'

He never has been able to lie. 'I'll wait outside,' he answers instead. Eyes fixed to the floor, he hurries on downstairs. Into the lounge – quick: swig from the flask, flames erupting in his chest. The TV's blaring loudly. Nathaniel keeps leaving it on, like some background noise in a dentist's surgery. Anything to divert them from what they're facing.

That Dad's brilliant brain was splattered over a coppice in Richmond Park.

Dad is DEAD.

But we can't talk about that.

A party political broadcast is on – the Progress Party. Tom strides across the room – he needs air – as Damian Price, the Prime Minister, fills the screen. All public-boy features and paid-for smile, congratulating his party for the successful part-privatisation of the NHS. Concluding with the same old trite that got them into government three years ago, 'Positivity yields prosperity'. Tom continues quickly out the opened French doors as the broadcast ends and the sponsor runs an advert. *Leata.* Of course, *Leata. Do any other sponsors exist these days?* The voiceover: husky and caramel-soothing, the kind to read bedtime stories. Even Tom momentarily feels compelled to listen: *I was often sad, and found myself thinking back to experiences from my childhood or imagining myself inadequate when compared with others . . . Just a year*

16

later, after taking Leata . . . my life is transformed. I am happy and striving for success. Bad thoughts no longer plague me!

Life's short. Enjoy it!

A super-fast robotic voice finishes with *Leata cuts off bad emotion. Proven: no side effects. Always read the label.*

Tom pulls hard on the French doors behind him, the glass rattling along with the pain inside his head.

Her

Both my phone and pad are vibrating on my bed like they're busy yakking to one another in my absence. Momentarily – yeah, yeah all right, *how very* unusual for me – I ignore them both and head to my dresser. With precision, I open my vintage jewellery box with its printed pink and yellow rosebuds. I use it solely to house my box of pills.

I look forward to this each morning. My ritual. *Leata*'s twenty-four hour effective, so by eight a.m. pill time: I am ready for it. I don't want to know what will happen to me if I let it slip for an hour even. If those adverts that show the consequences of life without *Leata* aren't enough (did you know 90% of pupils failing exams *don't* take *Leata*?), my friend Tara is evidence plenty of sporadic *Leata*-taking. She's über-miserable lately. Up and down like a yo-yo!

So the ritual, it goes like this: First, I take out the tray. Nine pills, three already gone. Next, read the message – today's: '*Anaesthetise emotional pain*'. Nice one. Some numbing is what I need right now.

Then: dig nail into foil. I like the sensation as it rips.

Pick out the small blue and yellow pill, '*Leata. Life's short. Enjoy it!*' inscribed in tiny print across it . . . onto my tongue, tasting sweet and shiny . . . and swallow; swallow again. Till it slides down my throat.

I've become pretty good at taking them without water.

Hey presto – *Leata* will start to work its magic.

Like it has for nearly five years. Ever since Mum and Dad put me on them. Which I'm forever thankful to them for – for *Leata* to be most effective you should start taking it after reaching double figures. Me – I stupidly resisted until I turned twelve. 'You're lucky,' Mum told me when I was still all uncertain about my first prescription, 'You get to bypass all those nasty teenage moods that wrecked me into adulthood. *Leata* will never work as well on me.'

In fact – yay – wha'd'you know, I'm feeling calmer already. *Leata*'s like warm water flushing through my arteries, lining every vein, eradicating bad energy from my blood, soothing me from the inside.

I really don't understand why people *choose* to be unhappy. When they can be happy!

The last stage of the ritual? Tweet the pill's message. Lots of people do this of course. But being who I am, mine always get retweeted thousands and thousands of times. Like the message's come from me personally!

My phone's stopped but my pad's still vibrating. I launch myself onto my bed: another DM . . . from . . . *Seth*.

I've re-jigged my schedule. Now free 2come 2Leata Blogger Quarterly Sat. U still going? If yay, why not come guest vlog back at mine after? Along with other things ;-)

My stomach tightens, knots, twists; tingles with excitement. Of course, we've messaged before about guest vlogging.

But – other things? My stomach flips and pinches dually. Well, it's not like we're not practically dating already. Right, so we've never physically met – but online counts for real time. We're virtual soulmates. And I *love* his channel. He's had this meteoric rise on YouTube in the last few months. What can I say? *Realboystuff* rocks positive vibes. And he's handsome, in a floppy-haired boy-band sort of way.

I've got to make it work. Like Millie says: 'Heth! Sope! You and Seth are a global brand waiting to happen! Think Posh and Becks. Brad and Ang. Romeo and Juliet without the tradge'.

But seriously: my followers do need to see me happy in a relationship. I must think of them, not myself. Some of them are old, like in their twenties. I've spotted some even Mum's age! I have responsibilities. I need my followers to see I'm always *evolving, growing, embracing life*. That's what *Leata*'s Marketing Director said at the last Quarterly.

I can't stagnate. *Livelifewithhope* as a brand must develop.

I bite down on my tongue. My pad finger hovering, ignoring the frantic butterflies in my tummy.

Hell, yes.

My heart's beating fast as I press return. Tingles turn into fireworks as Seth messages back instantly.

We will make fine music together.

Straightaway I Facetime Millie.

'Ready for our first year as human beings?' Millie's iPad is propped up at her dressing table. She must have just finished her tutorial. She does one for her channel *Makeupwithmillie* every day. I've not had to buy any beauty products since she started. Her haul is amazing. Her subscribers watch Millie put

19

on her daily make-up, with a few little words on how each product makes her happy. A little on the dull side (you didn't hear me say that), but Millie is unbelievably pretty. You can't blame her viewers for thinking they might look like Millie too if they apply the same brand of foundation. It is all about *hope* after all (see what I did there!).

'I'm just grateful to be out of that uniform,' I reply.

'Tell me about it. I'm free to flaunt.' She cocks a plucked brow down at her bra-boosted cleavage. Millie purrs like a cat when she talks. That and the cleavage is possibly another reason why she's picking up subscribers fast (you didn't hear me say that either).

'So Seth's asked me over to his to guest vlog.'

She lets out a short scream. 'Double date.'

'He lives in London, Millie.'

'Nearly sweet seventeen and never been . . .' Millie rakes a hand through her freshly highlighted hair, widening her eyes suggestively.

'And nor will I . . . yet,' I say primly. I start chucking stuff I need into my bag with my free hand so Millie won't clock I've gone red; phone, purse, hairbrush.

'Hey, you heard from Tara?' Millie's dabbing more pink gloss onto her plump lips. 'I'm using codename Misery for her on Facebook so we can discuss her.'

I sigh. I wish Millie wouldn't be mean to Tara. 'You shouldn't write things like that. What if she twigs? We're not bitches, Millie. We understand people. And we help them. Remember?'

'Did you notice – she didn't even bother to cover up her spots when we were out Saturday, Hope. It's disgusting. She never used to be like this.'

'Didn't you give her that great concealer you got sent from *JOLIE*?'

Millie makes a face. 'I didn't bother in the end, not after she said she doesn't have time to watch my *stupid* vlog!'

'Millie: we've just got to feel sorry for Tara. Not attack her.' Millie pulls her pouty face; I smile. *Meet trouble with a smile, ALWAYS.* 'We must try and laugh about these things. Like it's not Third-World poverty or anything.' (Err, like Third-World poverty would even exist if their governments would subsidise *Leata* or something. So Dad says.) 'And you know your vlog isn't stupid. Make-up makes girls happy. We simply need to convert Tara. A softly, softly approach. Beat her down with kindness.'

I force a bigger beam into the screen to show her I'm right. Millie might know everything there is to know about looking great on the outside, but I know everything there is to know about feeling good on the inside. Now and again we collaborate on each other's channels. *Inside and out. Beauty works both ways*, we tell our followers.

I go over to my windowsill to pick up some pens and stuff. Beyond the glass, the first autumn leaves are starting to conceal it, but I can still make out the treehouse in Tom's back garden.

It's hard to imagine that I used to spend my life there. The thought summons a strange sensation in the pit of my stomach, like staring at an old childhood teddy. If I allow it – *so, don't allow it!* – I can still picture Tom and me there, with his dad on the ground bringing us something to eat, using that basket we strung up with a pulley.

How can a person be there one minute, then gone the next? Puff. Like magic? Bad magic. I twist away fast from the window as it comes at me from nowhere. That feeling I've been getting when stupidly I let my mind wander to Tom and his dad – like there's something bad I need to run from. What? *There's nothing! Your life is great!* I take a deep breath, pressing a hand against my chest where it's starting to feel tight. Like my lungs are being squeezed of oxygen. *Stop thinking! Let Leata do its business.*

'I'm a-walking and a-talking, Millie.' I grab my stuff. I just need fresh air. That's all.

I gulp at it like a plant to water once I'm outside. Maybe I should start taking a double dose – just for now. I've seen lots of posts on double-dosers recently. *Leata* supports it. *'Because Leata has no side effects, quadruple dose if you need to: whatever makes you happy!'* Rumour has it the American President takes five a day to keep his spirits up.

'Kat reckons it's because Tara's parents are divorcing for real this time,' Millie's purring. She's back on Tara again. 'I said to Kat, what do they expect when her dad rejects *Leata*? I mean our parents never argue, do they!'

'No, they don't.' I take a deeper breath. Okay, I'm starting to feel better. *Leata*'s truly kicking in. Not before time.

'I mean, it's not rocket science,' Millie pouts.

'You're right.' She is. Even the government endorses the positive effect *Leata* has on divorce rates, same as it does on obesity, unemployment, crime. 'A cure for every social ill – but *only* if people will take it!' I repeat some headline I glanced on *Star* Media.

22

'Exactly! If *Leata* had been around ten years ago, maybe my mum would have never left! But do you see me moaning about that?'

'I never see you moaning, Millie.' Well, except about Tara.

'All I'm saying is Tara'd damn well better keep popping her prescription.' Millie is playing with her phone now, texting while she speaks to me. 'Hope, I won't have her round me until she sorts out that miserable face of hers. I'm *not* being a bitch,' she says as if I've just told her she is. 'Didn't you say in a recent post: "We have to safeguard ourselves from unhappy people?"' Millie's eyes flicker from her phone back to me, her forehead screwing up tetchily. 'Talk to her, Hope. Convince her to go to a PharmaCare Health Farm like Eliza Jenner did – it sorted her out! Make Tara see I can't be her friend if she continues like this.'

I inhale another deep dreg of air; it's summer hot for September. 'Of course I will,' I smile. 'It's what I do,' I'm saying, 'helping others back onto the path of positivity, that's –' when I catch sight of him. My lips keep moving, but my mind, like a dog sniffing out something alien, starts to drift elsewhere.

Where it really shouldn't.

Him

He sees her. As she sees him. They're both stood at the front now. Hope on her lawn bordered by colour-coded flowers; Tom on his white gravel driveway. Separated by a low level prickly hedge that's never grown as tall as both neighbours hoped it would. Hope raises a sprightly hand in acknowledgement.

Tom makes none back. She's caught him mid-swig. Quickly, he lowers the hip flask by his side, throat burning. His gaze holding hers with 'yeah, what?' eyes. It forces Hope's back to the screen she's holding out in front of her like a mirror.

He pushes his glasses up his nose, surreptitiously screwing the lid back on the flask, wishing she hadn't seen that. He stares ahead at their quiet private road with its line of neat, ranch-style houses. Then gives in. Slanting his view, he takes her in again. She's wearing one of those T-shirts that everyone seems to own a version of these days; it's taken over from Hollister or Superdry. His dad point black refused to buy any kind of branded fashion. 'Why offer rich companies free advertising space as well as buy their T-shirt?'

He can't read its yellow on blue slogan from here, but he recognises the curly *Leata* script. Below, her dark denim skirt is short, showing as much of her copper-tanned slim legs as Tom imagines her privileged school allows. When they used to play together, the Hope he knew lived in jeans, maybe that Muppet T-shirt she loved (Animal was her favourite; not that you'd guess it now). There'd be grass caught in her knotted short hair; her nails grubby and bitten ragged.

This version of Hope might as well have returned from Stepford. He imagines the nails are neatly cut and manicured nowadays, to go with the hair – dark as treacle, it hangs veil-like over her shoulders – and the manicured mind, and managed mouth. Yeah – no way would this girl be seen dead in a Muppet T-shirt.

Dead. A cold chill weaves through him as a car, shiny and black, pulls up at the end of his drive, its engine softly purring.

Close behind it: a longer vehicle, displaying a polished walnut coffin like some priceless artefact behind a museum cabinet.

For some reason Tom finds his eyes fly back to Hope; she's lowered her tablet. She is staring at the cars too. Her full mouth opened slightly. She glances at him. For a fleeting moment he thinks an expression chases across her face; the old Hope. The Hope from perpetual summers; warm bodies sitting close to one another on the edge of his treehouse. Legs dangling, discussing which Star Wars character they'd be (Hope: Han Solo; Tom: Obi-Wan Kenobi) or arguing over who was a faster runner (Hope, every time). Sometimes Nathaniel and a friend would be playing football beneath them (their mission: to annoy them). Other times Hope's sister Rose would come to find her for tea and they'd bombard her with spit balls.

'Are you okay, Tom?' Slowly, that adopted toothpaste-advertisement beam grows. As if she's in pain or needs the loo. The smile she's learnt like piano or advanced French at that exclusive school of hers. Nothing like the lopsided grin from when they were friends. In a flash the memories all fizz and dissolve.

Fuck it. Tom's fingers tighten round the hip flask. That version of Hope left as abruptly as his dad.

'Best of luck with today!'

Tom feels his face stiffen instantly. 'You what?' he shoots back. He removes his glasses then replaces them. Really? Did she really just say *luck*? He shakes his head quickly, breathing hard. *Go away; get lost.* 'Don't try talking about things you know nothing about, hey, Hope?'

It's the most he's said to her in five years. And it offends her – those Disney-wide brown eyes tell him that. *Never hold back from speaking your mind.* He hears his dad. *If the truth hurts that's their problem, not yours.*

Hesitantly, she wanders off. Tom draws his hip flask up again. Tips it back, staring over it at the panther-sleek cars. The two Dickensian-dressed men inside – they appear like apostles of Death itself.

2

Pull a mental fortress down
against bad thoughts
Leata

Her

My phone's vibrating in my bag as I pass through the wide glass doors into a swell of all-girl maroon. It rarely stops. Comments being made on my daily blog, or my last vlog; or a Facebook share or a like on Instagram. Retweets galore. And that's before we get started on emails and texts.

Having a *Leata*-sponsored blog means being on call 24/7 to check what people are saying. It's no different to being a doctor or something.

There's a tug on my elbow. 'I loved your blog over the holidays on starting Year Seven, Hope.' It's a newbie, wide eyes and fresh new uniform. 'It really helped.'

'Well, good,' I say, giving her The Smile. The one I've perfected for my audience like you practise an autograph (I've done that too. Well, you never know. Blog today. Book deal tomorrow).

Newbie's eyes turn more adoring. I toss my hair back. I get lots of comments from parents thanking me for helping younger kids find 'happy'.

'You know I wrote that post because when *I* first started school I found it *REALLY* hard.' Emphasis in your voice helps too. Make like you're singing almost! Spreading positivity isn't that hard, see! 'Poor me – *only* a few from my primary class *came* with me to Beaton High.' Not that I'd been friends with many others anyway. At primary, it had always been enough – me and Tom.

Tom. Oh, I could curse myself for bringing him to mind again. That fist is back in my stomach. Will his dad be buried by now? Tucked up in a box like some fairy-tale princess; *except he won't be woken up by a kiss*. I blink rapidly as if that might wash the image out of my mind.

'Gotta go!' I say brightly to the Year Seven. 'Tell *all* your friends to follow *Livelifewithhope*!'

I carve a path through girls squealing over new haircuts and holidays, past other sixth formers slouching in, proud and powerful in own-clothes. More voices send out praise for *Livelifewithhope*. I try and bask in it but my breath's still catching. *See* – proof why it does no good to entertain these kind of thoughts. Deep breaths. I've really got to get on top of this before I see the others. Millie especially can sniff out an off-mood like a foul smell. I start another countdown of positive things in my life. By *one* . . . I'm fumbling in my bag for the stash I keep there. Quickly break one out. I hear someone else doing the same near me. The snap and crackle of *Leata*; sometimes it's the only sound on a quiet bus or in a class test. It's a reassuring noise.

I swallow it back, skirting round the queue from the school nurse's office for the students whose parents don't trust them to take their *Leata* pill themselves. Honestly, some people really can't see what's good for them.

More shouts follow in my wake, 'Hey, Hope!'; 'LOVED yesterday's blog!' I catch more newbies doing WOW-eyes at me. A group stage-whispering, 'It's her, it is . . . life with hope girl. I recognise her from her picture.'

It's warming me back up. That and the extra *Leata* of course. I cast my smile about as a universal greeting back. *'Pull a mental fortress down against bad thoughts'*.

Maybe I *will* do like the American President. Multiple dose for a while. After all, I have the same responsibilities to other people like him.

Just until all this *death* is over.

Him

Early autumn trees surround the cemetery, their traffic light colours providing a garish frame for the assembly of grey and black on the other side of the hole to him. All of them: clasped hands and sorrowful, blank expressions, as if they've been choreographed that way.

Only Nathaniel and his mum have cheeks marked with tear stains. Even his grandmother's old milky blues remain dry, though she keeps dabbing at them with a tissue all the same: *the loving mother.* No one would guess she'd hardly spoken to his dad in a year.

Tom pulls at his tie. It's like he's a stranger at his own dad's funeral. There are cousins he hardly recognises; Dad's

29

stockbroker brother, who they only see at weddings, still wearing his *I've done better than you* face. Today he has. He's alive.

At the back is a man he doesn't recognise. Broad-shoulders and broken nose, he's standing next to DS Miles, the detective who's paid routine visits since Dad died. Somewhere in his late twenties, Miles belongs in an HBO police drama rather than the British beat. And doesn't he know it, the way his handsome features sit comfortably on his face, like they're relaxing on a summer's day. *What's he come for? To celebrate case closed?*

Closed. The familiar storm swirls in his stomach. Tom presses a hand against it. He can't run for a toilet now.

The vicar drones on. A light wind blows, causing the tree branches to creak and bow as if they're in mourning too. More empty words fill the sombre, warm air. July in September, his grandmother had muttered to them when they met at church. As if the weather's a more important topic.

Tom's eyes return to settle on Pavlin's bowed head. He'll admit it – after pushing his friends away these last two months, he's glad Pavlin's here, relieved for the comfortable familiarity of his friend's kind dark eyes; his long hair brushed and held tidily into a navy-blue patka. It's the first time he's seen him since before Dad died. BDD: Pavlin and him, watching films, talking music, slamming the school Neanderthals bothering them most. Right now, that version of his life feels like some grainy film he watched years ago.

More tears sting his eyes; he presses the heels of his hands into both, staring back at blackness. Dad would say, *let it out,* but he doesn't want to – he makes furious swallows to try and shrink the lump growing tumour-like in his throat – not here.

The vicar's tone hints at an end. Tom blinks open his eyes. A black crow squawks angrily overhead. A few people gaze up, as if relieved for a diversion, before a chorus of murmured Amens ripple through like a Mexican wave. Next, flowers and soil drum onto the coffin below. As if it's a curtain-call – Dad's last performance. Which makes them the backstage line-up. People start shuffling over. White noise of consolatory words begins, as if they're getting passed baton-like down the queue. *'Everyone reads from a script'*; he reckons Dad would sigh if he were here. Tom's hand gets stroked and patted as if he's some stone deity. A few dare to add a *Leata*-inspired quote, a *'life is for the living'* here, a *'bury your tears with your father'* there. No one stops and asks, 'but why would he do it, Tom?'

Really: why, Dad? A silent scream winds itself tightly for release: WHY?

In a breath the image starts to form, etch-a-sketch slowly, until Tom sees it in full. The picture DS Miles drew for them in politely professional, carefully approved words eight weeks ago.

Dad: found by some middle-aged dog walker; lying in a coppice, a gun they never knew he owned by his side. He had shattered his skull as families picnicked nearby and walkers paused to take in Richmond Park's brochure view.

He jerks his hand back from the next mourner pawing him. 'If you can smile your emotions will catch up.' Glancing up – it's the Wrights – he grimaces, Hope's mum and dad. Standing assuredly, as if *they're* the hosts at this death party.

Why are they even here? Jack Wright hated Dad. Dad hated Jack Wright more. As lawyer for PharmaCare, he led the team that sued Dad and the *Daily Herald* over his story five years ago. Ultimately ruined Dad's career. 'Hope not with you?' Tom asks facetiously; meeting their eyes like his dad instructed him to (*'eyes hold the lies behind the version of truth people want you to see'*). Right now, Mr Wright's gaze tells Tom he's only here for appearance's sake; Mrs Wright's – for the sandwiches after. Glamorous, but well padded, she's steadily put on weight since he's known her.

'It's not a place for a teenager,' Mr Wright answers, his eyes trailing off to the car park. Promptly, they steer off in that direction. Their vacant space immediately filling.

'Ralph,' Tom breathes out. Finally – a face other than Pavlin's Tom is glad to see. His godfather is probably the only person around this grave who was a real friend to his dad, going to university then the *Daily Herald* together.

Ralph's wife, Molly, stands neatly beside him; a pained expression tightening across her dark skin; her black hair twisted up tightly. They haven't brought their children either, though they are around Tom's age. Parents protecting their offspring. As if there's a sudden chill in the air, the thought makes Tom clutch his arms tight around his sagging suit jacket. 'Can I talk to you in private?'

Molly presses Tom's arm. 'I'll go and wait in the car,' she says to Ralph in a hushed voice as if they're still in church.

Tom draws Ralph back towards the older, moss-ridden graves in the cemetery. He's hardly spoken with him since Ralph accompanied Mum to identify Dad's body.

'You hanging in there, mate?' Ralph says, his faint northern twang trying to find a way out from the well-spoken London accent. His hair is just as red and thick as in the framed photo where he holds Tom, infant arms flailing, over the font.

Tom shrugs, digging his hands into his trouser pockets. 'Why d'you think he did it, Ralph?'

Ralph wraps a hand over his mouth, 'Tom, Tom, you're not still torturing yourself with whys . . .' He narrows his grey eyes with sympathy. 'Your dad was a mess . . . last time I saw him he was all over the place . . . nervy, paranoid . . .'

'I don't remember him being particularly nervy, paranoid,' Tom says quietly. *Why doesn't he remember that?*

'And nor should you. Hell, you only show your children the good stuff, keep your worst side hidden,' Ralph answers, pushing out each word like he's squeezing from a spent toothpaste tube.

'I knew Dad.' The hole in Tom's chest grows bigger.

'Oh, Tom, I didn't mean that. It's just . . . So you're seventeen in a couple of weeks, but you're still Matt's kid. Always will be –' Ralph sighs.

Tom bites his lip; the mourners have almost all left now. He can see his grandmother hobbling off on his uncle's arm, chatting away like she's leaving some jolly birthday party.

'If you want a reason – look to his work. The stories he was covering. "Nativity plays" or "20 is plenty" or "Not in my backyard". Matt never got over the fact none of the national papers would touch him after he got stung for that *Leata* story. You know this.' Ralph folds his mouth like he needs to tread gently.

'But he'd been doing articles like that for five years. He was frustrated yeah, but he was happy.' Tom shakes his head. He can see his dad clearly, playing video games with him, lounging around watching films together, kitchen dancing to The Stone Roses while he cooked dinner. 'He *was* happy.'

Ralph is staring at him with the same tired eyes as the school's career counsellor. 'Tom; don't. Don't try and understand it . . . None of us can get into another's head.' A sharp gust of wind whistles round them. It lifts Ralph's dark red fringe, revealing a purple-green bruise the shape of India.

'You hurt yourself?' Tom peers forward.

Ralph lifts a hand gingerly to his forehead. 'Yeah, the classic: walked into a door. Clumsy,' he mumbles, hesitating before he adds, 'It's knocked me for six too . . . your dad.'

Tom nods, this time he can't control the thickening of his throat; wetness slides down his face. 'I have to understand why he did it, Ralph, have to,' he gulps between tears, '. . . otherwise –'

'I'm sorry, Tom, I really am. It's not fair, and I miss him too,' Ralph cuts through him, a consoling hand squeezing Tom's shoulder, '. . . but we need to live, don't we . . . and the best kind of living is moving on.'

The tears slow. 'Isn't that a *Leata* slogan?'

'Is it?' Ralph laughs, rubbing a palm over his mouth. 'I dunno, maybe it is. Their messages are everywhere I suppose; they sink into your sub-conscious.'

'It doesn't mean you have to repeat them.'

Ralph opens his mouth, letting out a short, rueful laugh. 'You sound like your dad. Come on.' He starts walking away. 'We need to get back.'

'But don't you think it's odd?' Tom shouts after him; he really doesn't want this conversation to end. Ralph's all he's got to talk to, to try and work it out. His mum isn't capable of it; Nathaniel doesn't want to. 'Don't you think it's odd that his laptop and mobile disappeared from where he died? All his emails deleted? Like dad wanted to keep something from us?'

'Tom . . .' Ralph collapses his head to his chest. When he lifts it, his expression's considering something. Glancing over at Tom's mother, he steps back towards him. 'We all have our secrets, Tom.' He expels a short burst of air. 'Maybe – try asking your mum what your dad's were.' He holds Tom's eyes, 'I am truly sorry,' he says – but this time, the smile of sympathy, it seems to imply he's sorry for something else.

Her

After History, I find the others hogging the *Leata*-freebie yellow and blue beanbags in the Year Twelve common room. Millie and Bels and Kat. Hair long and L'Oréal full; faces perfectly made-up from Millie's haul. Tara's sat off to one side. Her auburn bob looks greasy and she's not got a scrap of make-up on. I put my smile on full-beam for her benefit especially. Return to the hive.

'What took you so long?' Millie punches me on the arm. It's her routine greeting. One day I will tell her it hurts sometimes, occasionally even bruises. But I don't like exchanging negativity.

Millie swings her hair round, exuding some flowery scent. 'Have you told the others about meeting *Realboystuff*?' she says aloud; she'll want the others to know I told her first.

'You're meeting Seth finally?' Bels squeals. Kat copies. 'Ask me anything you want to know,' Bels says suggestively. She's been sleeping with Sam for a year now.

I screw up my nose. 'I don't take advice, I give it,' I say. Besides, I don't need Bels' kind of advice. I mean, I can go back to his place just to kiss and hold and talk – can't I? My stomach skips – I can't tell if it's with excitement or nerves.

I edge over to Tara, bending low beside her. 'Hey, Tara, wassup!' I say in my sparkliest, life's the best, voice. 'Isn't it great to be in sixth form!'

Slowly she turns to face me. Her eyes appear nervous.

'Tara, are you even taking your *Leata*?' I cut to the chase.

'*Leata* won't help.' Her voice is strained. She pulls at her top; her nails look bitten raw. 'I need something else.' She looks like she's about to cry. 'I just want to stop feeling scared all the time, for no reason.'

'But there's nothing to be scared about, silly!' I put an arm round her. Now and again I tackle this kind of issue on my blog. The fact that doctors are fazing out prescriptions of anti-depressants or talking therapies. 'You *need Leata*, Tara. It's been proven to help with any emotional and mood issues. That's why there is no need for anything else. And if you still want extra help then you get signed up for a PharmaCare Teen Health Farm – that will sort you out. *Placing you back on the path to happiness*,' I recite the Health Farms' TV slogan.

'That's what my doctor wants me to do. He says it's all in my mind. I've just got to cheer up.'

'Then follow your doctor's advice.'

'Oh lookey what we have here.' I trail Millie's eyes. Frigid Fran has come in. It looks like she's pond-dipped her black hair over summer. The ends have this bluey-green hue to them.

'Has no one told you, Frigid? Halloween's not till next

36

month?' Millie shouts after her. Everyone except Tara laughs. Though Kat and Bels stop when they see I'm not joining in. I never would – I am so not a bitch. Plus Dad's told me to be friendly to Fran again. I'm honoured he's asked me. Like he did when Fran first moved here from America, last year of primary. Fran's mum is Dad's contact at PharmaCare. 'Nina Mitchell is worried about her daughter,' he said at the weekend. 'She wants you to look out for her. We do as my clients ask.' And err, yeah – I'm not surprised Fran's mother's worried. If I think Tara is bad – Fran virtually walks around in a sandwich board shouting: *NAD!* Negative Affective Disorder – the diagnosis of all non-*Leata* takers. It's no wonder she's ostracised.

Millie shouts out another insult as Fran takes a seat closer to us. It's the only one free; well, it was till two girls move away (hanging out with Frigid is not a good look). She does nothing to help herself – I mean, she could try *colour*? And does a smile cost anything? Hence the name see: Frigid's expression never changes from ice-cold miserable – it's not because we know anything about her sexual prowess (though Millie claims to, *'well, really, would anyone ever want to sleep with her?'*).

'Be nice, Millie.' I tug on her sleeve. Bels and Kat nod their heads in agreement. Millie has a gob on her, but the others respect my opinion more. 1,998,042 subscribers. Just saying.

Millie ignores me, 'But how do you do it, Frigid?' affecting her slow voice syrupy sweet. 'You always manage to work your clothes all Addams family.'

'Niceness meets with understanding. Nastiness meets with war, Mils,' I whisper.

'I like that,' Bels oozes. 'You're so good with words, Hope.'

37

'I'm not being nasty. I'm just speaking my mind,' Millie says. Turning back to Fran she grows her eyes horror-movie wide, making a vampire cross with her fingers.

Frigid does something worse with her own fingers.

Millie bristles. 'Frigid – you're like an infectious disease.'

'At least you can't catch me,' Fran sweeps her eyes over the four of us, 'you've all been inoculated against being human.'

I pull Millie back as she jerks forwards, her sticky lips stretching elastic band tight. 'Millie, feel sorry for her, not angry,' I say under my breath. 'Anger will only give you crow's feet.' That works. Millie views everything from a beauty perspective.

'Let me,' I say, thinking of what Dad wants from me. I head over towards Frigid – of course, I'd never call her that to her face. Name calling is low, we all just need to be *nice* to each other. I see others in the common room are watching, smiling over at me. Good. I need to show everyone how we can help each other. *Livelifewithhope* is all about leading by example.

I bend down till I'm level with Frigid.

'What do you want Hopeless?' she asks sulkily, her eyelids half-closing as if she wants to shut me out.

'Please don't call me names. It's not nice.' I pull a sad face to illustrate that fact. 'You know Fran, you shouldn't slate *Leata*. Remember, underneath our school slogan, "work hard and prosper", it thanks PharmaCare and *Leata*. Because they paid for our new sports building and all our new IT equipment. Like they pay for all those libraries and health centres and state schools that would've closed were it not for *Leata* sponsorship.'

'Oh, do me a favour. And quit making big eyes at me, Hopeless. You can't convert me however hard you try.'

I take a breath to stem my impatience. 'I'm just saying: remember your mum *works* for PharmaCare.'

'What is your problem, Hopeless? I mean, really, what is it?'

The way Frigid's looking at me, it's like she's genuinely trying to work it out. Damn her for her negativity. It does me no good to be around bad energy likes hers.

'You know . . .' Frigid is saying, 'Maybe it's time you start accepting there's no such thing as Father Christmas.'

It's like Dad says, some people just want to get hot-headed about anything for the sake of it. He's helped *PharmaCare* successfully sue lots of people for libel. He almost wins every case. One national newspaper even folded over court payouts last month because it was so horrendous about *Leata* all the time. *What does that say?*

I try a new tack. 'It's a new year, why not a new you? Join in more; you'll find we're all really fun. Millie can be your friend if you *make* friends with her.' *Big smile*. Come on, Fran, take the bait.

She stares at me, chewing on the side of her mouth. 'I heard about Tom's dad,' isn't what I was expecting her to say.

'Oh,' I say, instinctively reaching into my bag for my foil strip. I can sense my chest beginning to tighten again just with hearing his name. Pop one out; into my mouth.

Fran's looking at me with a sneer of disgust. 'What? You need help talking to me or talking about Tom? I thought you two were friends?'

I shrug. I never told her we fell out. That last year of primary, when Dad asked me to be Fran's minder, I took her over to the treehouse, four or five times. It wasn't hard to see she liked Tom. And when we started Beaton High and he went to Sladesbrook Comp, she asked for Tom's number. I told her bluntly: Tom wasn't interested in hanging out with her. I never asked him. I couldn't. We weren't talking by then.

Yes, *I know*, that wasn't very nice. And it would have played on my conscience ever since except that's not healthy. So I don't let it.

But I couldn't have it – Fran up there in Tom's treehouse. Without me.

'Tom's doing really well,' I reply perkily. 'It was two months ago now. He's had time to get over it.'

Fran pulls her head back. 'Really?'

I nod eagerly; broad smile. '*Really*.'

3

Don't ever go back.
The only way is forward
Leata

Him

The three of them silently tidy away the leftovers now that the last of the guests have left. The kitchen island and other surfaces are cluttered with empty wine bottles and half-drunk glasses; foil trays of sandwiches, crusts curling hard.

'I can't tell you how glad I am that's over,' his mum murmurs, passing behind him. Tom flinches as she strokes his back. He tries to rescue it with a smile her way. But his mouth won't work. As she joins Nathaniel at the sink, he grabs the nearest half-filled wine glass and downs it. *Over? How can it ever be over?*

He clears his throat, pushing his glasses up his nose. 'Mum? Ralph – he said to ask you – he said there was some secret, why Dad killed himself.' His voice amplifies in a way he doesn't mean. 'Was it something to do with why Dad left?' He regrets his last words as his mum lets out a short gasp.

Nathaniel whips his head round, his eyes creasing as if to say *shut up*. Tom shoves his hands into his trouser pockets, they're shaking.

Her voice when it comes is thick like pipes clogged up. 'Ralph had no right.' She runs a hand through her ragged bobbed hair, which is lined with grey like it never used to be. Before Dad died Tom only ever saw her power-suited and polished. She had to be for the city job that took her away from them five long days a week since Dad lost his *Daily Herald* job. So she could keep them living here, in a big house, in a nice area, near a good school. None of it was ever Dad's plan. His mum would've sent him to a school like Hope's if his dad hadn't put his foot down. 'I won't betray my Labour membership, Jean! Have my kids tidied and paid-for.'

'Tom, I didn't want to tell you yet,' his mum makes a hum of appeal as Nathaniel states, 'Mum wanted to protect you from it.'

'From what?' Tom looks between them both. 'You know something I don't?' he says to Nathaniel, whose expression is playing 'father' again.

'I'm three years older, I –'

'What's that got to do with anything, if –'

'Boys, please!' His mum's face has become more fog-coloured than pink since this morning, her forehead now permanently concertinaed. 'I should have told you, Tom. I just didn't want to hurt you more.'

Tom makes a face for 'go on'. He's not sure he wants her to now. He needs another drink first. He thinks of the hip flask in his jacket pocket.

'It . . . something was sent to me, anonymously on my mobile. Just over a week before your dad died,' she continues in a thin, sad voice. She turns to find her phone, holding it at a distance so she can read without her glasses, swiping and tapping until, 'Here.' She passes it to Tom.

Like her, Tom holds the phone away from his body, not because he can't see, but as if it's a bomb that's about to blow. He looks at his mum, at Nathaniel, then down again at the first picture on the screen, swiping through two further images.

A cold chill rises up his chest. 'Who sent these?'

His mum shakes her head briefly. 'I don't know. I tried calling the number, and got an out-of-service message.'

Tom's breath becomes shallow. Behind his skull, the pain is back, banging at the door. He stares down at the pictures again, his stomach sinking lower, to the soles of his shoes.

In the first, his dad's hands are fixed onto the arms of a woman – an attractive woman; an attractive woman younger than his mum by at least a decade. They both wear sunglasses; she has dark hair to her shoulders and a tight-fitting trouser suit. Tom flicks to the next one; his dad and the same woman, embracing, clinging to one another as if they are all that matters.

The third: kissing, passionately, like some still for a film poster.

He feels sick. 'This isn't Dad,' he says, knee-jerk words – because there's no argument – he knows it is, even before his mum utters an equally breathless, 'It's Dad.'

Clearing her throat, his mum adds, 'He didn't deny it . . . when I confronted him. He called it "work" . . . said I wouldn't understand.' Her voice has grown unusually icicle-sharp.

43

'How could kissing another woman be work?' Nathaniel chips in.

Tom sniffs, hands the phone back to his mum. *So this is what happened?* he has an urge to say aloud: *Dad had an affair, and you chucked him out, and Dad killed himself.* But tears are sliding down his mum's face. He can see she already holds that equation in her own head.

'It's not Dad,' he says again, but he's not talking about the physical likeness now. 'Dad was honest. The truth mattered to him.' Tom's eyes dart round the room as if he might find proof of that fact hiding on the cluttered countertops. Was Ralph right? *Parents keeping their worst side from their kids.* Did he not know his own dad?

Nathaniel's nodding his head meaningfully at the phone in Mum's hand. 'Clearly, he also cared for lies as well . . . Tom, he deleted his emails – to stop us seeing anything that –,'Nathaniel lets his words trail off when he catches the hurt intensifying in his mum's eyes. He turns back to Tom. 'Well, now you know. The rise and fall of Matt Riley.'

Tom screws up his face. 'Don't.' He clenches his fists, sucking in his cheeks hard. Nathaniel always took Mum's side against Dad. 'He's dead, isn't he?'

'Tom's right. Let's leave your dad be,' his mum intervenes, pressing a hand hard against her collar-bone. 'The best thing we can do now is put it all behind us. Remember the good stuff about your dad. There's lots to remember.' She nods encouragingly at Tom. Nathaniel scrunches up his mouth, as if he doesn't agree.

He doesn't care that they're both watching. Tom reaches for another of the used glasses, knocking back the wine left in it, then another; one more. 'Tom, what are you . . .?' His mum's shaking hands reach for him, but before they make contact Tom is leaving.

Her

I turn from the bus stop into Jubilee Woods, hugging gooey Seth thoughts to myself as if it's something cuddly I've just won at the fair. Usually I get too spooked taking the shortcut to the back of our road. But today: I am invincible. That third *Leata* sorted me out for the rest of the day. Even shrouded by light-zapping oaks, I am floating on a sunshine burst of happiness.

Seth's messaged me twice more today already. Our exchanges have flirted up a gear since I said yes. His last text: *I bet your lips are as passionate as your vlogs.* My stomach lurches like a toddler in the sweetie aisle. I can't wait to meet him, to – *oh no, come on, really?* I stop dead, glancing back at the road behind me. Back over at him. Tom.

He's walking fast through the woods towards me, as if someone or something's chasing him. That silver hip flask clutched in his hand. The suit jacket's gone, his shirt is open. His tie's round his head like he's a schoolboy playing combat. He's not seen me yet. I could still go the long way home. But – *he's just buried his dad, Hope! You should help him.* Right now, must I? That'll mean talking about the funeral . . . which will mean thinking death. Death and Life – they're as bad a partnership as Tom and Jerry or vampires and werewolves. Can't I just stay daydreaming about Seth and Saturday and vlog collaboration and falling in love?

Another time, I'm thinking, turning quietly away. As he looks up.

Our eyes lock. *Now you've got to say hello.* I take a deep breath. Trusting in *Leata* to stop my chest tightening again, as I walk over to him. Further into the wood.

Him

He wills her to turn and walk away. He can't be doing with this now. Shards of fuzzy light spray through the leaves, as if she's being spotlit for him, like some angel Gabriel. Come to tell him everything will be okay if he takes *Leata.*

'Hi Tom!' she says brightly, waving a hand.

He pushes his glasses up his nose. Yanks his tie off his head, feeling stupid. Somehow 'new' Hope always makes him feel stupid.

'"Hang the DJ?"' she asks, reading the T-shirt under his shirt.

'It was Dad's,' he says.

She tilts her head sympathetically, bites on her lip, takes a breath as if she's working up for the next question. 'Was the funeral hard?'

He stretches his eyes. 'Well deduced, Batman.'

Her

The boy needs my help. Seriously. He always did love the sarcasm. Back when.

Back when. 'Don't ever go back. The only way is forwards.'

'I am very sorry about your dad. He was awesome,' I reply. Well, I half-lie. I always preferred his mum. Yes, Tom's dad could be fun, plying us with juice and biscuits; swinging us about by our arms; grinning as he taught me the names of Socialist leaders, *don't tell your dad, Hope* . . . making sure we loved the old Star Wars episodes more than the new. He was

46

like a big kid. But it made me uncomfortable, all those times he hung around the treehouse just to sneak smokes of dope; his eyes going glassy, his mood growing unpredictable. Tom was more like his little mate than his son.

My phone starts ringing inside my bag.

'Don't mind me,' Tom mutters, a tired edge to his voice.

I check caller ID. *Millie.* 'I'm not going to answer it right now,' I say. I clear my throat, waiting for my phone's ringtone to finish, the tune from the most recent *Leata* advert. I love it.

'But at least a funeral brings closure?' I put a perky smile at the end of my question. *'Whatever you say as long as you smile, it softens it.'*

Tom kicks at the ground. 'Is empathy not on the curriculum at your elite bubble-school?'

'Is crap dry humour a specialism at your rough as chuff State?' I bite back without realising. Quickly adding a laugh, to show I'm making a joke. I'm here to help him, I hope he can see that.

'Remember Fran?' I say to change the conversation. 'She asked after you today.'

Tom makes a face like he's trying to remember. 'The American girl who joined Year Six?'

'That's her,' I say brightly, an idea starting to form in my head. Hey, what about it? Tom and Fran! I can help them both at the same time. Two negatives . . . into a positive!

Better still I can feature it on my blog! Tom and his grief will make a great case story! *Stateofhappiness* Emily won this year's *Leata* Bloggers' Award, all because she featured some self-harming kid. How she and *Leata* helped him turn his life around. How she encouraged him to go to a PharmaCare Health

Farm that cured him. They did an interview on Breakfast TV together and everything.

I'll change Tom and Fran's names to protect their identities of course.

'Yeah, the two of you should really meet up again. I think you'd be great for each other,' I say. Heck, I'm just too good at this. They should make me one of those UNICEF ambassadors. Move over, Angelina.

'I'm not feeling at my most sociable right at this minute.' Tom says each word like he's spelling it out for someone hard of hearing. Pulling another of his sarcastic faces at the end.

Well, no one said Angelina's job was easy.

'The death of a parent can do that to you,' Tom adds drily, holding my eyes for a second longer than I like. My eyes flicker nervously across his face. That white crescent scar above his eyebrow – I was with him when he got it. Sharing a skateboard, down Mason Hill. My idea. The bad ones always were.

I hurriedly divert my gaze into the trees. Note to self: The Past – it's not on your itinerary for life's journey, remember!

Clearly Tom thinks differently. 'You used to make a good Ewok when we pretended this wood was Endor,' he says suddenly.

'Daft kids!' I beam dismissively. Like I said: NOT on my itinerary.

'Yeah,' Tom sniffs and starts yanking off pieces of silvery bark. I can hear the tune of an ice cream van pulling up on the road behind us. 'Want one?' I ask.

I'm surprised – should I be disappointed? – when he follows me, his face darkening as if I'm leading him further into the woods, not out.

Him

He doesn't know what he's doing. Trailing peachy-perky-pumped-up-on-*Leata* Hope to the ice cream van. He doesn't even want a bloody ice cream. But he finds suddenly he doesn't mind her company. Maybe it's because Hope used to know his dad. 'Angelic rogue' Dad used to call her. She made him laugh. Before she made him pissed. When she told Tom 'you're not my friend any more'. *Like father, like daughter*, Dad had said.

He squints his eyes from the bright sunlight after the darkness of the wood.

Hope seems to be lingering at the back of the ice cream van. As if she wants him to look at the *Leata* slogan printed there in blue, *'Life's short. Enjoy it!'* It almost obscures *'Mind that child'*.

They're back in the wood. He chose a Funny Feet ice cream; she went for a Fab. *Some things never change then.* Biting off a big toe, Tom suddenly blurts out, 'Dad had an affair.' He stares at what's left of the foot, as if it contains some potion that makes him speak his thoughts aloud.

'Goodness, really?' Hope says uncertainly.

'*Leata* can't stop people from having affairs if that's what you're thinking.'

'Morals can,' she says, tipping her head thoughtfully.

'Forget I said anything.' He rips off the rest of the toes. 'I just found out. You're the first person I've seen.' *What am I thinking? Confiding in her?*

'That's okay. People often bring their problems to me. I'm known these days, for helping people embrace positivity . . . you might have heard of my blog, I –'

'Hope, nothing you can say will make me see anything positively.' He frowns. 'I've just found out life's a con. We're all in a wasteland. I just never saw it before.' He regrets talking again. Looking at her shocked face, he sniffs, 'Stay in your bubble though. If that's what makes you happy.'

Her

'I am happy. Very.' *Oh, dear, how do I steer this?* 'I believe you will be happy again soon, Tom. I really believe that.' I smile broadly.

'My dad had an affair, got found out, killed himself,' Tom says as if I've just contradicted him.

I keep my smile taut as my stomach stirs with some kind of dread. Is this the feeling Tara meant? About feeling scared for no reason? It doesn't help that the trees have become denser. Daylight banished, grey shadows loom all around us, the kind I'd imagine into the shapes of witches and ghouls as a child. It's colder in the shade; my hand's frozen from the lolly. I can't let Tom's mood affect mine, disrupt my dose. I start making harder strides towards the light, crunching twigs underfoot as I finger through the index of *Leata* messages I have saved in my head. Which one's most appropriate? I've not faced suicide before. Anyone on *Leata* wouldn't have to.

'The thing is: to think only happy thoughts, none of this "wasteland" – Negativity's a disorder,' I finally say, regretting it as Tom's face zips back up.

He bares pink teeth. 'Calling me a NAD, is that the best you can do?'

'Okay, well, how about . . . maybe we can just hang out. I mean . . .' I breathe out of my nose. I think of my blog. Tom, my case study. 'Be friends. Again.'

He looks like he's about to choke, or laugh. It's hard to tell which. 'You saying you want to go back to playing Star Wars and eating tea in the treehouse, Hope?'

'No. I don't mean . . .' I don't like his tone. 'Not like before.' No way, like before. 'You know, chatting occasionally. Maybe a feelgood film now and again?' Which thankfully is all that's being released these days. My blog and I totally backed last year's campaign for production houses to cease making *feel-bad* films. Funding's already been pulled on lots of horrors. And I heard that film where those boys make a suicide pact has totally flopped. I mean people dying in films is fine, as long as it's filled with hope and happiness for life. Die with a smile! People just don't want to see stuff that makes them sad. That's not what entertainment is for!

'Friends again? Really?' Tom's muttering away to himself, wiping his mouth like he's just been sick. He discards the rest of the pink foot into the undergrowth. A pigeon shoots out, flapping its way to the canopy above. Tom looks like he wants to follow it.

'I wasn't the one who stopped being friends in the first place, Hope. Adios.' He stalks off, raising the back of his hand in a wave of bye.

'Yes you were,' I whisper after him, before I've even realised the words have left my mouth.

4

If you don't have bad thoughts,
you can't have bad feelings
Leata

Him

Tom stands, frozen in the all-white, light-filled atrium, either
side getting pummelled by passing students. His head's hazy
from the glug of whisky he poured into his coffee this morning.
Dad: three days buried. It's how he thinks of time now, like he
hears mothers talk about their babies, 'five weeks and two days
old'. So his dad is eight weeks and four days dead. The ticking
clock of remembrance fills the future too. Dad's birthday.
Christmases without him. The anniversary of his death.

Someone shoves him with their school bag; Tom's woozy legs
lose balance. He stumbles towards the wall with its big banner
thanking PharmaCare for this atrium. '*Build better lives with
Leata*'. Maybe he should just turn round and go back home
– Nathaniel's driving back to university, his mum's returned
to work. The house to himself, he could just get steadily
drunker. A group of girls stare back at him, their mouths

forming whispers to one another. He sees it in their eyes – the latest label stuck to his forehead – 'The boy whose dad shot himself'. He's already seen the virtual nudging on Facebook. He's found it a strange distraction, to hover ghost-like at the edges of online conversations, watching virtual unknowns discussing his dad and why he did it and what an idiot he was, *cos he didn't take Leata.*

And now here Tom is, in the flesh for them all to see and discuss. Pushed onto the stage. The freak show more like. *Shit.* He was going to try and wait till lunchtime, but . . . He tugs out the Ribena bottle from Dad's ancient Puma record bag, taking a sip of the whisky he decanted inside.

'Hey, you're back, mate!' Tom almost spits it out again as Pavlin's arm slings round his shoulder. 'It's good to see you.'

'Hi, Pav . . . Not sure for how long . . .'

'It'll be all right – Lower Sixth, we get study rooms, remember? Away from the insanely happy riff-raff, yeah? 'N I bagged us a good one: Daisy, Alfie, Lyn-Mei. Miserable misfits together. It'll be cool. So you put a lot of thought into your first day of non-uniform, I see.'

Tom looks down at himself. He hardly recalls getting dressed. His green skinnies are stained from god knows what or when. The checked shirt smells of mothballs. The white T-shirt underneath yellowed from age; the 'i' and 'v' of Nirvana almost rubbed away. 'The top half's Dad's. Is that weird?'

Pavlin laughs, flicks his shoulder. 'Nah, you look cool. Retro, yeah? Anyway, here.' Pavlin pushes forward a thick, dull silver bracelet. 'From my dad. You know Mr Balil, not a man of words, but he wanted to show, you know, his sympathy, and all that.

It's a Kara. You wear it on your right wrist. In our religion it protects you from evil,' he winks.

Tom blinks fast, busying himself putting the bangle on so he doesn't have to say anything. Kindness from Pavlin's taciturn dad touches him more than those semi-strangers pumping his hand at Friday's funeral. He fingers the chiselled black inscription.

'Punjabi,' Pavlin says. '"There is no beginning. There is no end."'

Tom tightens his neck. 'Tell your dad, thanks,' he says, his voice thick.

They start walking towards the sixth-form block. Suddenly it seems possible to carve a path through all these people now he's got Pavlin by his side. 'And thanks for coming to the funeral, Pav,' he says looking ahead.

Pavlin wafts a hand in the air. 'Like I wouldn't.'

Tom turns, his whisky-clouded eyes trying to focus properly on Pavlin: smooth brown skin, dark eyes; the patka he wears despite its beacon for bullying. 'I respect my parents more than any nut-heads,' is how Pavlin sees it. That's why Tom's dad always rated him.

Something hard takes a punch at his stomach. He brings the Ribena bottle fast up to his lips.

Her
'I don't understand why we can't do Hardy any more.'

Ms Shone makes a tense shake of her head, her brown frizzy hair staying stiffly in one place. Millie's forever mouthing 'straighteners' behind her back.

'It's out of my hands, Fran.' Ms Shone blows her nose; the tip's red as if she's been crying. 'The new A-level curriculum was approved at the end of last term by the Education Minister. It stresses that more optimism is needed in literature and the arts.'

I'm surprised she's still got this gig; Beaton High has so much funding from PharmaCare now it's hypocritical for any teacher to turn their nose up at them.

'It doesn't stop you reading Thomas Hardy out of class, Fran. Independent bookshops are your best bet. I doubt you'll find him at the libraries these days.'

'Don't encourage her, Miss,' Millie shouts out. 'You need to get your head out of *The Bell Jar*, Fran, not further into it.'

'Enough, Millie.' Now Ms Shone really looks like she's about to cry. 'I want it known, I categorically don't agree with censorship.'

Trust Frigid Fran to start a row in our first English A level class. I tune out, not wanting to listen. I'm refuelled on feelgood. My blog was great this morning even if I say it myself. I wrote about NAD Boy who I'm determined to help out of grief and guide into positive thinking. And NAD Girl I'm going to set him up with. *Can I convert them AND bring love into their lives?* I asked my followers.

If anyone can do it you will, Hope. ☺
You're so kind, Hope x
U put others before urself, that's why I LOVE U

I tune back into Millie's Shone-baiting. I take it on myself to end it. 'It's not censorship, Ms Shone,' I pitch in politely, smiling sweetly so she can't take offence. 'It's merely taking out novels that are too bleak. Life is about hope and enjoyment. So our books should mirror that.'

There's a ripple of applause around me. I catch murmurs of, 'You're so right, Hope.' 'I'm with you, Hope.' 'You always nail it.' Maybe I should take over the class.

Ms Shone snorts into her tissue, mumbling to herself as she starts distributing copies of *Persuasion*. Millie leans over to me. 'Skinny jeans, my blazer. Casual smart, neutral colours on your face.' She's still answering my question from earlier. What to wear Saturday with Seth.

'Cleavage,' she grins cheekily, pushing out her chest as I fidget awkwardly in my seat. 'Oh and green sparkle eye shadow,' Millie continues. 'In fact I'll give you a whole truckload for free and you can guest post about it. I want to promote JOLIE to get more freebies from them.'

'I have to be ethical, Millie,' I state precisely, a little louder: others in class might be listening.

Millie makes an 'o' with her mouth, 'It's called *consumerism*,' she says, rolling her eyes. *The face of an angel*, Mum says. The face boys fall for. Millie. Me. Bels. Kat. Tara. It's a ranking we're all fine with.

Speaking of which, I turn round to smile at Tara, getting out the spare box of *Leata* I brought for her. My smile grows as she reluctantly takes it.

Yeah, the thing is to accept where you fit in life. Aspiration's the key. That's my fit. That's what I offer people. Hope!

Him
Tom returns from Economics to the shared study room. Someone's stuck a piece of paper up on the door: 'Warning: NADs bite.' He rips it off. Sometimes, BDD, he used to wonder

56

whether it'd be easier just to give in and take *Leata*, be forced to smile more and fit in. It sucks being in a minority.

Everyone's inside for lunch; better that than the *PharmaCare*-subsidised canteen menu: '*Healthy leads to happy!*' He loiters at the door for a little. Trouble is, he doesn't even feel he fits in here any more either. Pavlin, Alfie, Lyn-Mei and Daisy – they have both parents still. He's gone into another sub-group all of his own.

He moves past to the corner desk he bagged. Lyn-Mei's on the phone; Alfie is playing some black-listed game on his pad. The government's on a mission to ban violent gaming, but Alfie still finds them. Daisy and Pavlin are chatting serious-faced over her laptop. Besides Alfie's new earring and Lyn-Mei's choppy cut, the only other thing that's new is that Pavlin's become some superhero hacktavist over the summer. He's even wearing a PAL badge, Power Against *Leata*.

'How's Hari?' Tom asks, noticing they're on the home page of OpenFreeNet – the platform Pavlin's cousin's part of. In his final year at Bristol University, Hari shamed his family by spending last May in prison for leaking classified information on how the government sold-off all Mental Health Trusts to PharmaCare without a proper bidding war. Tom's dad got involved campaigning for Hari's eventual release.

'He has to keep his head down till he finishes his course. Which means he's relying on the PAL network to spread and share the news OpenFreeNet find, before they release it. That's what Daisy and I are doing now – OpenFreeNet have uncovered this story on how the government is covering up an increase in student suicide. They're passing deaths off as accidental rather than – ' Pavlin stops abruptly, eyes turning regretful. 'Oh, sorry, mate, I didn't think.'

'Don't sweat it.' Tom tries to break a smile. Fails.

'We can work on a different story if you want to join us,' Daisy says, earnest eyes under a thick dark fringe. They went on a few dates BDD. The way her mouth tugs at the corners, Tom supposes he should tell her he's no longer interested. But he hasn't got the words for that either. If he just stays quiet, hopefully that'll be message enough.

He mumbles a 'no, you're all right,' sitting down and unscrewing his Ribena bottle. He drains the last of it back till his body grows sluggishly warm. He already fell asleep in Economics. Mr Jones must have noticed, but he said nothing. He closes his eyes. People are generally keeping their distance. He can't blame them.

Her

'I despise trolls. Have they nothing better to do with their small lives?' Millie sniffs, swiping through comments from her morning vlog. 'Can't they see, I change people's lives for the better!'

I peer over her shoulder. Most of Millie's comments are giving her love, telling her 'you're so beautiful.'

I wait for Tara to catch up, looping my arm through hers to walk down the corridor to the dining hall. 'As long as you don't think bad thoughts, you'll be fine,' I tell her.

She nods. 'Mum's looking into the PharmaCare Health Farm my GP recommended,' she says quietly.

'Yes!' I nod enthusiastically. 'Remember how Eliza Jenner went last year. She's not had a panic attack since.'

58

'She looks spaced out.'

'She looks happy,' I beam. We catch up with the others as we join the dinner queue.

'How could anyone find fault with your saying *JOLIE* Plastic Pink makes you happy every time you apply it?' Kat's widening her eyes, 'I mean OMG!'

'Some people just get off being nasty,' Bels shrugs. 'Implying you get paid to promote *JOLIE* make-up is pure evil.'

Taking a tray, I agree with Bels. Even though, okay, it's true. *JOLIE* do pay Millie to publicise their products – but hey, Millie's still spreading happiness even if she does get a salary out of it!

Millie pouts, puts her phone away, starts applying more Plastic Pink. 'Why can't people see we do it for them? To make others happy.'

'Sure, you're Mother flipping Teresa reincarnated.'

'NAD! Take that back!' Millie slams her tray heavily against Fran's chest behind us. 'You're probably one of my trolls! The look fits!'

Fran whips Millie round, pinning her against the metal counter. Millie's pink gloss mouth starts chomping, as if she's trying to get to a piece of Fran to bite. It would be humorous if it wasn't so hateful. 'Stop it, Fran! Millie!' I exclaim. Students are stopping to watch. No! Someone's got their phone out. I can't have a photo of me next to this!

'Tell your dog, apologise, Hopeless,' Frigid hisses. She looks close to crying.

'Fran, don't be like this,' I say. I smile because another girl looks like she's taking a video now. I step closer to Fran. 'Listen: I saw Tom and he would love to see you. Let Millie go and I'll tell you more.' Operation Love Match might as well continue now.

Fran's looking at me suspiciously. But it works. She loosens her grip on Millie, and Millie fidgets free, catapulting into Bels and Kat.

I pass them a look for 'rejoin the queue', pulling a reluctant Fran away.

'Really. Tom would like to see you again. He remembers how well you got on, when you came round to mine those times. Doesn't that make you feel better?' This will make a good piece for today's blog. *From violence to victory.*

Frigid's still passing me a look of disbelief, but I recognise it in her eyes. Hope.

Now I just need to convince Tom he wants to see Fran.

Him

Shit, he's glad that's over. Tom stumbles home with a hangover. His head bowed, working out ways to leave school altogether, he doesn't see him until he's almost at his front door. Small and slight, with tight black curls and a leather-tanned face.

'Mikey?' Mikey: the ex-convict, with a past more colourful than the Kray twins, transformed into a man who lives to help others.

'Tom!' Mikey starts towards him, limping. 'I was shot by a mafia man,' he told Tom as a wide-eyed ten-year-old. When his dad worked at the *Daily Herald*, he wrote loads of stories on the plight of the homeless. That's how he and Mikey met. Religiously, Tom and his dad would serve food at St Patrick's homeless shelter every Christmas and Easter. His dad said

60

it made more sense than sitting stiffly in a pew mouthing Hallelujah.

Mikey grips a strong hand around Tom's arm, pulling him forward to slap his back. Tom inhales the familiar scent of tobacco. It instantly makes him want to cry.

Pulling back, Mikey's wizened features turn sympathetic. 'Listen, I'm sorry I've not called to pay my respects before . . . or come to the funeral . . . personal reasons,' he says in his gruff voice. 'But . . . I thought you'd want Matt's stuff back.' He stares down at the grey holdall by his dusty black boots.

Straightaway, Tom recognises it as his dad's. 'How come you've got his bag?'

Mikey rubs the stubble on his chin. 'Didn't Matt say? 'E'd been stayin' with me the week before 'e died. Only just come across 'is bag in a locker 'e were usin' at St Paddy's.'

'You saw him then? . . . Before . . .?' Tom's throat thickens, his voice coming out choked. 'How was he?'

Mikey takes a roll-up from his top pocket, leaving it unlit in the corner of his mouth. 'He was a mess, Tom,' he sighs. 'Cut up over 'im and yer mum.' Mikey pans callused hands. 'I couldn't even offer 'im a bed. Only floor space. We're chocka right now – all these cuts the Progress Party are makin' to benefits and fundin' – lots of other shelters are closin'.'

'The Progress Party sucks.' Tom gives in. He crouches down and unzips the holdall, his stomach aching like it does whenever he sees Dad's belongings. His dad's favourite khaki army jacket is packed on top; it jolts him away again.

'Aw, I'm sorry, Tom.' Mikey screws up his face. 'Your dad was one of a kind, you remember that. These days, no press

61

will cover issues like 'omelessness like Matt did. Cos papers have their Pharma-bloody-Care advertisin' revenue to think of.' He lights his roll-up, taking a deep drag. 'Bloody government would ship every 'omeless person on a boat to Australia if it were still a colony.'

Tom inhales deeply. 'Every NAD with them. My mate Pavlin says university admissions are checking Facebook to track applicants' levels of cynicism. Whether you're pro- or anti-*Leata*. It's what makes a good citizen these days.'

'Ain't that right – join the club or yer out on yer ear. And they call it democracy.' Mikey's voice trails off. Leaning on his good leg, he's staring over at Hope's house, at her dad jumping into his navy BMW.

'You know Jack Wright?'

'I know Matt 'ated him.'

Tom adjusts his glasses. 'He came to the funeral. Even though he only ever spoke to Dad to complain about his loud music.'

'Dick. He 'ated yer dad for slatin' PharmaCare, not for playin' loud music. Their fight was that black 'n' white.' Mikey hides his face as the BMW passes by.

'You don't want him to see you?' Tom asks quizzically.

'He's the type that can cause trouble for me and St Paddy's, get my drift?'

Tom opens his mouth to ask what he means. 'Gotta see a man about a dog an' all that.' Mikey taps his nose and starts limping away fast.

'Keep out of trouble, Tom. That's the best bit of advice I can give you. Yer dad never heeded by it.' He smiles crookedly, showing graveyard teeth, nicotine yellow.

Mikey gone, Tom lifts up the holdall, staring down at it as if it's a small kid holding his hand. He takes it into the hall before he properly searches its contents. Picking out a handful of clothes, he holds them to his nose, inhaling deeply, trying to locate a hint of his dad's aftershave, his favourite mint shower gel beneath the musty damp smell. He opens his washbag – his toothbrush is still here? He bites hard on his lip as longing digs deep into him, like a bulldozer is scooping out his insides, every muscle, every sinew. Fumbling towards the bottom of the bag, his hand hits something hard.

He takes in a sharp breath. *Shit.*

His dad's laptop.

He's grappling it out, as the doorbell rings.

Her

'Hi!' I say über-brightly, recalling what I just told my followers: *I'm going to suffocate NAD Boy's grief with happiness!*

Tom ticks his head back at me.

'It's so hot today, isn't it! Going to get hotter still apparently. I *love* Indian summers, don't you?'

He looks at me as if he can't focus. Silence. God, he's hard work. Was he always this hard work?

I sniff the air. 'Have you been drinking?'

He doesn't answer, changes the subject. 'A friend just left me some of Dad's stuff.' He indicates the laptop cradled in his arms. 'It's Dad's.'

I swallow back my immediate thought, *what if there's a suicide note on it?* It won't do to ask such things. I've got to get Tom to think positive. 'If you hang onto your dad's belongings you'll

63

keep the past present. And that means there's no space for a future.' Seriously, did I just say that? Never mind paying me to advertise on my blog, *Leata* should pay me to write their messages! 'I've googled grief and –'

Him

'What d'you want, Hope?' He cuts into her speech, hugging the laptop tighter. Her pale blue top hangs loose off one shoulder. He tries to look anywhere but at the tanned skin there.

'Just to talk to you, Tom.'

'It takes my dad's death to get you to my front door again?' He bites down on his lip to stop himself from saying anything more. He can feel the whisky stirring his tongue. He doesn't want to be mean.

She shrugs, pulls her plastic beam tighter. 'I think I can help you . . . move on.'

'What are you, the Avon lady? I'm not buying happiness today.' He closes the door with an apology. If he doesn't close it now he *will* rip into her.

The other side of the glass, Hope says, 'Have you thought any more about you and Fran? Getting together? I think it'll be a great distraction . . . and Fran always liked you and –'

Her voice trails off as Tom takes the laptop and holdall up to his room, leaving Hope's lecture to an empty hall.

Alone again with the laptop, he opens it, half-regretting it as he does. Does he really want to see what Dad was up to? Letters between him and his lover? What if there's a diary?

He needn't have worried. He can't even get past the password. Dad must have changed it. He tries every combination of their

64

family names, birthdates, his dad's favourite bands. Nothing works.

Remembering the pocket on one side of the holdall, he unzips it. Inside there's a notebook, cold and damp, filled with shorthand Tom can't decipher. Seeing his dad's handwriting even in code makes his insides churn, like he's communicating from beyond the grave.

He tugs out his dad's army jacket and puts it on, even though it's as hot inside as out. Pushing his hands into the pockets, his fingers meet with a crumpled piece of paper.

His forehead furrows deeply as he unfolds and reads it. It doesn't make sense.

It seems to be a police incident note. The handwritten scrawl from Epsom police station records a statement made by his dad, alleging that someone paid for a gun with his credit card.

Tom checks the date at the top.

Two weeks before Dad blew his brains out in Richmond Park.

Her

I stand there yakking away like an idiot for an age until it finally dawns on me – Tom's not there any more. The sermon I've just given, the one I rehearsed, has completely fallen on deaf ears! Suddenly I know what a Jehovah's Witness feels like. He could have at least heard me out!

I crunch back over the gravel, the noise reminding me eerily of the time I came to deliver my letter. The stupid little Hope of five years ago. I'd spent an age decorating it with stickers and drawings. My stomach twists. I stop and stare back at Tom's front door, swallowing back a memory of a feeling. God, where would I be without *Leata* . . .

I'm turning from Tom's drive into my own when I see him. A man in a beat-up Range Rover. Staring directly at me. He must have driven in past the gate (that clearly says Private Road) and parked up while I've been at Tom's door. He starts getting out. Dirty stubble and deepset eyes; his features thin and twisted on a long face. He wears a silver tracksuit that shines like foil in the afternoon sun. The way he looks at me, head tilted as if he's examining me, makes my heart drum faster.

'Your dad in?' he shouts after me as I head quickly to our front door.

I say nothing, panic rushing me inside, wishing for once Rose and Lily didn't have clubs every night. After checking all the external doors are locked, I head upstairs, straight into Dad's study. It has a window directly over the drive. Peeking round the curtain, I check if shiny tracksuit-top is still there. He is, leaning against the car. I go and sit down in Dad's chair, picking up the phone on his desk to call him. It goes straight to voicemail. I put it down again, telling myself: chill. Mum will be home soon.

I swing the chair side to side, trying not to let that man's mean face preoccupy me. I've always loved it in Dad's study. Mainly because it's out of bounds. Even the cleaner's not allowed access. Maybe that's why it smells different to the rest of the house, musty and lived-in. Often, when we were younger, I'd pass by and Rose would be sat in here on Dad's knee. I'd wait ages for my turn, hanging around for Dad to invite me in too.

Rose still comes in a lot now. *Rose is the academic one,* Mum always says, *she needs your dad's input.*

I make a smile, a big one; it always dispels any bad thoughts before they can form. *'If you don't have bad thoughts, you can't have bad feelings.'* I like that one.

I lift up in my seat; he's still there. At least he's not moved.

Sitting down again, I nudge the mouse accidentally. The thin computer screen in front of me flashes on. Dad can't have turned it off. The screensaver comes into focus. A picture from our summer holiday in Spain. Dad hugging Lily dripping wet from the pool. Rose laughing wide-mouthed over his shoulder. You can just make me out . . . yeah, that's my leg I'm sure, on the sun lounger behind.

I sniff; bigger smile! And run a Happiness Countdown. To one: *Nearly two million followers, Hope!* I click the mouse quickly to get rid of the picture. It switches to a home page of yellow folders. Almost immediately, my eyes fix on one.

Why would Dad have a folder with Tom's dad's name on it?

I shouldn't. *No you really shouldn't!* I'm doubleclicking on it when I hear the sound of feet on the stairs. I bolt upwards as he enters the study.

'What do you think you are doing, Hope?'

5

Only question what
you can answer
Leata

Her

His voice is level, but tight. 'Are you snooping on my computer?'

'I . . . no!' I look down, ashamed, shaking my head. I hate, hate, making Dad unhappy. It instantly takes me back, to the bad times. To the days before *Leata*. 'You'll give him a heart attack!' Mum used to say every time I made him cross.

It would panic me. The thought I could actually kill my own father.

But now I please Dad. And that feels good.

I take a breath. 'I'm sorry. There was a man, he –' I stop; noticing a pair of dirty white trainers beyond the gap in Dad's legs. I glance up.

The man from outside. Inside.

'I needed printer paper,' I end prematurely, as Dad steps aside, beckoning shiny-tracksuit in.

'This is Hope.'

The stranger glares at me as if I'm some drink he wants behind a bar. 'All right, Hope.' He flicks a glance at my dad.

Dad twists his mouth. 'He says he saw you at the Riley house. What were you doing there?' He's using his lawyer voice. Was I not supposed to be there? I take a deeper breath, trust in *Leata* to keep me calm. 'I'm trying to help Tom. He needs my advice to find a way out of his grief.' I'm about to add, my blog post about Tom has already got three hundred thousand retweets, when Dad balls up a fist and knocks it gently on his desk.

'Has Tom said anything about his father?'

I try and think of the answer that will please him. Shiny-tracksuit's still glaring at me. I pull my arms over my chest. 'No nothing, but he was clutching his dad's laptop like it was a comfort blanket.'

'His dad's laptop? You sure?' Dad's eyes have widened; he moves his face closer towards me as I nod eagerly. He looks tired, there are bags under his eyes. 'Right.' He makes a grunting noise, flicking his fingers for me to leave.

'Sorry, Dad,' I say again. 'I won't come in here again.' He doesn't answer, he's reaching for the phone. Asking for Nina Mitchell. Fran's mum.

Shiny-tracksuit is blocking the doorway. I have to rub against him just to get out.

'My name's Slicer by the way,' he leers at me. He's well spoken despite his scruffy appearance.

I walk fast down the corridor, closing the door to my room. If he's one of Dad's clients, I hope his case ends soon.

Him

His mum's car is on the drive, a black Merc alongside it, when he makes it back from visiting Pavlin's. If anyone will know how to access his dad's laptop, Pavlin will. He'd avoided Mrs Balil's insistence to stay for dinner – now he wishes he hadn't. He's not in the mood for visitors.

He hears his mum approach the moment he opens the door. Dressed work-smart, she's hugging herself as if she's cold, despite the heat. Her skin tone ghostly pale today; even her lips appear colourless.

'School go okay?' she asks in a weak voice.

'Fine. Work?' It's like looking in a mirror, the desperation he sees reflected there.

She's reaching out a hand towards him when DS Miles starts striding into the hall. She drops it back by her side.

'DS Miles,' Tom says.

'Hey, Tom. What've I told you? Call me Ethan.'

Tom rushes a hand through his hair; takes his glasses off, wipes them on his T-shirt; puts them on again. He just wants to get to his room; he needs another drink. The pain lodges heavier in his chest without whisky.

'Ethan,' his mum says precisely, her lips trembling slightly, 'was just passing. Wanted to see how we're doing. Isn't that kind?' She begins to edge towards the lounge. DS Miles extends an arm after her, like he's inviting Tom into his consulting room. A U-bend smile slowly forms on his face, pointing up to his eyes. Everything about the man is buffed and preened. His dad wouldn't have liked him. That's all Tom needs to know.

He goes in, joining his mum on the sofa.

DS Miles sits in a chair opposite. He fills the silence with another of his slow, vertical smiles, before *How've you been? Can I do anything? You getting any external help?* starts slipping out smoothly through perfect lines of polished teeth.

'I'm not talking *Leata* if that's what you mean.' Tom eyes his mum. It's not like it seems to be doing her any good.

'What other help is there?' Miles nips his trousers over his knees, leaning forward. 'But you know we're here to help too. Any problems – or if you hear anything about your dad's suicide, you report it to me, okay?'

Tom adjusts his shoulders as if he's been caught out in a lie he hasn't made. He doesn't lie. He takes a breath. 'There is something.' He looks at his mum – he should tell her first, not the detective. 'Mikey brought Dad's bag back. Clothes and stuff.'

'Who's Mikey? Why did he have your dad's bag?'

Tom keeps his eyes on his Mum as he answers DS Miles. 'A friend of Dad's. He was staying with Mikey, the last week of his life.'

'Can you give me Mikey's surname? Address?'

'Jones,' his mum says quietly. Tom's insides tense when she adds, 'St Patrick's in Vauxhall.' Something tells him Mikey might not run the shelter completely within the lines of the law.

'There was something else though.' Tom has it re-folded back in the pocket of his dad's army jacket. 'Dad reported some kind of credit card theft.' He hands DS Miles the incident note. 'So what does it mean? Dad shot himself with a gun that someone else bought on his credit card?'

'Whoa there, Columbo!' Miles laughs, stretching his hand out into a stop sign; the vertical smile shooting up to chiselled cheekbones. 'What's that *Leata* message? "*Only question what you can answer*"?'

'Someone else bought the gun?' Tom's mum says, panic flashing in her eyes. Instantly Tom regrets mentioning the note.

'It's all right, Mum,' he says. He needs to do better at filling Nathaniel's shoes now he's gone.

DS Miles' vertical smile still holds like a capital 'U'. 'Don't worry, Jean, I'll investigate this. The likelihood is,' he adopts a sympathetic face – a priest to a dying man, 'it was a mistake, by the gun dealer . . .' He looks calmly between Tom and his mum. 'Maybe his credit card went through twice. There'll be a logical explanation. Always is.'

His mum is nodding her head vigorously. Tom can see she wants to believe that. Maybe he should too.

Right now, he just wants a drink; obliterate his consciousness. 'I need to do school work.'

'Tom.' Miles puts a hand out to him. 'I sympathise with the situation you're in, believe me I do.' He thumps his chest, an ape in the jungle. 'I have a dad.'

What? Tom stares vacantly back at him. Shit, he really needs a drink.

'Before you hit the books – can you show me the belongings this Mikey brought back? I suppose I'd better just check over it.'

Tom presses the heel of his hand to his head; it's banging as if it's trying to get his attention. 'Sure, I'll fetch it.'

* * *

He stands watching DS Miles root through the holdall. His mum's gone to finish making dinner. From the clashes of pans she's not having much success.

The slow smile ascends. 'His personal things weren't in here? His laptop or stuff?'

Tom tries to think, as much as his muddled mind will let him. 'His laptop was in there. But I haven't got it.'

'Where is it, Tom?' Miles straightens up, exuding a waft of lemony aftershave. He pushes forward a perfectly shaven jawline, smooth as pink marble. There's a twitch of cheek muscle as his blue eyes pierce Tom's.

'In my school locker.' Tom has to force the lie out of his mouth – the police only need to connect Pavlin with his cousin Hari to start asking other kinds of questions.

Miles has a disbelieving look on his face. The thin mouth drops to horizontal, the eyes turn serious. Tom starts biting his thumbnail. 'I had to go back to school for something, so I left it there to show an IT teacher. Don't know Dad's password, see.' He never realised how much easier it is to lie, once you start.

'Let's go get it then.'

'School will be locked up now. It can wait, can't it?'

Miles eyes him, digging a tongue into his back teeth, before he says, 'I don't want you sharing that laptop with anyone. You hear me? I need to check it out first, Tom. Cross the Ts, dot the Is in my investigation. You understand? It's imperative.'

'Sure. I'll bring it home after school tomorrow.'

Miles makes a kind of salute. 'No, that's okay – I'll call you in the morning, swing by there.' The smile's back. 'It'll all be okay, you'll see. What doesn't break us makes us stronger, right?'

Tom fiddles with his glasses. That's just it, he feels like answering, *I'm already broken*.

Her

I'm trying to sleep; I can't sleep. My mind jumps from that man Slicer to Seth, to Tom, and back again. Their faces whizzing round till they almost become one. I try and stay fixed on Seth. His flat. What will he expect us to do? Do I get it out there, straight away – I'm a virgin and intend to stay that way, at least for now? That starts making me nervous too, so I skip instead to our future – if our collaboration is good enough, we might get a TV deal, magazine column. I start drawing a promo portrait of Seth and me together – when the light flicks on. Dad fills my doorway.

I shuffle up in bed, blinking against the brightness. 'What is it?' I ask groggily.

My bed bounces as he sits on the end.

'I need your help, Hope.'

I love the sound of those words. *Dad needs my help*.

'I'm very worried about your friend, Tom.'

I start to correct him – *Tom's not strictly speaking my friend* – but he talks over me. 'You know how his father was very anti-PharmaCare, led a smear campaign five years ago that we completely squashed in court?' I nod solemnly, like I see Rose do, as he continues, 'I have concerns Tom might be getting led down the same path, by friends of his father's.' Dad tips his head, smiling cautiously at me. He looks genuinely worried. 'You mentioned you were trying to help him? Well, I'd appreciate if you keep a closer eye on him. Shadow him. Make sure he stays out of danger. He's already at a disadvantage, not taking *Leata*. The last thing he needs is to be used as some vehicle to spread negativity by people who want to harm PharmaCare. Will you help him?'

I sit up straighter, nodding vigorously. 'Of course I will. I was already trying to do just that in a way. I mean, I want to help Tom, I think I – '

'Good girl,' Dad interrupts me. For the first time, in I don't know how long, he bends over me, kissing me briefly on my forehead. I breathe in the comforting scent of a hard day's work: faded aftershave and clammy skin.

He turns off the light. His kiss stays with me. Within seconds, I'm asleep.

Him

Friday at school passes pretty much the same as Thursday. Tom's refilled his Ribena bottle from the whisky bottle he bought at the supermarket, using Nathaniel's ID – the provisional licence that Dad sneakily kept back from the DVLA to pass to Tom, *'To use in pubs and clubs. Don't tell your mum'*.

He's taking small sips, sitting in his corner of the study room as Daisy laughs quietly to herself. She's hacking into other pupils' Facebook accounts making anti-*Leata* statements. Now and again he looks over to catch her staring at him. She flushes and retreats behind her laptop. Lyn-Mei is tapping her phone furiously and Alfie's playing a game. Pavlin is trying to get into his dad's laptop. He's using some hacking program for guessing the probable combination of a password. Tom just had to supply a long list of words and numbers.

'I think we've nearly cracked it,' Pavlin says, getting excited, as Tom's phone starts buzzing. It's DS Miles again. He's already had two missed calls from him this morning. He sighs, answering this one.

'Tom – I'm going to swing by your school now to pick up the laptop,' Miles says cheerfully, 'I happen to be going that way.'

Tom looks over at Pavlin. He wants to give him a bit more time; see what's on it first before the police bag it and file it, and reassure themselves: case closed. 'Can you make it right at the end of day? I'm busy with classes.'

Miles reluctantly agrees and Tom ends the call – just as Pavlin's hands spring off the keyboard. 'Got it!'

'Shit, yeah?' Tom rushes over as the home page comes on. Something snaps in his stomach as he stares at the familiar background picture – Tom and Nathaniel as round-faced little kids beaming into the camera as if everything is right with the world. 'What was the password?'

'Truth89.'

'Figures,' Tom makes a half-smile, almost laughing for the first time in months.

'89?'

'The best year of his life, Dad always said. His first year at university. The Stone Roses played live.'

A distant bell sounds; Daisy, Lyn-Mei and Pavlin start moving to their next class. Tom decides to miss History. He's more concerned with right now. Alfie has a free but he's too distracted by Zombie Attack to notice Tom clicking through his dad's stuff.

He trawls through pictures from over the years, files of research notes and articles for the type of stories his dad said sucked out his soul. His dad's recent internet searches have been cleared like his emails. The only thing that leaps out at Tom is the title of a document recently saved onto an external file. 'Cloud 9'. He makes a note of it and starts to log off, stopping when he remembers his dad's calendar. His heart accelerates as he scans the month leading up to *that* day. Blinking hard, he stares at the screen. He fumbles for his phone.

'Mikey? It's Tom. I've got a question,' he spits out soon as Mikey answers the shelter's phone.

He sounds like he's sucking on a cigarette before his gruff voice answers, 'The feelin's mutual, Tom. You tell the police about Matt's bag?' He sounds pissed off.

'What? Well, yeah.' Tom pushes a nervous hand back through his hair. 'The case detective made one of his friendly visits. It just came up. Why?'

'Didn't your dad teach you? Never tell the police anything. If I got stabbed, mugged, thrown off a cliff, I'd never report it. They came round this mornin' botherin' me at St Paddy's of all places, didn't they. Askin' about why I had Matt's stuff.'

Tom rubs his head. Why would the police be *that* interested in Dad's bag? The same reason DS Miles wants the laptop urgently? The hairs on the back of his neck prick up.

'I don't need this shit, Tom,' Mikey continues. 'See . . . they'll think I was researching the story with your dad, it's – '

Tom catches the tone to his voice. 'Researching what story, Mikey?'

He listens as Mikey starts to backtrack, saying, 'I didn't mean nothin'.'

Tom inhales deeply. 'I just got into Dad's computer.' He pauses. 'On the day Dad died – he was meeting someone. *At Richmond Park.*'

It's Mikey's turn to draw breath.

Her

On the bus home, I take a gamble that his number's the same as it was when we first got phones the summer five years ago. *Want to hang out tonight?*

Him

He arrives home. His mum said she'll be back to make dinner. He told her she doesn't have to. Dad always did the cooking. Besides, they will only sit there silently shovelling food round the plate. Whisky's the only thing that fills him. Speaking of which. He gets his hidden bottle and pours a mugful in the kitchen. He's taking a first glorious sip when his phone buzzes with a text. What the fuck is Hope up to now?

Can't. Busy sleeping.

She responds in an instant.

Coffee tomorrow morning?

Catching first train 2London. A genuine excuse this time. Mikey had relented, inviting Tom to help serve breakfast at the shelter. He knows more, Tom's sure of it. There's more to why Dad killed himself.

Like there must be more to why DS Miles was so keen to get to the laptop. More behind that U-bend smile, when he arrived at school to pick it up, pressing on Tom the fact that, 'Yeah, your dad didn't need to press charges over any credit card fraud. Like I thought, it was the shop's fault – they mistakenly duplicated your dad's gun purchase.'

Her

Cool! I've gotta go 2London Sat! I'll come with u!

Him

It's not your thing. I'm serving food at a homeless shelter.

Her

ALL people are my thing! I LOVE the homeless! ☺ ☺ ☺

6

Every hour you spend on
negativity is a wasted hour
Leata

Her

The train carries that morning-of-the-night-before-stench. I
pinch my nose as I lead us down the aisle searching for seats. Tom
behind me, no doubt still wearing that gobsmacked expression.
Clearly he never thought I'd turn up at far-too-early-o'clock. I
squeeze past a group of chattering Spanish students into two
free seats across a table. A seriously overweight man is already sat
there, wedged in by the window and gorging on a paper-wrapped
pasty like it's his final meal. Millie always says it's not hard to tell
who's on _Leata_ and who isn't. Like that T-shirt slogan popular a
few years ago, 'Choose _Leata_, choose life'. I sleep in mine now.

Tom's staring at me like I'm some puzzle to work out as
he collapses into the seat opposite. He's wearing his usual
uniform of grunge. Today's anarchic T-shirt reads, '_Burn, burn,
burn_', red on black.

'Why are you even coming to London?' he asks suspiciously.

'I have a bloggers' meeting at PharmaCare later.' Fingers crossed Tom won't require too much babysitting and make me late for it . . . for Seth. My stomach collapses into a pile of goo. *Seth*. I'm ready for him. Millie's make-up bag of JOLIE, check. Powder-blue blazer and sexy leather leggings, check.

Check: this morning's blog teaser post. *Today I'm helping out NAD Boy I told you about. And later on meeting A.N. Other. Yes! HIM! Thank you gorgeous followers for shipping me with Realboystuff. Back laters for an update on both boys!*

Tom fixes his eyes out of the window. His hair always falls over his eyes, whatever length – which right now is too long. I tilt my head; you know he might be considered vaguely hot if he bothered to look like he knows it.

'Do you need to wear them all the time?' I ask, pointing at his glasses. It was a few years ago I noticed he got them.

'Not all the time, no,' he answers bluntly, adjusting them. '. . . just like to,' he chews on his mouth, taps his knuckle on the table agitatedly.

Cue a sympathetic smile from yours truly. Time to get working. 'Speaking of which, my pill message this morning was, *"Adjust your focus from microscopic and life will appear brighter."* Broader smile. 'Things are never as bad as they appear, right?'

'Hope,' he says, in the manner of an exasperated teacher, 'if you hadn't noticed: things *are* as bad as they appear for me. Don't you get it?'

I tip my head. 'Of course.' *Do I? What if my dad died?* 'It's just,' I take a deep breath. I must help Tom find positivity. '*Every hour you spend on negativity is a wasted hour.*'

He forces out a throttled, dry laugh; starts pulling out a bottle of Ribena from that seen-better-days Puma bag on his lap. Only when he's taken a drink do I smell it. It's not any blackcurrant goodness he's just knocked back.

'Really?' I whisper. 'At this time?'

Tom takes another, noisy, slurp as if that's his answer to me. 'It takes the edge off.'

'Well so does *Leata* but it doesn't give you a hangover.'

'No, you just turn into an extra from the Matrix. And not the ones in the black outfits.'

I make a sigh of *what's the point*, reach for my tablet from Millie's oversized handbag. I think I hear Tom murmur, 'That's it, plug in the pacifier.' Okay, I do hear him say that. But I choose to ignore it. Switch it on all the same. I feel a kind of relief when – yay – I have plenty of messages and comments to trawl through.

Aaaah, one from Seth – butterflies, go! He's sent me a selfie; one brow cocked up. *Can't wait 4our minds n mouths 2finally meet. 6hrs & countin.*

Mouths. I swallow back a tidal rise of nerves. Silly. You're nearly seventeen. You've kissed loads of boys.

I flick over to Facebook. Millie's tagged me in some charity-awareness thing. She's always seeking sponsorship for some cause. 'How you're seen on social media, is how you're *seen*,' she says.

'Look,' I say to Tom. 'Shall we do this? I've been nominated to video myself shouting out three things I love, in a public place!'

Tom enlarges his eyes like I've just suggested we jump from the moving train.

'Everyone's doing it!'

'So says the lemming.'

I don't know why – I should be offended. But the way he says it, that dry edge to his tone, there's something nostalgic about it (is nostalgia even healthy? Google it) – and without meaning to, I laugh.

And my laughing – that makes him smile. *Yes*, Tom Riley smiles . . . a real smile, from years back.

And for just a moment there, a knife twists inside me: *what am I doing?*

Him

The train announcer broadcasts Vauxhall next stop. Tom starts to get up, watching Hope put her tablet and her phone and her make-up bag away. As they wait by the train doors, he questions for the millionth time why he's letting Hope and her plastic positivity, *Life's great!*, accompany him.

Does she really think she can save him?

Worse – why does a small part of him feel pleased she wants to?

He glances at her sideways as the train slows into the station. She's holding that fixed smile on her round face, stretching her lips so it emphasises the dimple in her chin. Dressed so bloody inappropriately for serving breakfast. The Hope he used to know dressed more like a boy than a girl. Is she in there somewhere? The Hope whose dad was always having a go at her; teachers forever telling her off? The Hope who once turned her mum's washing line into a zip wire?

He hears her draw a sharp breath as they step out onto the busy platform. Her eyes darting behind them as if she's seen someone she knows. She says she's fine when he asks, but she grabs on tight to the side of his dad's jacket until they reach street level. He almost regrets it when she lets go.

They cross the junction under the shadow of the MI6 building, looming like Oz's Emerald City. His dad said it was his dream place to get locked in. 'All those secrets, Tom.' He said that the last time they came here, to serve lamb roast at the shelter over Easter. Tom's stomach clenches. *Was Dad having his affair back then?*

He can't bear it; he reaches back into his bag for his Ribena bottle.

Her

Tom's drinking again. His eyes are going glassy, his walk's turning into more of a shamble. I'd be lying if I don't admit I'm starting to feel a little panicked. Especially after thinking I spotted that nasty Slicer man at the station. The same straggly hair and foil-shiny jacket. It can't have been him. Or if it was, it must be a coincidence.

'Over there,' Tom slurs, pointing at a wide green door in the arches beneath the train tracks. There's a whoosh and rattle of metal as carriages travel overhead. Pigeons coo noisily once the train passes. It's dirty and smells of wee. And there are horrid posters stuck to the brick wall that the street cleaners must have missed. Anti-*Leata* propaganda from that crazy PAL network.

We're buzzed in via a security door. Down a corridor, past slim cabin-sized doors. 'The pods where residents sleep,' Tom explains as I peer into an open one.

'I thought they slept in dormitories.'

'It's not the army,' Tom answers, moving through another door into a canteen area full of people. I hold my breath readying myself for a stench of the unwashed. Releasing it, the air smells normal. Of food mostly. And I'm pleased it's clean. And bright. Apple-green chairs and pale blue walls, as if it's mimicking nature. Shame then about the occupants. They couldn't be less cheerfully dressed if they tried; clothes dark and well worn. Most sit alone; a few coupled together, talking quietly. No one seems to be having much fun. There's not a *Leata* poster in sight to inspire them to change their lives. *Positivity yields prosperity*, someone should remind them. If you're negative, you'll never get out of here!

I stay close to Tom, weaving through white wooden tables. I wish he wouldn't keep stopping to shake someone's hand; scratch that Labrador's chin. Now he's pausing to chat with some man, asking him how he's doing. As if he's one of them!

A girl with blonde dreadlocks tugs on my sleeve. Her eyes are more glazed than Tom's. 'Hi, I'm Aggie. Who are you?' she says. She can't be much older than me, but her skin's almost grey, weather-beaten. 'Hope.' I smile, tight-lipped. I don't want to get caught in a conversation. Though maybe I should offer her a strip of my *Leata*. They'll be good for the messages even if she doesn't take the pills.

Tom's on the move again. I trail him into a kitchen out back. It reeks of grilling bacon. A large woman with purple hair and a ring through her nose is cracking eggs into a pan on an industrial-sized oven. Wearing a black apron with CREW written in pink, she greets Tom like he's a long-lost relative,

85

'Stranger, where've you been all my life!' pulling him to her, squashing him against her sizeable chest. I can hear her mumbling things about his dad. How sorry she is. *Etcetera. Etcetera.* I wonder about intervening – *isn't that my job here?* Tom's protector? Because, really – it's not helpful, people reminding him about his dad. When what Tom needs to do is forget.

'Mikey! Tom's here,' the woman yells and a slight, dirty-tanned man in a denim shirt appears from another door. His small, crinkly eyes mimic the tight black curls on his head. He walks with a limp, one leg dragging stiffly behind him like a punt. If I'm honest, he looks like he should be telling fortunes, not feeding the homeless.

I step back a little, feeling even more out of place.

This Mikey greets Tom with serious eyes before he turns to me. 'Well, what d'we 'ave 'ere!' he says, a sandpaper voice, the kind ravaged by tobacco.

'Brought yer girlfriend, Tom?'

I'm not sure who flushes a deeper red, me or Tom.

'This is Hope Wright,' Tom shrugs. 'My neighbour.'

Dirty-tanned man sucks in his breath as if my name offends him somehow. Lines appearing fan-like around his mouth. I look at Tom quizzically.

'I won't bite, girly,' Mikey laughs, revealing yellow teeth and a stench of cigarette smoke that almost makes me retch. I don't know anyone who smokes these days. 'How about you get an apron on and help Tammy 'ere?' He points at the woman with purple hair who's started singing along to some country tune on the radio. 'Tie yer 'air back, yeah?'

He steers Tom towards the door he came out of. 'Come and 'elp me with stock, Tom.' Making it pretty clear, I'm not welcome to follow.

Him

Mikey pulls an arm round Tom's shoulders, guiding him into the room of supplies just beyond. 'What've you brought 'er for?' he says as he shuts the door behind them, tugging him over behind shelves with giant tins of baked beans. 'Jack Wright's kid? Really, Tom?'

'She's harmless. We used to be friends. She thinks she's helping me "find happy", that's all.' Tom pulls a pretend frantic face. Relaxing it, he adds, 'Why didn't you want Jack Wright to see you yesterday?'

''E's the lawyer for PharmaCare, in't 'e? I just don't want to go causin' trouble fer St Paddy's. Things are bad enough. I'd be shut down like the rest if I didn't get my money from other means,' Mikey pulls a roll-up from behind his ear, curving his hands round to light it as if there's a wind about. 'My residents rely on me, I'm all they've got, yeah? What with their meth no longer being prescribed. Or any benefits they can get being cut. They're being cast off, unless they sign up for some PharmaCare mental health treatment.'

'You mean taking *Leata*?'

'I mean gettin' serious treatment. PharmaCare own all of the country's Mental Health Trusts now, 'aven't you 'eard? And as they see it, those who *Leata* can't work on, drug addicts and the like – or those who won't take it but need welfare 'elp – they get a different kind of treatment.'

Tom pulls his face back. 'What kind?'

Mikey shrugs. 'I dunno. Any of my guys who've signed up for it, I've never seen again.'

'I've not heard of this going on.'

'Of course you ain't. The press ain't reporting it. Who wears what at the Oscars is of more interest to the public than how the government are sellin' out the 'omeless, drug addicts, those who live on the edges of society. It was this kind of dirt yer dad was always trying to kick up.'

'Things are messed up, Mikey.'

'Tom, my boy, everything's always messed up. That's why I provide a roof and warm dinners.' Mikey takes a deep inhale, blowing out smoke in a straight line. 'Listen, I don't know anything about yer dad meetin' someone the day and place 'e died.' He pulls small pieces of tobacco from his mouth. 'But I do know 'e was treadin' in some serious shit. You've got to watch yerself, Tom.'

His words set Tom's heart pounding; igniting the sleeping headache in his head thumping behind his eyes.

'What story was he doing? I mean, he was forever tweeting anti-*Leata* stuff, but no national newspaper would pay him to do a story on *Leata* any more, not since he was gagged by the libel trial five years ago.'

'Maybe,' Mikey waves his cigarette. 'But that didn't stop Matt poking deeper in the dirt. ''E thought 'e was gettin' to the truth at last.'

Tom makes a confounded face. Blood pumps faster through his body. 'The truth?'

Mikey sucks hard on his roll-up, exhaling smoke sideways. 'You know I 'elped yer dad from time to time, with information yer might not get from usual means – way back when he was on the *Daily Herald*.'

Tom nods, even though he didn't know that.

'Right. Well, 'e'd still bounce things off me now and again, ask me to do some diggin' with 'im. I never made it my business to ask Matt questions. Only ever asked for a donation to this place, all right?' Mikey looks around as if he's checking for anyone listening; takes a hard drag from the roll-up, his mouth puckering. '. . . 'E were startin' to investigate another theory. One that's been kickin' around underground for a while. The possible long-term side effects of *Leata*.'

Tom swallows, his mouth is going desert-dry. He ticks his head for 'go on'.

'Yer dad thought, if people won't listen to 'ow the drug's alienatin' the vulnerable, doin' dodgy deals with government, maybe they'll listen if they find out it's directly 'armful to them.' Mikey rubs at his stubble. ''E seemed to think 'e were on the cusp of revealin' summit big . . . but you never knew with Matt. 'E could get all excited like a big kid one moment. Deflated the next.'

Tom nods. He remembers that.

'And then this contact in PharmaCare who 'e were hasslin' for information.' Mikey crosses himself across the chest, his expression darkening. 'The bloke died suddenly, didn't 'e.'

'What do you mean "suddenly"? Like suspiciously?' Tom almost chokes on the idea.

'Matt thought so. He was nervous. Paranoid. Said it were because 'e were finally gettin' proof about *Leata*'s dark side.' Mikey looks at Tom thoughtfully. 'That crash yer dad 'ad, you remember?'

'Yeah, he got banged into in London.' He remembered his dad getting tetchy with his mum for complaining about garage costs. He'd originally thought that was what had sparked his dad leaving.

'Nah.' Mikey shakes his head thoughtfully. 'Nah, Matt didn't reckon that were any accident. 'E thought it were a warnin': to back off. Soon after, yer mum got sent those photos. Okay,' Mikey puts his palms up, 'so yer dad was a naughty boy. But someone sent those photos on purpose an' I don't believe it was the lady's angry 'usband.'

Tom starts chewing on his thumbnail; his heart's beating double fast. 'So who was Dad's PharmaCare contact?'

Mikey shakes his head. Flicks ash onto the floor. 'Like I said, didn't ask questions, did I. Matt said the less I knew the safer it were fer me. 'E was hopin' the *Daily Herald* would buy it if 'e got more evidence. Talked about givin' it as an exclusive to some journalist mate of 'is.'

Tom's breath is coming fast. 'Ralph,' Tom almost whispers. 'It'll be his friend Ralph.' He digs his hands into his hair. 'So you think PharmaCare was threatening Dad? What if they *were* behind those photos sent to Mum? And this dead source – what's that about?'

'Oi.' Mikey lifts a hand, tapping it against Tom's cheek lightly as if he's trying to wake him up. 'Don't go addin' up two and two and makin' five. I don't know what was real, and what was your dad's paranoia. I dunno what 'e found out. Better for me and you that way . . . you and I don't want to be wadin' through that shit. Not if you value yer life, and I value St Paddy's. Get me?'

Mikey's features soften. 'Listen, I'm only tellin' you what I know because chances are PharmaCare'll be watchin' you and yer family, checkin' the dirt your dad kicked up 'as settled. So watch your step. Yeah? I'm not tellin' you this stuff to start you down the same path 'e went on. I'm tellin' you so you don't step on to it.'

'But what if . . .?' Tom can feel his whole body trembling.

'What if, what if . . . if you say it enough times you start to fear things that aren't there.' He puts a hand on Tom's shoulder, staring directly into his eyes. 'Uncoverin' people's secrets is a dirty business.' Mikey draws a long smoky breath. 'People don't like bein' stripped bare. Especially when there's money and power involved. We don't know anythin' really, Tom. Except your dad was scared.' Mikey plucks the end of his cigarette out of his mouth, flicking it on the floor and grinding it with his thick boot. 'Right now – we've got important people to feed. Cos whatever yer dad found out about *Leata*, I know this much: if you 'ave problems but you don't take that drug, this government don't want to know you. I've got me 'ands full now other shelters are closin'.'

Dazed, Tom starts following Mikey back into the kitchen, two giant bean tins in either arm. The shutters are up between the canteen and kitchen ready for serving. Mikey nudges him. 'Do me a favour, if the police come callin' again – don't mention what I said. Better still, don't talk to anyone about it, yeah? Certainly not girly over there.'

Tom glances at Hope. Her hair drawn into a ponytail, she's wearing a 'crew' apron, loaves of bread and a toaster in front of her, but she's staring at her phone rather than working. Still distracted by her screen life. A small rage sparks inside him.

Her

I am exhausted! Thank god I brought my make-up bag with: my whole face has slid off with sweat from serving hot food.

'I like your jacket,' the girl called Aggie says after I reluctantly agree to wipe down the tables after the food's finished. 'Where's it from?'

I don't want to make her feel bad so I lie and say somewhere high-street cheap. I speak in a tone especially perky, because it might rub off on her. I consider maybe taking the blazer off and giving it to her. It would be the nice thing to do, if I didn't need to wear it to meet Seth. I give her one of my blog cards I had made up instead. 'Follow me,' I say brightly, giving her benefit of my full smile. She'd probably best get her teeth fixed before she copies it though.

'Will I see you again?' she says as I finish working.

I make a happy face. 'Maybe!' I lie. I mean, I can't come here again. Isn't it best I don't think about this kind of stuff?

Tom pulls away from talking quietly with Mikey as I head back into the kitchen. Mikey puts a thin cigarette in his mouth and leaves, muttering, 'Fag break'.

'Everything all right?' I ask. Tom's looked sort of cross since he came back out of the stock room.

He fidgets his shoulders. 'Yeah. Everything's fine.'

Well that's something at least. There's nothing more to report to Dad since I texted him earlier in the kitchen. Though Tom still looks like he's got some crime scene to resolve. But right now, I can't be of help to him. 'I have to go, sorry,' I say. I need time to re-apply and re-brush. Thinking of my promise to Dad, I add, 'Can we get the train home together?' using a tone that implies Tom'll be helping me out. 'I'll be done for the 7.10.' Done? Will I have a status change for Facebook? I giggle nervously in my head.

I leave some of my blog cards at the security desk. Snapping a selfie of me doing this to include in my post update later. Maybe I should do more of this – community help – though not with homeless people. Vulnerable children maybe – they are always happy.

7

If you think you're the best,
others will too!
Leata

Her

I'm so glad to be out of that place. Back into life, sunshine
and smiles. Okay, admittedly, there's not a lot of either on the
underground to King's Cross, but there are PharmaCare adverts
all over my carriage to reassure me. '*Leata. Because we all need
help on life's journey.*' I like that one. Another's promoting a
PharmaCare Health Farm. They run all kinds. Mum went to
a smokers' one; Tara's at the teen version. She should be back
at school by Monday. Happy again!

I twist my neck: the picture above my head advertises
PharmaCare Aesthetics. '*Stay young. Stay happy.*' The
small print recommends you book a consultation after you
turn twenty-five. I remember Millie saying she's made her
appointment already!

A smartly dressed woman across from me is popping a pill.
I reach for my own. Why not? I need a little extra to get over

this morning. Tom, those people at the shelter, how can they get life so wrong? It's like they *want* to be miserable.

At King's Cross station, heaving with travellers, I cross the concourse to the toilets. Facing myself at the mirrors, I have to virtually re-do all my make-up! Spray on perfume (to cover up the smell of bacon); brush my hair till it's glossy again. I straighten my back to walk tall as I leave. *'If you think you're the best, others will too!'* Big, big smile for the toilet attendant to cheer her up, because, let's face it, she looks depressingly glum.

I head towards the station exit. A group of tourists rush past me talking excitedly about platform nine and three quarters. And that does it – Tom rudely nudges his way back into my head space – it was the last thing we did together, to come and pay homage here ourselves, aged eleven. I squeeze my mind shut. It's Seth I've got to think about now. My future. I walk out onto the pedestrianised strip where nursery-age children are squealing as they jump and dart through water fountains like it's a second summer. They wear high-vis vests with *Leata* messages. If *Leata* could sponsor the weather, it would be summer all year round. I keep smiling to set my mood perma-happy, and make my way towards the glass building beyond. The silver sign of PharmaCare glints in the sun, *Leata*'s familiar blue and yellow branding beneath. I feel so proud to be a part of their corporate family.

I get my phone out, pretending to talk into it, as I pass through the revolving glass doors – as one of their sponsored bloggers I need to look *in demand, ever-busy!* I love this foyer; it always makes me feel like I've arrived. Dorothy at Oz! Charlie at the Chocolate Factory! Everything about it shines and brims with happiness. The receptionists, all blue and yellow uniforms, look as if they've just been taken out of their wrapping.

In fact I adapted my new smile from theirs my first visit. I've been here about eight times for the Blogger Quarterlies now. When I first got my sponsorship two years ago, they did a little ceremony for me and other bloggers like me. So cute. *Realboystuff*'s meteoric success has meant Seth's only recently got their sponsorship.

After badging me up, one perfectly manicured nail points me to the seating area of funky blue and yellow chairs. There are beanbags too, like the ones they have at school, and video game consoles and table football. Piped *Leata* radio ads compete with live news from Star Media, on the super-giant television above the reception desk. I'm home.

Him

His mind's jumping all over the place on the train ride over to Clapham. Images whipping round like a tornado in his mind, fear rippling under his skin: Dad maybe knew something big about *Leata*? And his PharmaCare source died suddenly? Does that mean . . .? He takes another slug from the Ribena bottle to stop that one spinning on a cycle in his head – he can't think like that. Not yet.

The Tube stops. *And why did Ralph not tell me about Dad's Leata story at the funeral?* storms his head as he drifts along in the swell of passengers from the platform to the exit. Outside, he sucks in warm air. The weather's become almost prickling hot. His skin's already damp with sweat, but he doesn't want to take Dad's jacket off. His head aches from too much whisky as he stumbles his way round the edges of the common towards Ralph's road. Still, he keeps drinking more.

At the door, he drains the bottle. *Why would Ralph not tell me?* He flexes his fists, trying to put a lid on his frustration. Rings the bell.

Ralph's older son, Ollie, comes to the door. They used to hang out lots when they were younger, camping trips, weekend barbeques, but they hardly know each other now, except for the odd 'like' on Facebook.

'Hi.' Tom tries to check the slur in his voice. 'Your dad in?' He pushes a hand back through his hair, suppresses a belch. His insides feel raw.

'Hey. Yeah – Dad! Tom's here. Hey, are you all right?'

Tom tries to nod, but it makes Ollie spin and multiply. He bends over, hands to knees, gulping in breath. Tears start to roll down his cheeks.

'Tom, what you doing here?'

Tom straightens up at the sound of Ralph. Too quick. His stomach replies for him.

A bucketful of what looks like orange Tango shoots out of his mouth, drenching Ralph's trousers, splattering his shoes.

Until everything goes fuzzy, grey . . . black.

Her

A few others have joined me till we're a group of about forty or so. Some I've met at past Quarterlies, a few I've done guest vlogs with. I recognise the *Positiveandperky* girl and, oh look, that's *Bestthingsincehappymeals*.

My heart's been steadily thumping harder against my ribcage,

97

waiting for Seth to arrive. He's still not here by the time two executives come to collect us, high patent heels clipping across the floor. Perfect lipstick on perfect smiles.

'Hi, great to see you again, *Livelifewithhope*,' the taller one says. They like to name us by our blogger titles. Today I *am* my blog not me. What am I talking about – my blog is me!

The group separates into two lifts. I *so love* their mirrored doors dotted with little messages. '*You have beauty in all kinds of ways*'. '*You can be as great as you want to be.*' '*Reflect back what you want others to see!*' They appear written over your clothes, your face. They have the desired effect. As the lift doors ping open at the penthouse floor I am (ha, literally), on top of the world.

And then I see him.

And my stomach shrinks in a sudden, unexpected panic.

Him

He opens aching eyes to meet another's, grey, searching his from above.

'You feeling any better, Tom? I thought it was best to let you sleep it off on the sofa,' Ralph says, 'Molly and the boys have gone out.'

Bolting up – head banging violently from motion – words rush out. 'Why didn't you say at the funeral when I asked?' His vision blurs. 'Dad was writing a *Leata* story? He was involved in some heavy shit? Knew something big? And his car bashed into? His source dead?'

'Hey, slow down, slow down.' Ralph pushes his palms out. 'Where d'you hear all this from?'

He remembers his promise to Mikey. Shakes his head. 'Doesn't matter who. I just did. And I know he spoke to you about it!'

'Ah hell, Tom,' Ralph pulls his palms back and drags them down his red stubble, stretching his face into a hound-dog. 'Your dad was filled with crazy notions. Was always sniffing around for a *Leata* scoop ever since that story five years ago got him sacked. Listen to me, first,' he adds as Tom jolts forward to speak. 'I know all about your dad hassling a *source*.' He makes speech marks in the air. 'A source who subsequently had a heart attack. A heart attack, Tom. I also know your dad was never that good a driver. That he had a prang on the A3. Your dad made the choice to come up with a mad theory about it.'

Tom collapses his head into both hands. Inside, a fierce battle is ensuing from either side, meeting in the middle. Neither side winning. He looks up again. 'Okay, answer this one then: Dad's calendar had an appointment to meet someone at Richmond Park, the day he died.'

Ralph's face screws up. 'Who?'

'There was no name.'

Recognition passes slowly across Ralph's face, loosening his muscles. 'Tom, kiddo, I think you just found your dad's appointment with himself. It's like your dad, to write down the time and place . . . that he was going to . . . his final headline.'

Something hard and sharp grips Tom's insides. *Why hadn't he thought of that?* Already he can sense the surrender in his guts.

Ralph releases a long sigh, slumping down on the sofa next to him. 'Here, I got you these.' He passes water and aspirin from the coffee table.

Tom takes both, knocking the pills back with a large gulp of water – too fast, his stomach curdles again. He takes short breaths to stem another rise of nausea. 'Sorry about your clothes.'

'Don't sweat over it,' Ralph cuts his hands through the air. 'Where've you been drinking though, Tom? Who serves a sixteen year old?'

'Seventeen tomorrow.'

'I know, the card's already in the post. But that doesn't mean you should be drinking like this – alone? In the daytime? It's no way to deal with grief, Tom.'

Tom's hands grip round the water glass like he might crack it. 'Last thing – "Cloud 9". Did Dad send a story to you with that title?'

'No, it doesn't ring any bells. I never received any stories from Matt. Only the occasional email with some outlandish theory. I never took any of it seriously.'

'But Mikey said Dad was going to give you his story as an exclusive?'

Ralph looks startled. 'As in Mikey Jones at St Patrick's?' He swings his head low. 'Hell, Tom, don't trust a word that man says. He used to fleece your dad, getting him to make donations for his shelter just to ask some dodgy questions of shady people. Ask your mum, she knows all about that. It was her well-earned cash your dad used. Mikey's out for himself, a troublemaker.'

Tom squeezes his eyes shut against this new version of Mikey. He remembers his mum and dad rowing about regular payments Dad gave to St Patrick's. 'But Mikey said Dad was getting to the truth – about the side effects of *Leata*.'

'What?' Ralph jumps up like he's fidgety. Going to the mantelplace, he adjusts the photo frames of his sons there. 'That nasty rumour's been doing the rounds for a while. There can't be any truth in it.' His expression is worried when he turns. 'What did Mikey say about that?'

'He didn't know anything more.'

Ralph chews on his mouth as if he's contemplating something. He sits back down. 'I dunno, Tom. Your dad was hell-bent on revenge against PharmaCare since they sued him at the *Daily Herald*. You know he was always spouting that stuff about government being in bed with *Leata*. Money passing hands.' He pushes both hands back over his hair, forcing his fringe up. The bruise from the funeral has faded to a faint yellow-green. He lets out a rueful laugh. 'PharmaCare has a defence wall thicker than Windsor Castle. How would Matt have got through it to find out any *truth* about side effects?'

Tom swallows; his throat feels scratched and raw from being sick. His body's aching like he's coming down with something. What Ralph's saying is starting to make more sense than Mikey.

'You're hurting, Tom. That's all this is. I feel your pain, you know.'

Tom pinches the skin between his eyes as Ralph's arm comes round his shoulders. His mind feels like it's gripped in a vice. *How can anyone feel my pain?*

Her

'Be the person you want to be, and you'll end up her.' That was what I lived by from Year Seven on. I would be that girl. The popular girl. The girl who wouldn't piss people off any more.

101

The girl Dad would praise and cuddle like he did Rose and Lily. That girl. The girl I'd never been when I hung out with Tom.

New school. New me.

And I've become *her*, haven't I? I please everyone now. Everyone likes me. I'm loved and I look and sound good.

So why, right now, standing here, almost stuck to the back of the lift doors, do I suddenly feel like old me? The troublemaker, the antagonist, the girl teachers and parents always found fault with?

The girl who was Tom Riley's best friend?

Staring over at Seth, surrounded by other bloggers like a celebrity, I can't stop picturing Tom.

I try counting down, numbering each of my blessings. But it does no good. I grapple inside my bag, take another *Leata*. Close my eyes tight shut, willing it to kick in. I've got to get a grip.

When I open them, he's stood in front of me.

'Having a moment?' he says, his mouth opening in a half-smile. Striped top and dark blue skinnies, his fringe flicked just-so, he might have strolled straight off a magazine shoot. '*Livelifewithhope* . . . in the flesh. Looking good.'

'Hey, Seth!' My voice comes out like a squeak. 'Yay, we meet at last!'

He tugs his phone out of his back trouser pocket, hugging me to him, arm out as he points it at us. 'Let's share with our followers: "*Realboystuff* and *Livelifewithhope* together at last".'

He smells nice up close. Hair gel and soap. But my stomach's still twisting. There's a fog in my head.

'I'll send it you now.'

He starts tapping onto his screen. So I do the same; receive the photo; share it on Twitter, Instagram, despite a tightening in my guts.

OMG! Guys I have finally met Seth Tuck!! Squeeeeeee!

I wish I could feel anywhere near as excited as my tweet. Tom has to exit my head. I need to salvage this moment! My future!

We're being called into a meeting room. There's about a hundred or so of us here. I try to keep smiling. Last resort – I repeat the Smurf song on a loop in my head, drowning out all other thoughts. Seth continues to get mobbed as we claim front-row seats. He and Emily, aka *Stateofhappiness*, are the ones the other bloggers want to collaborate most with.

Yet it's Livelifewithhope Seth's chosen to guest vlog today! I've got to relocate that excitement. I hear my phone going mad in my bag – that'll be my followers, my fangirls, my subscribers emoticon-screaming at the photo, sharing that Seth and Hope have met in the flesh at last!

The Marketing Director, Sofia, comes in, medieval-long jet-black hair and large thick-rimmed glasses. The kind you wear even if you don't need them. Because wearing those sort of glasses are so in. I make a mental note: buy some. Sofia's enthusiasm is feverish, though I can't quite be sure what she says, before she hands over to Toby, the Social Media Manager. The guy who sorts out our contracts and keeps a check on content. Since I last saw him, he's grown one of those cool beards boys in their twenties are wearing. His skinnies hang off his hips so I can see the top of his underpants. They're branded at the top with the *Leata* slogan. How cool is that?

103

He speaks as if he's talking in capital letters, starting nearly every sentence with OMG or LOL. He's such fun to listen to. I sneak a sideways glance at Seth. He's taking notes of everything Toby says on his iPad. I pull my tablet out, smile wider, harder as I start doing the same.

'LOL, look at my all singin 'n' a-dancin PowerPoint, people,' Toby opens his mouth dramatically. Everyone laughs. I join in a little too late.

Seth elbows me. He's written on his pad, *Can't wait for the Hope and Seth show*.

I make my smile girly sweet; widen my eyes as my stomach creases. Now I'm here, I'm not sure I'm ready for showtime.

What is going on with you, Hope Wright?

This morning . . . Tom, going to the shelter . . . it's messed with my settings. I just need to reboot.

'Yay, we love all these guest vlogs you're doing, people.' Toby is dancing about in front of us. 'Build a better platform for one another. Working together, in turn builds a better brand for y'all individually. Remember what we are about . . . '

Seth shoots his hand up into the air. 'Spreading happiness globally in ways other young people can relate to.'

'Yes!' Toby points his hand out as if Seth's just won the jackpot. 'We rely on you as *Leata* ambassadors to be the trendsetters. Look right, talk right.' He starts giggling. 'We *love* the geeky faces you pull; keeping it real. People LOVE attractive people pulling ugly faces, we've got statistics that prove that – it makes ordinary people feel connected to YOU. Oh and we'll soon be sending you more *Leata* branded clothing for your wardrobe. Do try and wear it on your vlogs. Run competitions

104

to win pieces on your blogs too. Even film yourselves chatting as you take your pill. *Leata* – it's an every day thing.'

His face turns mock-serious. 'Now, the bad news. There are still many bloggers and channels out there trying to bring the positivity down. Power Against Leata – it's an oxymoron, people! Still, the PAL network appears to be growing, and lately, growing fast.'

I tip my head in an intent-listening pose. I tend to block out the negativity so I've never looked at any PAL blogs. I don't even give trolls head space.

'Be aware of the enemy, guys.' Toby's face lights up again, 'Okay, special mentions!' he says. 'It goes without saying, all hail to *Happyaslarry*. He's too busy with his book tour to make it today, but let's show him some LOVE with our hands, people.' He star-jumps, pointing dramatically at *Jumpforjoy*. She's the workout queen. 'Your total has hit three million, girlfriend!'

Next, Toby leads *Positiveandperky* in a round of applause, before doing the same with 'fabulous newcomer *Realboystuff*. People behind slap and nudge Seth's shoulders. I try to look proud. I jump when I hear my name next. '*Livelifewithhope* – checked in with yours today. LOVING the case story.' Toby blows me a kiss. 'NAD Boy – that's what we want! Living proof how sad people are who are not on *Leata*. You HAVE to convert this NAD. Your followers expect it.' His eyes intensify as if he's ordering it like Dad. My chest tightens. What if I can't make Tom happy? I'm starting to think it's impossible.

I tune out, in . . . out again. My mind feels a muddle. It keeps darting back to the shelter, to that girl Aggie. What could have happened to her to become like that? Lurching back over to

Tom. He was looking so wired. What's he doing now? Maybe I should have stayed with him. Dad wanted me to. Dad cares about Tom more than I do.

Toby is wrapping up. His PowerPoint is switched off. 'Remember, guys: you are the best social creators out there but more follow in your wake. Don't get lazy,' he adds with a big smile and a wink. 'You WANT *Leata* sponsorship? Then keep what you put out there FRESH, relevant – even happy people can get bored easily – we need entertainment as well as education.'

There's lunch before we all leave, and a chance for a tour of the offices, but Seth turns to me the instant we move from the room and says, 'Shall we skip food and go make our video?' I'm struggling to think of an answer. Mainly because the right one's 'yes', but it's not sitting right on my tongue. He tucks my hair behind my ear. Wow. He touched me. Seth touched me. So shouldn't my stomach fizz? Butterflies, where are you?

'I'm only a ten-minute taxi ride away.' He holds out a hand for me to take, his fingers weaving with mine, palms pressing. He's so handsome. I really should be fizzing and fireworking now.

I notice the vlogger *Happythoughtsonly* nudging Seth as we pass towards the lifts. Seth winks back at him; winks again as we say goodbye to *Stateofhappiness* Emily. She's really pretty. She guest vlogged on Seth's channel last week.

Outside, he hails a taxi smoothly. We get in; he shuffles closer to me after giving the driver his address.

'So my agent –' he speaks low, softly.

'You have an agent?'

'Sure. Most successful vloggers are going down that route now. You not got one yet? Come on board with mine. It'll make it easier if we do end up getting any TV deals.'

I nod, try and smile. It feels crooked on my face. Seth touches my knee; slides a hand up my thigh. I wish I'd worn something less skin tight. I wish I was feeling something inside. Millie says her stomach goes crazy when Ryan even looks at her.

I try and talk to distract him, but he's on me before I see it coming. His lips pressing against mine. His hand up against my bum. Tongue now poking and gliding around as the taxi jerks forwards in heavy traffic. I've kissed plenty of boys since Tom. Loads. Tom again? Now? *That childish kiss between you two meant nothing!*

I try and pull away. 'I can't breathe,' I say.

Seth tugs me back closer. His hand now clamps to my breast, massaging it like it's dough. I don't like it. I really don't like it. His tongue's moving faster. 'Wait till we get to mine,' he mutters.

'No,' I shoot back. I'm breathing hard. His hand's still on my breast. I stare down at it. 'I can't . . . I can't.' That feeling is back, like someone's playing an accordion with my lungs. 'I think I need to get out.' No! You need to pull yourself together!

Seth removes his hand, his smile tugging downwards. 'What're you talking about? We've got a video to make. My subscribers are expecting you, waiting for me to post it. *Leata*'s Toby is well behind us. He suggested it. What are you playing at?'

Toby suggested it? I try and suck in air. The taxi smells of cheap pine air freshener. I'm starting to feel sick.

'I think we should do this another time. I'm not feeling well.' What am I doing? This is career suicide. Seth's going to be the biggest thing on the internet soon and he's picked me over *Stateofhappiness* or *Positiveandperky* to do his vlog with today.

He scowls. 'Your time is now, Hope. What are you: some sort of internet tease? All mouth no action?'

His hand grips my thigh, pinching it. It hurts. 'I thought this was what we were sharing today?'

'I just want to do this another time,' I plead. This isn't the same boy from *Realboystuff*.

'I'm here now. Take it or leave it.'

I have to take it. I lean into him, pulling him back, opening my mouth ready. I can do this. This is what I am about. I please people, don't I? I make people happy. I stopped being friends with Tom. I began taking *Leata*. I re-invented myself. I can't unravel all that hard work now!

Seth's hand is back groping my chest; the other up and down my leg. I have no butterflies; I have no fizzing in my stomach, no tingling in my groin. I just feel scared and empty. And ill.

I jolt away again. 'Stop the car,' I shout at the taxi driver. 'Now, please!'

It pulls into the side of the road. 'I'm sorry about this,' I'm bumbling.

I don't dare glance at the expression on Seth's face as he snipes, 'WTF?'

I stumble out of the taxi so fast that I trip over the kerb. I go flying. Sprawling half on, half off the pavement. I twist round, hearing my leather leggings rip on the bum. Seth's getting out

108

his phone, pointing it at me. No – is he really taking a photo? The taxi door slams; it drives away.

Him

He's been sat waiting at the agreed coffee shop at Waterloo for over an hour, facing a *Leata* banner advert above the platforms: '*Don't make any stops on the happy train!*' Propping up his aching head, he continues writing countless questions in his notepad, based on what Mikey and Ralph have said. He's already trawled the internet on his phone, but there are no real answers there except Ralph was right – his dad's 'side effects' accusation has already been made by the PAL network. Thousands of other anti-*Leata* voices across the globe spout fears over PharmaCare funding government, bribing doctors . . . Dad could have got any of his theories just from a few clicks on his computer. Some of the PAL members have been successfully sued like his dad and the *Daily Herald* were five years ago. Jack Wright's name appears a number of times as the lawyer winning cases for PharmaCare. They win, because there is no proof that substantiates any of these theories.

Tom sits back in his chair. *Does that mean the theories can't be true? Or they just have the best lawyers?*

He scans the concourse for Hope. His body itches to get home; to try and translate his dad's shorthand. To see if that reveals anything else. He takes a slurp of cold coffee and starts tapping out a text to Pavlin. Asking him to check with his cousin Hari on any *Leata* side effects threads he trusts. His mouth feels swollen on the inside from puking. His stomach still aches. He feels crap over what Ralph said about Mikey. But Ralph knew his dad best. *He was delusional* . . . A whole new image of Dad is starting to form, one at odds with the enthusiastic, passionate man Tom loved to be around, broken and beaten and possibly beside himself with revenge and paranoia.

Looking up again, he spots Hope walking towards him. She seems a faded version of the girl from this morning. Her hair is all over the place. Her pale blue blazer tied awkwardly around her waist. If it's possible for Hope, she looks upset. The forced smile has been wiped.

Unfortunately it grows again the minute she sees him; like she's putting a mask back on. Plastic perfect.

'Tom! Had a good day?'

He shrugs. There's no point telling her any of it. She'll only spin it positive. 'Did you?'

Her

What do I say to that? Flippin' awful? I lost it and made a fool of myself and I didn't like how Seth touched me and yet at the same time I'm mad at myself for jeopardising my collaboration with him? And my legs hurt from where I hit the pavement and my best leather leggings are torn in the worst place and I suddenly feel like crying, even though I haven't cried in years, except for happy tears at films and weddings.

'Every day's a good day!' I answer in the end. Smile über-brightly. Tom has to keep seeing me happy if he's ever going to embrace the light side himself. Even if I have to make things up (what are my ethics on that?). There are too many people expecting me to wave my magic wand over NAD Boy.

* * *

110

For once I'm pleased for Tom's sullen silence on the way back. Both my phone and tablet have run out of juice, which I'm glad about, as I won't be able to check on my followers waiting for further feedback on Seth. I've got to work out how I'm going to pitch that first.

I watch Tom scribbling furiously in his notepad. Paper and pen, like some ancient scribe.

The edges of my smile keep pulling south.

I really must be losing it because I even start thinking about blogging honestly when I get home. *I messed up with Seth because I didn't like the way he groped me* and *I don't know how I can help NAD Boy. What do I know about grief?*

I almost laugh out loud. How can I admit to that? When I'm the *Livelifewithhope* girl?

Him

He stares at his notepad. Writing down more questions on the train ride still isn't bringing answers. What about this source of Dad's who died? Was Mikey dramatising that? He glances up at Hope. She's smiling fixedly out of the window as if she's the Queen inanely acknowledging a stream of fans outside. Except there are only cows in the dusk-filled fields they're passing.

'Your dad – was he still on my dad's case over things he said on social media about *Leata*?'

Hope looks round. Her smile looks superglue-stuck to her face. 'What?'

'You heard.'

She makes a face as if she's pitying him. 'I very much doubt it.'

'But he didn't like Dad.'

'That's not true,' she seems to bristle, before correcting herself. 'I mean, your dad could infuriate him, playing his music so loud and letting his grass get overgrown. But the *Leata* libel case thing, that was water under the bridge. Dad was just doing his job.'

'As mine was doing his.'

Hope makes a pacifying face.

Tom adjusts his glasses. What he needs is a source like Mikey said his dad had. He needs an insider who can supply him with concrete answers. 'That girl Fran you mentioned . . . didn't her mum work for PharmaCare?'

'Still does. Nina Mitchell. She's Operations Director. She's Dad's main contact there.'

Tom tries to make a smile that looks natural. 'All right, tell Fran I'd like to meet her, if she still wants to hang out.'

He can't tell if Hope looks overjoyed or unsure. 'Yay. Great idea, Tom.' But her tone sounds excited. He feels a stab of, what? Disappointment? *Well, that'd be stupid.* 'I'll DM you her Facebook page. Get in touch with her ASAP. I *know* Fran will be super pleased to hear from you.'

'Super pleased,' Tom sounds back sarcastically, but with a smile after, because Hope doesn't seem to get he's joking. Or maybe it's just that there's something else going on – she still looks spooked. He'd offer her a slurp of whisky, but he's got none left. And after today, he's not sure he can touch the brown stuff again. Not for a day or two anyway.

Besides, now he's got another narcotic to distract him; it's starting to run through his veins, fill the cavernous hole in his heart. Even if Dad *was* delusional, he has to retrace the last steps of his life.

He has to make sure . . . PharmaCare had nothing to do . . . with why he killed himself.

SECRETS

Secrets are the stuff that sits quietly between lies and truths. People learn to keep them so that we protect the truths that matter and lie about what hurts.

Matt Riley

8

Your expressions are your gearstick.
So smile and get in the fast lane!
Leata

Her

Hope wakes suddenly as if a hand has come out to shake her.
Her heart beating fast for some distant reason. Getting up,
she switches on her tablet and phone from where they're
charging on her desk.

Straightaway, they start vibrating, buzzing, pinging with
incoming.

She opens the most recent text – it's from Millie. The latest
in a whole load of messages.

& u don't want 2even lk @Twitter

It's enough for Hope to go there first without reading any more.

A hard ball takes a slug against her stomach, as she stares
at Seth's feed.

Why would he post that?

Above a link to his channel is another to a photo of
Hope, sprawled over the kerb; her expression horror-struck.

Twisted. Ugly. The tear in her trousers revealing pink knickers beneath.

Already it's been retweeted thousands of times since last night. Tears pricking her eyes, she clicks around. It's being shared on Facebook. Instagram. Pinterest. Discussed on Tumblr. Comments are appearing thick and fast . . . people calling her what the trolls do, what Fran did this week . . . *Hopeless*. Many call her worse. Four-letter worse.

She clicks through to Seth's channel. Her breath is coming in short bursts, drying her throat. The vlog he posted last night has 1,538,351 views so far . . . and counting.

Something inside her head says, *Don't watch it*, but her finger taps 'play' all the same.

'*Livelifewithhope* or *Hopeless*?' he's saying. *The name-calling starts with him?* Her hand clasps her mouth as her windpipe fills with nausea. 'Funny how some people are not what you expect when you meet them in real life. And I don't like that!' Seth jumps around on screen, pulling 'cutely vexed' onto that handsome face. '*Livelifewithhope* is one fast girl. Seriously folks, she wouldn't take NO for an answer. Desperate or what? She *fell* from a great height.' He grins cheekily, pushing his phone forward with her photo that's fast going viral. 'Showed her true colours, you know!' He spreads his arms out. He's wearing a *Leata* T-shirt. The message: '*Your expressions are your gearstick. So smile and get in the fast lane!*'

'We don't want to make social media false, do we? We want to keep it real. Take me – what you see is what you get!' He pulls another cute face for the camera. 'Guys! Ship me somewhere finer next time!

'Like. Ship. Me. To . . .' He pulls someone onto screen. *Stateofhappiness* Emily. She's giggling away next to him. Hope's hand tightens round her mouth. The tears start to rush out. He must have gone back to get Emily after leaving her sprawled on the kerb.

A direct message flicks up in the corner of her tablet. Millie again.

Damage limitation Hope. You're losing followers.

She swallows back the tears, swiping hurriedly over to her own channel. Her subscribers . . . they're starting to decrease. Tapping onto her blog. The same there.

Followers who only yesterday were brimming over with love, calling her beautiful and the best, like loyal subjects to her royalty – now they're making comments as if she's failing them. As if she's not who they thought she was.

She breathes slowly, counting down from ten . . . but only gets to six before she moves over to her jewellery box. Manic, trembling hands pick out the silver strip. For once, she doesn't take time over the ritual, swallowing back two – fast – without even pausing to check the messages. Her hand pressing against her head as if she can contain her panicking thoughts somehow, she starts pacing her room, trying to work out *how* she limits damage. Picking up her phone, she thinks about calling Millie for more advice, but something tells her Millie might be enjoying this. Why else add smiley faces to her messages? By tonight Millie could be ahead in follower totals.

'You need to update me. Now.'

Hope glances round sharply. She didn't hear him come in. Frantically, she rubs tears away from her face in case he asks.

She doesn't want Dad to know she's failed. She doesn't want him disappointed in her.

'I'm in a hurry,' her dad says, his eyes fixing on her impatiently, before grazing her room as if it displeases him somehow. She looks around with him. It's tidy. It's always tidy now. Like *Leata* advises. Ordered house. Ordered mind. She's not the messy girl she used to be. She hasn't been that girl for five years.

His eyes fly back to hers, serious, yet distracted. It makes her exam-nervous; she can't fail him. Her words tumble out after one another. 'Sorry –' she stutters, 'you weren't here last night. There's not much more to add to what I texted. Tom went to see this man Mikey – a friend of Tom's dad. And I had to feed homeless people and –'

'Slowly, Hope! And I'm not interested in the homeless.'

'Sorry.' Her phone's vibrating in her hand. Her tablet making noises on her desk. She switches both off. Takes a breath. 'This Mikey – he seems to care about Tom. Nothing more. Though Tom seemed agitated the whole time. But that could be because he's drinking lots. He needs help, Dad.'

Her dad bites down on his mouth, hands on hips, staring at the floor like he's deep in painful thought. His eyes register hers again. 'We're aware of this Mikey fellow. He's a nasty piece of work by all accounts. You need to keep a close check on any dealings he has with Tom.' He walks over to the window, staring out onto the Rileys' back garden. 'Mikey Jones's got a list of criminal prosecutions bigger than your mother's credit card bill.'

Hope forces a laugh. He makes a face as if it's no laughing matter, stepping back closer to her. She breathes in her favourite aftershave and wonders if she can tell him about Seth after all. He'd be mad, wouldn't he? That someone had treated his daughter like this? She wills his arms to lift up around her as he continues, 'You see, Matt Riley, he was a troublemaker. Inciting terrorism – of the emotional kind. We were building a case against him. Tom's very vulnerable right now. People like Mikey might try and use Tom to carry on his dad's work, to gather libel against PharmaCare.

'When you're not at school, you shadow Tom from now on. You hear me? I want to know where Tom goes and who he sees. It's your job to keep Tom safe.' He makes a small, serious smile.

It soothes Hope's shredded stomach. She's starting to assemble the words to tell him about Seth. But he's already turning, walking out the door as if he has somewhere to go fast. 'Make me proud, Hope,' he says on his wake.

'I will, Dad,' she shouts after him. She will. Proud. Like Rose makes him.

She turns her tablet back on. She should do something; hair, make-up . . . video herself in her cute kitten PJs her followers always say they '*love!*' Laughing, big grin, 'oops' eyes . . . 'Look who forgot to take her *Leata*, yesterday! What a ditz!' Then turn it serious, like a public information broadcast: 'Warning to you all – this is what can happen when you forget!' Take the blame – don't turn it back on Seth. Who would believe her now anyway?

She wipes fresh tears from her eyes. First, she needs to calm down. No way can she look like she's been crying, like she's sad. She stares at her home screen. Something about today's date pinches inside her mind. Until it hits her. It used to be a date she remembered like Christmas. Exactly a week before hers, they used to plan a private celebration together midway between.

Her mind jumps in a new direction. Making Dad proud – that's all that matters, isn't it? She starts getting dressed.

Him
'Again? It's Sunday, and you went in yesterday.' I stand in the kitchen doorway, watching Mum rush round the room, shoving stuff into her bag amongst the debris and dirty dishes that never gets tidied or cleared up these days.

'I have so much to catch up on, Tom, from being off for two months. I won't be long. You just relax. Order take out, watch films. Get your friends over.' She stops and gives me that appealing face she wears a lot these days. The one that says she *has* to go into the office, because she *has* to get away from this house – and its memories of Dad, everywhere.

'It's just you're going in earlier all the time, and getting back later.'

She comes over to me, placing a hand on my chest. 'You mustn't worry about me.'

I stare back at her gaunt, grey face, into the eyes that are permanently bloodshot. I want to help her.

I have no idea how to help her. I'm trudging through the same sinking sand.

All I can do is not remind her, it's my birthday (I scooped up all the cards on the doormat when I got back yesterday). And not weigh her down with what I've been up to. Keeping more of Dad's secrets and lies to myself. That's what I can do.

We're swimming apart in the deep blue sea. But at least I've found a new way to keep afloat.

'What's this you're wearing?' Mum's fingering my jacket before backing away as if it's contagious, blinking furiously.

'It's Dad's,' I answer, though she knows that already. 'I can take it off if you prefer?'

She shakes her head, but speeds up getting ready to leave.

Once she's gone, I start tidying up the kitchen a bit. Anything to distract me from thinking about the fuss Dad would make over birthdays. Mum was conservative: a card and whatever you asked for. Dad was the balloons and surprises and cake for breakfast and daft extras from those innovation catalogues that advertise gifts you really don't need. Like the universal remote control or the sofa arm drink holder.

I finish washing up and get a mug of coffee, trying to resist adding whisky to it. My hands shake from sobriety, but my head still hurts from yesterday's binge. I glance at the clock. I'm not sure how long I'll last without it. I'll try and give it till lunchtime at least. I need to keep my mind clear to think. *Think*.

Last night, I started translating Dad's notebook, using some shorthand translation on the internet. It took bloody ages to do just a few pages, only to find out that a local youth centre had closed because it refused *Leata* funding. Hardly a big secret.

I'll go upstairs soon and translate the rest. That's all I can do right now. Until I hear anything from Pavlin's cousin Hari. Or meet that Fran girl – she's already messaged me back on Facebook, *I'd love to meet with you, Tom*. I slot some bread into the toaster. I feel suddenly starving now I've not started the day with alcohol. Waiting for the toast, I retrieve my notebook from yesterday. I flip through the notes I made as I butter; start eating. And stop. *Was Dad's crash an accident?* I've written.

What about Dad's car? I throw the toast down. It was at the garage getting fixed from Dad's bump – did it ever even come back? I think I've got a vague memory of Nathaniel driving it into our garage during the worst of the fog, a few weeks after Dad died.

I go into the hall, searching the bowl where we keep all the keys. Something inside of me lifts when I find they're there. I head outside fast, across the driveway to the garage. Only Dad used the garage because he hardly drove his car. I've not been inside since.

Swinging up the doors, my stomach jumps and dives simultaneously as I stare at Dad's silver Golf – sitting there as if Dad's just turned up home. A blast of yearning for him charges into my chest. The last time I was in his car was a couple of weeks before he died. It was one of the lessons he'd started giving me. Dad was determined I take my test the minute I turned seventeen. 'Taste the freedom of a set of wheels as soon as, son.' Empty car parks, wastelands . . . on the driveway and even up and down our private road until one of the Neighbourhood Watch mafia complained. Probably Jack Wright.

I unlock the door. Sit down in the driving seat; shove the key into the ignition. Dad's The Smiths CD kicks in. '*Heaven knows I'm miserable now*'. But the rest – it's been cleaned out – did the garage do that? The mess Dad left like a trail of destruction in his wake, is all gone. They've even removed the smell of Dad, the faint whiff of a sneaky cigarette, the mints he always had on him. *Keep your breath sweet and people will want to listen to you, Tom . . . and your mum won't get suspicious about my other habit.* I can picture Dad's half-smile as he said it. I think of the affair – just how much of himself did Dad hide from Mum with mints and clever words?

Ah shit, Dad. I rest my head on the steering wheel. *I don't want to think badly of you.* Not now.

I jump as a knock rattles the glass.

She comes into view, bending down by the passenger window, hand waving manically, mouth sounding out-of-tune Happy Birthday lyrics. Her eyes look a little red, but aside from that she's her usual perky, fake-smiling self.

She climbs in without an invite. 'Confession! I only remembered when I looked at today's date! Sorree – *no* time to get you anything!'

I pull my body away from her exclamation overdrive. 'Hope, you've never got me anything for my birthday in five years.'

'Past is past. We're in the present now.' I almost expect her to chime next: 'and the future's bright'. But instead her expression turns sorrowful. 'How are we after yesterday?'

'Royal "we"?'

'How are *you*, Tom?'

I don't answer. She's clearly taken her happy pill recently. I don't talk pill language.

'So what're you doing in here?' She gazes around. 'Garages are such gloomy places. This music doesn't help. Shall we change it?' She starts fiddling with the wrong knobs. The sat nav blinks on.

I glance sharply at Hope, back to the dashboard. 'Shit, why didn't I think of that?' I lean over, hurriedly tapping to recent

125

destinations. There are only two plugged in. The top one is dated. 10 June. Three weeks BDD. I tap it and the red arrow hovers over some place near Windsor.

'Who'd your dad know there?' Hope says idly.

I turn the key in the ignition, the engine hums awake.

'Tom, what are you doing?'

The sat nav woman tells us to turn left at the end of the driveway. 'What does it look like I'm doing?'

'It might be your dad's chiropractor, for all you know!'

'Dad only ever used the car when he had to. He was an environmentalist.' I balk at the patheticness of that statement – Dad was lots of things I thought he was. 'When he used the car it was always for a good reason. It's not like I'm asking you to come with.'

Her

She slams a hand against her chest. *What is Tom playing at?* 'You've only turned seventeen *today*, Tom. You can't drive.'

'The things Hope Wright doesn't know about me because we've not been friends for five years,' he breathes out, hurriedly jamming in his seatbelt. 'Starting with: I *can* drive. It's just a matter of a test, and I'll prove it by dropping you off at yours.' He starts reversing the car out of the garage, swinging it round.

Sat nav woman repeats her instruction, competing with the music. Something depressing from Tom's dad's era. 'Tom – you can't just drive there. We'll get the train.'

'We?'

'Tom, it's illegal to drive without a licence!'

126

'Thank you for the reminder, Constable Wright.' He stops the car, extending his arm, palm flattened for 'get out'.

Hope looks back over at her house. She thinks of the spectators crowding round on the internet – readying to watch her go under the guillotine. She thinks about what Dad said. Shadow Tom, take care of him. He needs taking care of. 'What if the police pull you over?'

He shrugs. 'I'll lie, pretend to be Nathaniel. I already have his licence.'

Hope laughs instinctively. 'When did you become the bad boy? I thought it was me who was the wayward one.' She bites down on her lip. Did she really just say that? *The past is past, Hope. Don't let what Seth's done unhinge you!*

She catches Tom staring at her like she's just spoken a foreign language. Her stomach curdles. He seems different today. His eyes don't look as glazed over from misery; his breath doesn't reek of alcohol.

'Fine, let's go,' she says pertly, just to stop him looking.

He makes a face back as if to say 'do whatever you want', and jumps out to close his front door, then the garage. She twists to watch him as he jogs back to the car, like a man on a mission, alive again. What's got him so stoked? Just the idea of his dad's last drive? That's morbid.

'You'd better be a bloody good driver,' she says as he climbs back in.

He looks at her curiously again. 'I thought happy people didn't swear?'

She fidgets in her seat. 'I'm a little off this morning.' She clears her throat as he pulls out of their road. 'I think I've just committed blogging suicide.' She winces, realising what she's said too late; starts to apologise.

Tom laughs. 'Don't worry about it.'

'You seem better?' she says as he glances at her fleetingly.

'I'm glad . . . to have a lead . . . I just want to find out what made Dad do it.' His lips tighten like he's fighting something. 'Because I keep getting this weird feeling . . .' He rubs at an eye. '. . . Dad never meant to leave me.'

Her body goes rigid in her seat. She has to say something, put him straight. *I mean, WHAT is he implying by that?* But when he pulls his hand away she sees a tear escape. So she stays quiet, reaching out a cautious hand to his shoulder.

It's the first time she's touched him in five years.

So why does it suddenly feel like just yesterday?

Him

'So tell me about this internet suicide.' I use her phrase once we've made it safely onto the M25, and I'm feeling better about driving. Dad taught me well.

'Oh, you don't want to know. You'll think it's ridiculous,' she answers.

I glance at her after I've changed lanes. Now she looks like she's about to cry.

'It's clearly bothering you, so tell me.'

She blows out through her cheeks. 'It's just . . . well, someone I thought was a friend . . . he's sharing this vlog he's made slating me. You're known by your numbers. And mine are going down. My blog, my channel; Twitter, Instagram – my followers are deserting me, and . . . I don't know . . . what I want to say to them.'

I shrug. 'Just be honest.'

'Honest?' she says, almost laughing. 'No offence or anything, but what do you know about maintaining a blog brand?'

'Not a lot. But my mate Daisy has this book blog – she reviews the books *Leata* advise against reading.' I make a face as if I know she won't condone that. 'And in her posts – she always seems to speak from the bottom of her heart.'

'The bottom of her heart?' Hope repeats the words slowly.

'Yeah, like – stop saying everything's awesome.' I glance at her again. 'Everything isn't.'

'Keep spreading the joy, Tom. Keep spreading it.'

The dry tone of her voice makes me laugh suddenly. 'You sound like old Hope,' I say, without thinking.

Abruptly, we both go quiet.

Her

She can sense her body tightening again. She doesn't quite trust herself to speak right now. Pulling off the motorway, Tom comes to a stop at a set of traffic lights. He turns to her, letting out the kind of sigh as if he's something to get off his chest. 'When we used to hang out, you never gave a toss about what anyone thought about you – that's why you were always getting us into trouble ...'

His mouth and his eyes seem to be stretching like he's reminiscing. Like he's seeing her, right now, as she used to be.

'The past is the past,' she mutters to herself, staring out of the passenger window to avoid his gaze.

He goes quiet too as the traffic moves again.

She rests her head against the glass for the rest of the journey. She's really regretting coming. She's got a headache from crying this morning. And she's still waiting on this morning's two *Leata* to kick in. Why aren't they working yet? She's not even got her bag with her to take more. Or her phone to update Dad.

Staring back out front, they've started driving down wide streets with houses tucked out of view behind grand gated entrances. Another fifteen minutes later and 'You have reached your destination,' sat nav woman announces.

They both stare over at the tall wooden gates, the top of a grey slate roof in the distance beyond them. Tom pulls the car up against a security buzzer on the wall. The nameplate reads simply, *Blythe*. With a security company listed beneath.

Tom winds down his window and glances at Hope before he presses the button.

After a short while a terse voice answers 'Yes?'

Him

The authoritative tone throws me. I instantly begin to stutter, 'Err, I'm here, because –' I lose my voice. This was a stupid idea. I'm about to wind the window back up when I hear Hope tut. She leans across me, confidently shouting into the buzzer, 'Did a Matt Riley visit here June tenth?'

There's muffled silence the other end, then a noise that sounds like a huff before, 'Who?'

'Matt Riley,' I say, finding my voice again. 'Your address was in his sat nav. He must have come here.'

More silence. And, 'Oh wait, wasn't he the journalist who killed himself?'

'Yes.' Tom's voice wavers.

130

'Yes, I was doorstepped by him a few times – I never let him in, mind you. We spoke just as you and I are speaking now. I sent him away. I didn't know what he wanted. But I don't talk to press.'

'Can we ask who you are?' Hope leans across my lap again.

'I should ask the same of you. Please leave my premises now.' The buzzer clicks off.

I bite down on my nail, then roughly drag out my phone, tapping Blythe and PharmaCare into Google. It comes up with nothing. Turning to Hope she has those sympathetic eyes on me.

'What next, Starsky?'

'I'm going to try the next place,' I mumble, scrolling down the sat nav to the second postcode. N6 4TR. 'You don't have to come. I can drop you off at a train station.'

She chews her mouth and shrugs. I take that as my answer.

Half an hour later we're crossing Hammersmith, onto a road clogged with city traffic. A red bus pulls up in the lane next to me. A *Leata* advert on its side. Someone on-board is taking a pill right under it, like it's been choreographed that way.

Her
It's taken them over an hour just to get from west to north London. She sits her arms folded; she's starting to feel like a petulant child, forced to go visiting grandma. She should have agreed to getting dropped off at a station. She should be at home, reuniting with her phone and tablet, rectifying her screen life. At Archway, they follow a slow queue up the hill towards Highgate, taking a series of right turns until they

131

arrive at the point of the arrow on the screen. Tom turns the engine off and gets out.

Hope stays in the car, watching him stride up and down the few paces that will be covered by the postcode. It'll include at least fifteen, maybe twenty of the tall Victorian terraces either side of the leafy suburban street. He can't go knocking on every door: *did you know Matt Riley?*

Another disappointment. She softens, feeling bad for Tom as the look on his face begins to mimic hers: this was a stupid plan. She's thinking about suggesting they do something nice for his birthday before they go home – when Tom freezes.

She follows his gaze. A woman with dark bobbed hair is coming out of one of the houses. A little boy with butterscotch corkscrew hair and apple-round pink cheeks bouncing around next to her.

She gets out of the car. 'Do you know them?' she asks as she reaches Tom.

He ignores her, crossing the road, going straight up to their gate like he's in a trance.

The woman glances round as she locks her door.

'It's you,' Hope hears Tom say, in a voice that breaks.

9

Picking at scabs
will only make you bleed
Leata

Him

'You and my dad,' I say plainly, fidgeting my hands, in, out of my pockets.

She looks over abruptly, confusion registering across her face. It's her. I know it's her. She can't be more than thirty. Dark hair tucked behind her ears. I can almost see why Dad would fall for her.

She shakes her head, 'Who are you?' before her eyes harden. 'No. No, I can't do this. Come on Benny.' She reaches out for the little boy, who's looking mesmerised by Hope behind me.

'I really need to talk to you,' I say urgently. I feel Hope put a restraining hand on my arm. Did I say it too loud? I take a breath, start again. 'I'm not here to blame you or anything. I just want to find out about you and my dad.'

'That's really not possible,' the woman says, 'you have to leave.'

'I am Benny, who you?' the little boy starts saying to Hope, proudly sticking out a round tummy. 'Why do dogs like bones?' he asks straight after she tells him her name.

'Please.' I look back at the woman, searching her eyes – to communicate that I don't mean trouble.

She blinks as if she doesn't like what she sees back. 'I can't help you. Really, I can't.' Despite the heat, she starts doing up the buttons on her cream mac with clumsy fingers.

'My mum got sent photos of you with my dad,' my voice croaks, and my hands are shaking. I fiddle with my glasses to occupy them.

'I heard,' she says, struggling with the last button.

'Dad told you?' I rush out. 'Do you know who sent them? Was it anything to do with some story he was writing?'

Hope glances up sharply while little Benny asks her, 'You ever met a bear?' with a pretend growl.

The woman's mouth fidgets nervously. She steps closer. I can see blue flecks in her brown eyes. She smells of sweet perfume. '*Some story*? I *was* your dad's story.'

Her
The woman – face flushed – she's grabbing cute little Benny's dimpled hand again, dragging him away from Hope even though she's not answered his question about bears. She tries to hold Tom back as he starts to rush after them. He can't go harassing this woman. 'She looks upset, Tom.'

He just shakes her off, continues. Hope stands there for a minute, not knowing what to do, before she follows after them.

Catching up, she can hear Tom begging the woman to

listen. He rounds on her so she has to stop, taking off his glasses, as if he wants the woman to really see him. His face looks bare without them; his eyes a deeper brown, smaller, almost marsupial. Something in Hope's heart seems to plunge with an unfamiliar longing. For a time. *Don't think about the past*, she tells herself harshly. Pulling her arms in tight as if to keep herself safe, she quickly covers the last few metres between them.

Spotting her, Benny launches himself over, exchanging his mum's hand for hers, as if they're old friends. Hope smiles down at him, meeting his upturned face. 'I met a bear in Canada once,' she tells him, half-listening as the woman speaks quietly to Tom.

'I'm Imogen. Are you Tom or Nathaniel?' She must be relenting because she adds, 'We're going to the playground just up there. You can walk with us.' She puts a hand out for Benny but he clings more fiercely to Hope's hand. Imogen smiles at him and continues walking beside Tom. Benny starts singing the Batman theme, bobbing his curly head in tune with it. Hope strains to hear them talking over it.

'You look a lot like him,' Imogen's saying.

Tom replying, 'That's what everyone says.'

'Matt and I finished a month before he . . . ,' Imogen pauses. 'I never meant that much to him. It was casual. He would never have left your mum. He loved her. You and your brother, you were his world.'

'You don't have to say that.'

'It's true,' Imogen says, 'I was just "work" to your dad.' She stops abruptly.

'Mama's sad,' Benny says, pushing two fingers into his mouth. Hope watches. He's right, Imogen is quietly crying. Tom looks uneasy. His hand goes as if to comfort her, but he can't quite seem to do it.

Hope tries to distract Benny, pointing out two fighting squirrels in a tree as she listens.

'I have a track record with letting men dupe me,' Imogen is saying shakily, flicking her gaze at Benny.

Tom stutters something incoherent back and kicks at the ground, staring down at his grubby Converses. Hope's stomach dips for him. Bad enough talking to your dead dad's lover for the first time, but when they talk like this? Though she can't say she's surprised at the revelation. Yeah, Matt Riley could be fun, but he could be an irresponsible idiot too. All that spliff smoking and cursing and *don't tell your mum, Tom*. Tom was always proud to be his accomplice.

He doesn't look proud now.

They resume walking. Hope swings Benny's hand, pretending to hum along with his 'na-na-na-na Batman!' He gets more excited as they begin to hear the sounds of children's cries and squeals, following a storybook tree-lined path to a clearing in a wood. There – a large, multi-coloured playground, heavy on the blue and yellow. The gated entrance holds a board advertising *Leata*'s help with purchasing new equipment. Lucky children, Hope thinks.

The playground is mostly empty, just a few parents clustered round a sandpit, coffee cups in their hands, chatting vigorously to one another. Hope spies a couple popping a *Leata*. Comparing messages on the foil. She wonders if she can scrounge one.

'What did you mean before: you *were* Dad's story?' she hears Tom cautiously asking Imogen as Benny scrambles onto a swing.

'Want me to push you?' Hope asks, one ear trained for Imogen's answer.

'Go really high, high, Hope,' Benny cries, his little curly head bobbing with excitement.

Hope starts pushing him gently, tensing as she hears Imogen say, 'I worked for PharmaCare. For John Tenby. Your dad – he only wanted to get . . . intimate with me because he wanted access to John . . . to *Leata*'s secrets.'

Him

'John Tenby,' Imogen says again, as if the name should mean something to me.

Hope is twisting round. 'John Tenby, Tom,' she says too, 'the man who discovered the formula for *Leata*.' She moves her eyes to Imogen. 'I interviewed him once for my blog . . . he's a really great man. It must be amazing to work for him.'

'He was Dad's source?' I cut in.

'John reluctantly spoke to Matt,' Imogen says tightly, 'I don't believe he told him anything.'

'Were you his source too?' I ask.

'Me?' She slams a hand against her chest, surprised eyes. 'I was only John's PA. I didn't know anything. Like I said: your dad just wanted to use me. To get to meet John. It just took me a while to realise that. I'm sorry,' she adds when she catches the look on my face.

I make a hand signal that it's okay and start fumbling for my notepad in Dad's bag.

'I recognise that bag,' Imogen says sadly. She makes a strangled laugh as I start to write. 'Your dad was always scribbling away.'

I glance up. I don't know what to say to that. Her face seems to be showing she had real feelings for Dad once. 'Pen and paper helped him think,' I shrug.

Imogen taps the pad. 'Then maybe write that John Tenby meant the world to me. He doted on me and Benny.'

A coldness starts creeping up my spine as I suddenly clock something. 'Why do you keep talking in the past tense?' I sense Hope glance sharply around again.

Imogen puts a hand against her mouth as if she's about to be sick. Tears flood her eyes again. I see an answer there.

'Someone told me Dad's source died,' I say, my voice tight and fixed. I'm not sure whether to scream hallelujah – a breakthrough – or curl up and tremble.

'Imogen – is John Tenby still alive?' I ask.

'Of course he is!' Hope twists round, answering for Imogen. Her mouth gaping open when she catches the look on Imogen's face. 'I'd have heard if he'd died!'

'The news hasn't been released yet.' Imogen's face flushes before it pales. 'You can't tell anyone I admitted to that. It's really important no one knows. PharmaCare don't want anyone to know. Not until *they* release it.'

She draws a long breath as I ask how he died.

'I can't tell you any more. I'm putting myself at risk just telling you he died.' Her face seems to run a gamut of emotions, from fear to surrender. Finally she adds, 'John lived alone. The police found him . . . heart attack, they say. He was sixty-four. But he was healthy,' she adds as if she's impeaching me over the verdict.

'When?' I catch my voice as it breaks. 'When did he die, Imogen?'

Imogen eyes me then darts her gaze away. Pushing a thumbnail into her mouth, she bites down on it. 'The day before your dad.'

Benny has stopped swinging, he's tugging Hope over to a little wooden house nearby. I drop down onto the empty swing before I fall over. My head is spinning; facts colliding.

Hope is walking back over as I try a new tack. 'Do you know if John Tenby said anything to my dad about *Leata*'s side effects?'

Imogen squints her eyes as if the warm sun's suddenly become too bright. She shakes her head again. 'I don't know what they talked about.'

'Is *Leata* harmful?' I ask.

'God, no!' Imogen shoots back at me. I hear a wide-eyed Hope let out a long exhale. 'No, John would never create anything harmful. He was a good man. The best of men. With *Leata* he's done the world no end of good. Just look around you.'

'It is a lovely playground,' Hope says.

'I mean globally,' Imogen cuts in. 'It was John's only solace – the way it clearly helped people find happy. Because being the inventor of *Leata* – it was an albatross around John's neck.' Imogen looks directly at me. 'People like your father forever hounding him for how he created *Leata*. His secret recipe for the artificial plant source used in *Leata*.'

'The secret about the plant source. Was that what Dad was after?' I almost spit it out, my mind clouds over, like it's hit a dead end. Is that the big secret? Dad was searching for the components of some lab-grown plant? To see if it was harmful?

Imogen is calling over for Benny. She looks back at me. 'I really don't care what secret your dad was after. All I know is Matt destroyed John.' Her eyes seem to be answering a more distant question. 'I've said more than I should already. Please tell no one about John Tenby being dead.'

Her

Hope can't think straight. She feels suddenly cold despite the warm sun. *John Tenby's really dead? And no one knows?* Imogen's voice wavers as she calls again for Benny. He darts out of the playhouse and into Hope instead. 'Come play, Hope!'

'We need to leave you and your mummy to have fun,' Hope says, stroking the top of his warm, curly head. 'Tom and I have to go.' She tries to catch Tom's eye. Imogen's looking too fragile for this. She recalls a *Leata* message from the other day. *'Picking at scabs will only make you bleed.'*

Tom is getting off the swing, fumbling his glasses back on. His face fidgets and twitches as if he's trying to say something. Eventually it comes out. 'How could my dad have destroyed John Tenby, just by asking questions? He was a journalist.'

Imogen remains silent.

Tom steps closer to her. Hope can hear him breathing heavily. 'And isn't it too much of a coincidence? John Tenby and Dad, dying a day apart?' His tone sounds both accusatory and deflated.

Imogen simply shrugs; her eyes refusing to meet Tom's.

'Imogen, please, tell me: *was* there anything suspicious about John's death?'

Hope catches the look Imogen throws at Tom, like he already knows the answer to that question. 'Your dad hounded John. And he wouldn't take no for an answer.' Her voice breaks, gulping air. 'And then John died.'

'What do you mean by that? Are you saying it's linked?' Tom is glaring at Imogen. Her mouth is fixed shut again. The warm air around them fills only with the screams and cries of children, happy and sad; with Benny tugging on her arm. 'Play, Hope. Hope, play with me.'

Eventually Tom shakes his head. He starts walking off.

Hope watches him before turning back to Imogen. She's crying again. 'I'm sorry. Tom's all over the place since his dad died,' Hope tries to explain.

'It's not his fault,' Imogen gasps between tears. Benny stumbles back towards the playhouse, solemnly shaking his head like he's mimicking his mother's mood.

'We should leave you both alone,' Hope says softly.

Imogen makes a grab for her as she turns to leave. 'Take care of him, watch over Tom,' she says. 'He'll get himself in real danger if he keeps asking these kind of questions.' Her brows crease, and she wipes a hand under her nose. 'Tell him – I can't give him the answers he wants.' She adds sadly, 'Everyone has something or someone they're trying to protect, don't they?' Imogen looks across at Benny's head bobbing in and out of the playhouse window.

Hope knows she should ask what Imogen means. But she's not sure she wants to know. 'Do you want my number?' she says lamely instead. 'I mean, if you need to speak to me or Tom again?'

Imogen hesitates before she answers, 'Okay, yes, maybe I should take that.'

As they leave, Hope gives Benny a quick hug goodbye; he smells of sunshine.

Him

I can hear Hope shouting for me to stop, but I don't. I sprint down the park's path, as if distance can make sense of the things Imogen said. Sweat forms a layer over my body, but I wrap Dad's jacket round tighter. Questions whirl like a twister inside my head. My dad used Imogen? Left Mum, broken and guilt-ridden? All for a story?

And John Tenby, the *Leata* inventor? Imogen was implying Dad had something to do with John's death! Did Dad cause his heart attack or something? The day before *he* died?

What if, what if, what if . . .

'I think Imogen's scared,' Hope says, catching up with me, out of breath from running. She pulls on me to slow down, biting her lip, like she's about to cry too. Her face is devoid of its usual glowsome positivity. Like even Hope . . . has lost hope.

'Tell me what you're thinking, Tom?' she says, digging her eyes into mine.

I glance at her like she's asking me to strip nude. Hope? Wants to know what I'm thinking? I take a deep breath. The only insight I have to give her right now echoes Ralph's.

'I'm thinking I never knew my dad.' I pull Dad's jacket even tighter. 'I'm no longer sure . . .' I say, stumbling on, '. . . if he was even a very good man.'

Her

She walks a little behind Tom. She doesn't know what to say to him. He's started swaying a little, like he's drunk again, even though she's not seen him drink anything. He looks hot, wretched in that jacket, yet he tugs it closer around him as if he's frozen.

Her stomach's in her throat; throat in her mouth; she doesn't know what to think. How to act. How is she supposed to act? A clump of teenagers around their age barge carelessly past on the pavement, phones out, swigging Coke cans, talking loudly. Girls piggybacking boys. Another pair have their arms round each other. Carefree, happy. One girl wears the *Leata* T-shirt Hope has. From behind, Hope can see her taking a pill. She reads out the message aloud. Some of them whoop in response.

'OMG I must tweet that one. That's like the best message ever,' her friend shrieks happily.

They round the corner, Hope walks on. This morning's the first time in a long time she hasn't tweeted her message. Friends. Parties, vlogging; fashion; FUN – that's *her* life. Right now – she should be working a way to save it, rescue herself from a public hanging on social media. She wipes her forehead, it's clammy. The air's so hot, and the sun keeps shining brighter. Excited screams erupt in the distance, probably from the same group. *Everyone else is happy right now.* Her chest's growing tighter. Quickly she starts at *Ten: I have a great family.*

Before she can think of nine, she hears Tom utter a 'fuck'. White-faced by his car, he's staring fixedly at something on his phone.

Him

'Dad. It's Dad's number,' I say to Hope, in a ghost of a voice. 'How can it be Dad?'

I feel Hope take the phone from my hand, but the message stays in my head as if it's become tattooed there.

Advice: Stay away from people your dad knew – you'll only cause trouble for them and urself. Ur dad wld want u to just get on with life.

'Someone knows we're here,' I say to Hope. I start circling the pavement, my hands burying in my hair. 'Someone has Dad's phone. *How?*' I'm breathing hard, like I'm in pain.

Hope has the phone pressed to her ear. I hear a voice come on. I cup a hand over my mouth to steady my breathing, whispering hoarsely, 'Is it my dad?' *How can it be Dad!*

'It's an automated voicemail,' Hope shakes her head. 'Who are you?' she says into the receiver before passing it back to me.

I spin round, checking the few faces on the street around us, families strolling; lone bodies fixed on where they're going. 'Are they watching us now?' My throat thickens. I want to cry, or scream. Or hit the lamp post. This is messed up! 'Why? Why would someone have Dad's phone? Someone's following me! It has to be PharmaCare!'

Hope puts out a hand, touching my arm as if to remind me she's here. 'Don't jump to conclusions.'

'What other conclusion is there?' I snap. I tighten my face to try and keep in other words. It's not Hope's fault. More softly I add, 'Can't you see? It's all connected. John Tenby was Dad's source and he told him something bad about *Leata*.'

My phone buzzes in my hand. We both look down sharply.

A text message from Dad's phone. *A friend*, it says, in answer to Hope's voicemail.

I text a reply quickly. *I want to speak to you.*

We wait. Neither of us talking, eyes fixed on the screen. Nothing.

I can hear Hope now breathing as hard as me. 'Maybe it's someone who's got your back?' she says in a weak voice.

I give her a look as if she's just said the sky is green. 'Give up with the positive spin on everything! Someone knows we're here! Wants me to stop asking questions! Someone. Has. Dad's. Phone!'

Her

Neither of them say much on the car journey home. She managed to convince Tom not to go racing back to the park to interrogate Imogen some more. 'Let's sleep on it first.' She thinks of little Benny's innocent, grinning face. She wants Tom to leave them alone, whatever Imogen's part in this.

But she has to agree. It doesn't look good. She needs to talk to her dad. She wants her dad to make sure Imogen's not messed up in something scary. Have him explain why PharmaCare are covering up John Tenby's death. Reassure Tom, it has nothing to do with his dad's death.

She turns the CD on. She'd rather have Tom's dad's dated taste in music than this loaded silence.

Tom eyes are fixed on the windscreen; his brow permanently twisted. Every now and again he rubs his face. She wants to know what he's thinking. And she doesn't want to know what he's thinking.

She tries to close her eyes, wishing herself asleep for the hour or so it will take to get home, so she can block out the pain and fury and confusion playing across Tom's face.

Instead, seeing darkness, she recalls Imogen's distress, Benny's excitement. *What's Imogen protecting Benny from? Who rang Tom? Why don't they want Tom asking questions?*

Her eyes zing open, back onto Tom's face. It's still held the way she left it. She doesn't want anything bad to happen to him.

Her heart beats faster as Tom pulls into their road. Dusk forms a grey veil over the smart beige houses and meticulously planted autumnal trees and neatly shorn green hedges. Home again. It's only now they've arrived, she realises: she's not sure she wanted to be back this soon.

She readies herself for seeing her dad waiting on their driveway for her, or Tom's mum angry with him for taking the car. Instead, someone else is standing on Tom's drive. The only car on it – a black Mercedes – isn't one she recognises. Nor is the man. He's good looking, like really good looking. Grey tailored suit, open-collared white shirt. Trousers tapering to polished shoes. Leaning against the car like he's just passing time. As they pull in he straightens up, smiling pointedly at Tom.

Hope glances at Tom as he switches off the engine. 'Who's that?'

Tom stares ahead, his hands gripping the steering wheel tightly till they're almost the colour of bone. 'Police. The detective assigned to Dad's suicide.'

Hope looks between them as the detective rounds on the Golf. She has an unexpected urge just to grab Tom and take him somewhere safe. Take him to the treehouse. Hide out there until years have passed, like in fairy tales.

The treehouse was always the place they'd run to when one of her schemes went wrong. To get Tom out of danger for the ticking off she was due.

Except, Tom can't really be in any danger – *can he?*

'Tom?' The detective is knocking on the window, doing a motion for 'wind it down'.

Hope can see the gum he's chewing as he opens his mouth wide to say, 'I'm not going to ask to see the licence you clearly haven't got.' He makes a smile, the ends of his mouth pointing directly up to his eyes. A smile that sits comfortably on his face as if it's reclining lazily on a chair.

'And who do we have here?' he says, talking in words drawn out like Millie does.

Hope annoys herself by blushing as the intense blue eyes round on hers.

'My neighbour, Hope,' Tom answers for her, a curt edge to his voice. 'Are you waiting for my mum, DS Miles–?'

'*Ethan*, remember?' The detective runs a hand over his crew-cut. 'No, in fact it's you I'm here to see; we need to have another chat. Come and get in my car. It's comfier.'

Tom finally looks Hope's way, his brow furrowing like he's asking her to intervene somehow.

She shakes her head. She doesn't know what to do. *NAD Boy.* She was wrong, stupid, *idiotic!* to think she could ever help him.

'You'd probably better get off home, Hope,' the detective says like he's thinking the same thing.

147

She gets out with Tom, tossing out a quick 'bye', trying to make a face like there's nothing for him to worry about. The detective's already said he doesn't care about the licence! But her chest stays tight as she walks away, counting down in her head just to stop herself running back and doing something stupid.

By *one*, she pauses, glancing back. Tom's being steered into the black car.

'*It pays to forget; hurts to remember,*' she hears chant in her head, as if a *Leata* advert's just come on to dissipate all her bad thinking.

The thing is, she finds . . . she can no longer remember why it pays to forget. All she wants to do, is remember.

10

Keeping busy blocks bad thoughts
Leata

Him
'Hello, Tom.'

'Afternoon, Tom.'

I freeze, my whole body going rigid with fear. In the back of the car sits a smartly dressed woman, slim legs crossed; short brown hair, a bit older than Mum. Up front in the passenger seat: a broad-shouldered man with a bent nose; his dark suit jacket straining over a barrel chest. Recognition punches me hard in the stomach. 'You were at my dad's funeral.'

The man makes a face as if to say, 'So?' Pin eyes, set in a doughy round face, are impenetrable as he flashes a heavy badge my way, muttering in a low, nasal voice, 'I'm DS Miles' boss.' He doesn't offer a name, besides saying, 'The Commander. And this here is my colleague.' He ticks a finger at the woman, before folding his mouth assuredly, as if it's my turn to go next.

My turn – I twist to move away. I'm not doing this, whatever *it* is. But DS Miles stays behind me. He presses a hand hard

149

against my lower back, pushing me further in. 'We just want a chat, Tom.'

Miles shuts the door before climbing into the driving seat, continuing, 'We got a call that you've been making door-to-door visits.'

My mind flies between the house near Windsor and the anonymous caller. 'Were you following me?'

The Commander adjusts his position, flicking at his jacket. The woman beside me coughs. DS Miles laughs, eyeing me in the rear view mirror briefly. 'Tom, Tom, stop with the tone of suspicion. How many of those teenage dystopias you been watching?'

'No one's following you. A lady, Imogen Poole, reported you to a police contact of ours, okay?' Miles replies airily. 'Why did you go and see her, Tom?'

Imogen went to the police? Hurt pulls at my stomach – that she would betray me like that. I tug on my neck, staring between them, unsure of the best way to answer. I suddenly find myself wishing Hope had stayed with me. When we were kids and we got in trouble, Hope was the one who lied for us. Between Hope's talent for it and my parents never giving me any need to – unlike hers – I always fell on the truth or silence. I don't think truth will serve me well now. I don't think they'll accept silence. 'Why do you ask?' I choose evasion instead. 'Are you here because of Dad?'

The Commander scratches his head, adjusting his hefty bulk in his seat. 'Imogen Poole is a vulnerable person right now.'

'You didn't answer my question.'

The woman next to me lets out a tight shriek of a laugh. I recognise it from some of the teachers at school. The kind that says *who do you think you are?*

The Commander continues, 'Yes, we're here because of your father. Ms Poole was . . . shall we say, romantically linked to him . . . before he took his own life.'

I nod, to show them I already know this. 'Does this have something to do with the fact John Tenby is dead?' I blurt out without thinking.

It's their turn to look uneasy.

'Is that what Ms Poole told you?' The woman re-folds her legs the opposite way, twisting her body closer to my side of the car, her mouth pinching into a strained smile. 'John Tenby's death has not been announced. And we've been instructed to keep it that way. For the time being. Ms Poole had no right to tell you about it.'

'Why?' I balk. 'Why hide his death from people?'

'Leave the management of the complicated things in life to the professionals,' the woman answers in a clipped tone.

The Commander gives her a look. 'The boy deserves an explanation, doesn't he?' He turns his pin eyes back to me. 'Most of the stories you hear are only half the news. For the last century, the police have worked with government to keep a check on what gets out, what stays contained. Like John Tenby's death. Too many bad news stories and we'd all be buried in misery!' He makes an effort to laugh, but his mouth doesn't oblige.

'Everyone does it these days: school with exam results; hospitals with operation success. And us, the police: children found, criminals arrested. Crime decreasing. Society is all about the positives. People just never realise – what goes on in the background to maintain happiness in society!' He speaks proudly, as if it's all his doing.

'You can't hide news from people,' I say, exhaling deeply. It's nothing Dad hasn't spouted before – but from the opposite side of the fence. *The State controlling the way people feel*. 'But to be honest, right now, I don't really give a toss what the police spin or don't.' Deeper breath. 'Is John Tenby's death connected . . . to my dad?'

'John Tenby *died* of a heart attack.' The Commander pauses, clearing his throat. 'Whether a gun wound brought that on, the coroner couldn't tell us,' he finishes, staring out the window.

'A gun wound?' I shout out. *A gun wound?*

I can see DS Miles eyes fixing back on me in the rear view mirror.

The Commander shakes his head slowly. 'So Imogen didn't tell you that bit?'

My mouth seems to be filling with cotton wool. I recall Imogen's expression as I struggle to get the words out. 'Are you saying . . . do you think . . . my dad shot him?'

'We do,' the woman says. 'And then your dad took his own life a day later.'

The back of my throat makes a noise. I collapse my head into my hands. I have to get out of here.

The Commander's saying something quietly, but I can't hear him over my own thoughts. Bit by bit Dad's being erased. The arm curled round me, reading me bedtime stories; inventing games on rainy days; sneaking out with a cheeky smile for puffs on his spliff. The man who was always there, to listen to me, and tell me what to think, how to behave. *Be truthful, Tom, always, most importantly, to yourself.* What did the truth even mean to Dad?

My voice comes out in a whisper as I lift my head again. 'Why would my dad want to shoot John Tenby?'

The Commander re-adjusts himself in his seat. 'Because he was angry that John Tenby wouldn't provide him with the information he was after. Your dad was deranged, by all accounts, with falsehoods about PharmaCare he wanted substantiated,' the Commander is continuing. 'If the gun did go off from his hand . . . we are sure it was by accident. We don't wish to pursue that line of enquiry unless we have to. Negative news and all that as I was saying. John Tenby is like a saviour to many people. PharmaCare want to manage the release of his demise carefully. I hope you understand, Tom. We are asking you to say nothing . . . to anyone. Think of it as protecting your father's reputation.'

I look up. My head is banging even without alcohol in my system. 'He was being blackmailed too.' I'm not sure why I feel the need to stick up for Dad in some way. 'Did you know photos of him and Imogen Poole were sent to my mum?' From the looks on their faces, I see instantly that they do. 'Plus, DS Miles, there's the fact Dad reported his credit card used to buy a gun!'

Miles frowns. 'And I told you, that all checked out.'

I take a breath, making sure I want to share it first. 'Someone just texted me . . . from Dad's phone.'

This time it's news to them.

'Okay, mate,' Miles says, though he's staring at the Commander. 'Can you show me the message?'

I dig my phone out of my jacket pocket, tapping to the first text, showing it to them all.

'Your dad's phone, huh? Leave that with me. Let me check that one out,' DS Miles nods, smiling.

'You must know there are people who want to bring *Leata* down,' the woman says to me. 'The PAL network, for instance, will stop at nothing. Maybe they see you as a way to stir up trouble. The best thing for you is to go back to your studies. What A levels are you doing?' She makes an attempt at a smile, acting like she's actually interested in the question all adults ask.

So I don't bother answering. I open the door to get out.

'Tom, we need you to let us do our job,' the Commander's saying as I climb out. 'Keep out of it, leave it to the police. Don't add to your mum's stresses, yeah?'

I look between him and the woman. 'I don't tell my mum anything right now.'

'Good boy,' the woman says as if I'm a pet dog, 'We want to keep a lid on this . . . ' The ends of her mouth turn down; her hands retreat to her lap. 'For now . . . until we know what we're dealing with . . . until the time is right for announcing John Tenby's death. Understand?' She gives me an *I know best* smile. 'Besides, your mother doesn't need further heartbreak, until we have all the facts.'

The Commander tilts his head round. 'Just play nicely, Tom and we'll all get on.'

I've had enough. 'Okay,' I get out.

'Paranoia, Tom,' DS Miles says out the open window. 'Don't give into it like your dad did.'

I grind my teeth as the engine purrs awake.

'Have a good evening,' I hear the Commander chime as the shaded windows wind up, blocking them all from sight.

I stand alone on the driveway as the Merc leaves. My whole body is shaking. Staring over at Hope's house, for a moment, I think of calling for her, like I did as a child. When things were simple.

Her

He hasn't spotted her hiding in the porch. She watches him stare up at her bedroom window, and wonders if she should go to him. But by the time she's decided she should, he's disappeared behind his own front door and her mum has opened hers.

'Hope, there you are! Where've you been all day?' Her mum doesn't wait for an answer. She rarely does. 'I'm just dropping Rose off at a friend's, then taking Lily out to the shops before they close. Fancy it?' she asks breezily.

Hope couldn't smell drink on Tom's breath, but she can detect it on her mum's. 'No thanks. You sure you're okay to drive?'

Her mum jangles her car keys in the air as if that's her answer, adding, 'Your dad had to go out to meet a client . . . He doesn't stop, working too hard, "*Keeping busy blocks bad thoughts*", there you go!' she says as if she's hardly noticing what she's saying. She starts rushing Hope's sisters out of the house; Lily pirouetting; Rose's head stuck in a book. 'Tell him not to eat if he gets home first; we're due out at the Chichons for a Neighbourhood Watch supper.'

'Course,' Hope smiles. A smile that feels alien on her lips after today. But it's what Mum wants from her. It's what everyone wants from her.

Except Tom.

Him

'Happy Birthday,' I say into the empty house, anything to stop myself incessantly repeating the same words in my head. 'Dad shot John Tenby?'

Because there's nothing I can do with that question. I either believe the police or not.

For the hell of it, I open the drawer in the hall where I chucked yesterday's card haul. I used to get excited by a doormat piled with cards. Now I feel nothing. Nada. The one on top is stamped from the doctor's surgery. Putting the others under my arm, I open it, walking into the kitchen. It's the same as they sent last birthday. Front cover: *Your birthday can get happier with Leata. Make an appointment for a healthier you!* Inside, it notes I'm not yet on *Leata*, reminding me I can get a prescription without parental approval now. And if I start my prescription *'within the next two weeks!'* I'll get discounts *'from your favourite stores!'* Smiley face. Smiley face. Ecstatic smiley face. Before it signs off with a printed signature from my own doctor.

My doctor knows my favourite stores? I crumple the card up in my fist and chuck it in the direction of the kitchen bin.

It's my birthday. And I've just discovered my dead father's a murderer.

Sod it. I need a drink.

Her

She heads up to her room, throwing herself down on her bed. The cleaner must have made it. Nothing can be left in disarray for long in this house.

She used to like mess.

She used to make mess.

Mess used to get her into constant trouble.

Hope lets out a silent scream, burying her face into the covers. Closing her eyes, the question is no longer haunting her from the shadows of her head, it's out there, lit up like a neon sign. *Why did Tom and Hope stop being friends?* The past is doing what it shouldn't, what she's banned it from doing for five years. It barges on through. Memories start assembling in her mind's eye like a chorus line entering centre stage.

It was her fault.

She sent the stupid childish letter that asked Tom, *Marry me?* Nearly twelve, they'd kissed, properly, for the first time. She was elated, ecstatic . . . she was serious about her proposal. It was a serious time. She can still recall the weighty feeling of fear for the future. She was about to go to a new school. A different school from Tom. Mum and Dad pressing her to start the school year on *Leata*. Insisting she stop being Tom's friend after what his dad wrote about PharmaCare.

She handwrote the letter, even though they were on email by then. She drew pictures and carefully selected stickers for the envelope. She popped in two love hearts with carefully chosen messages.

It was his fault.

The email he sent back. A blunt *What? Was that supposed to be a joke? As if – don't be stupid, Hope.*

<u>It was her fault</u>.

She emailed back. She told him he was horrid. She told him he wasn't her friend any more. She told him, *Just as well we're going to new schools*, and, *I never want to see you again.*

<u>It was his fault.</u>

He never replied.

Hope lifts her head from the bed. The past clinging to her like oil on her skin.

She gets up, going over towards the black screens of tablet and phone on her desk. She has half a thought to chuck them both in the bin. She doesn't want to talk to anyone. But what does she have left? If not *Livelifewithhope*?

She switches both on.

Her followers and subscribers have gone steadily down all day. She glances over the insults and jokes and cursing. Her insides chilling as she reads comments from fangirls and fanboys who overnight have become mean girls and nasty boys.

Flipping over to Facebook, she spies an exchange between Millie and Bels. *You have to cold-shoulder people who dark cloud you.*

She's not sure if it's paranoia that makes her think they're talking about her. *Would her friends really want to see her fall?* Millie did it to Tara; why not her too?

She still hasn't the energy to defend herself. But she wants to post something. If only to take her mind off Tom.

She decides on blog over channel. Not just because she looks a mess. She wants to keep things plain, honest. Not a happy emoticon in sight.

When she's finished she scans back over it. Without realising it, she's written a story. A true story. About a boy and a girl. A girl who could be bad-tempered and mischievous and impatient and passionate. And a boy who thought lots, who was shy and quiet, yet also so goddamned chilled out.

The girl loved him, for being what she wasn't. Like he loved her, for being what he wasn't. As well as all the bits in-between where they were the same. They spent every free hour together in the treehouse.

Until they fell out. Because he wouldn't make her unhappy happy.

She knows her followers will think she's gone mad. She's throwing kindling onto the already roaring fire of disapproval.

She signs off with a question. *Is it possible to have happiness . . . without unhappiness?* and taps 'publish'. She shares it on Twitter and Facebook, posts it to Tumblr, and leaves her room before she can delete it all. Going downstairs, she freezes on the top step.

Daddy's home.

Him

I've chucked all the cards in the recycling, collecting the loose cash and cheques from Grandma and the same aunts and uncles I've not heard from since the funeral. Commiserating, celebrating . . . I'm not sure I know the difference between the two any more. Aren't they both just doing what's expected of you?

I'm getting up to pour myself another whisky from the hip flask when Mum rushes in with a flurry of apologies. 'Oh,

Tom, I'm so sorry, so so sorry. Sorry, Tom.' Her thin arms are labouring under blown balloons and bags of sweets and a boxed cake as if I'm eight. Or she's Dad. 'Really sorry, Tom. I only remembered on my drive back. I stopped at Sainsbury's. I got cake. I didn't know what to buy you for a present. You know how bad I am at choosing gifts. I'll give you the money instead.' Her gaunt face amongst the plump balloons might seem comical if she didn't look so lost, mingled in with a fierce attempt to look happy for me.

'You really didn't have to, Mum,' I reply truthfully.

Her body slumps for 'of course I did'. She comes over, releasing the balloons flying over the kitchen, kissing me lightly on the cheek. 'Happy birthday, darling.'

I nod my head in reply. She starts busying herself with the bags of microwave food she's bought, probably so I won't see the tears in her eyes.

She doesn't ask what I did today, so at least I don't have to lie to her.

Of course, I could tell her the truth – about Dad and John Tenby – but as I watch her, head bowed over the microwave instructions for ready-made lasagne, she looks as fragile as a tower of ash. One poke and she might crumble. Disappear forever.

It's my job to protect her, isn't it? Now Nathaniel and Dad aren't here?

The sky's setting scarlet and orange by the time I excuse myself, patting my stomach from one meagre slice of shop-bought chocolate cake, to go upstairs to the guest room. To log onto

160

the internet. I have an email from Hari, saying he hasn't heard anything new about *Leata*, besides the rumours already out there. But he gives me a number to call him.

I search for anything on the death of John Tenby first. Even though I predict it will be futile. Which it is. Even on PAL-linked blogs and threads, there's nothing. All I can find are a couple of general news stories describing John Tenby as a recluse who won't do media interviews. Besides that, the press is generally positive, lauding him as some kind of societal saviour with his 'wonder' drug *Leata*. No surprises there – when the police are clearly working with government to block bad news. Happy. Happy. I switch off and reach for Dad's hip flask again. In-between sips, I continue with translating the rest of the shorthand in Dad's notebook.

Her
She sits on the top stair, trying to identify the other voice with him. Gruff and low like you might imagine a storybook wolf's. Yet well-spoken.

It doesn't take her long to realise – it's that man, that Slicer.

'PharmaCare pay you to do a job,' her dad is saying.

Pay him? Hope twists to stare through the gap in the stair bannister, like she used to do when she was younger, to eavesdrop on the many, many conversations Mum and Dad used to have about her and her wayward behaviour and what they should *do* about it.

They walk further into the hall. Slicer is wearing ill-fitting blue jeans beneath the familiar silver tracksuit top; his features thin and twisted on his long face.

161

'I have nothing to do with the money. Your contract is with PharmaCare.' Her dad has his hands up as if in surrender. His forehead shines with sweat.

'But they get you to hold my leash. You're the go-between, aren't you? So go-between – tell them, if they want to keep clean by getting me to do their dirty work, they need to pay me more.' Slicer stabs his chest, spittle collecting at the corners of his dry mouth.

Her dad lets out a long sigh. 'Fine. I'll see about a raise. But meantime, you keep squeezing this Mikey fellow about the information he's trying to sell you. PharmaCare think he's bluffing.'

'I've told you, I don't like that job. Mikey Jones has friends in the kinds of places I don't want to mess with. You hear me? You get me that raise first before I go hassling him again.'

Hope sucks in her breath – so it *was* Slicer she saw at the station when she visited the shelter?

'How about you pay me to photograph that woman again? One with the curly-haired kid? I liked that job. She's a looker.'

Her dad lets out a sigh as Hope's body's goes rigid. She thinks of this monster trailing Imogen and Benny. The impression claws at her insides. As Hope's phone starts ringing in her room.

Damn it.

'Rose? Hope?' In an instant Dad is hollering up the stairs. 'Are you in?'

Hope stands up, trying to look like she's just arrived there as she starts down the stairs.

'Hope. When did you get back? Where have you been?' Her dad's eyes look hostile, but his voice is calm.

She swallows, picturing Benny's curly head – squeezes out a 'with Tom.'

'Yes? Where did he go? What did he say?'

Hope hesitates. She flicks a glance at Slicer. He's by the front door, eyes on her, scratching his neck as if he's only half-interested in her answer.

'Don't mind me,' he says. 'Your dad and I have no secrets.'

'Where did he go?' She repeats her dad's question back, to buy herself time.

Slicer buys her more. He saunters over, between her dad and her. His breath is stale as he interrupts, in that voice incongruous with his appearance. 'You look like a daddy's girl. How about you tell your father to keep his promises?' He flicks a finger out, a thick gold band round it, stroking it slowly under her chin. 'Always so pretty at this age, Jack, aren't they? Need to take care of her as the dogs assemble.'

Hope glances urgently at her dad. She can't understand why he's not telling this man to leave her alone. She holds her breath till Slicer moves away again.

'I'll be in touch,' he says stiffly to her dad, before the door closes behind him.

Hope stares at her father. 'Is everything all right, Dad?'

'No,' he snaps quietly. 'I'm under a lot of pressure from work. Tell me what happened today with Tom.'

Hope slowly shakes her head. 'Nothing really,' she says with forced certainty. 'We just had fun. It's Tom's birthday.'

'But did he *say* anything?'

Hope tries to think on her feet. Something is burning up inside her, the 'old' Hope, Tom called it today – the Hope who used to regularly lie to Mum and Dad, who came up with schemes for fun, who liked nothing better than annoying their Neighbourhood Watch brigade.

She needs to know first he's not following Tom on behalf of PharmaCare, before she trusts him with more information.

Eventually she says, 'Yes. He said he'd spoken to John Tenby this morning. The *Leata* inventor.' She checks her dad's face. *Is he in on it – this John Tenby secret? Is that why he got Slicer to photograph Imogen?*

'Yeah, someone gave Tom his number,' she continues when he says nothing. 'I don't know who. Tom said he was a lovely man. He told Tom that he should just move on with life. Forget about his dad's death.'

Her dad's eyes search over hers. He's opening his mouth to say something when her mum comes tumbling back into the house with Lily and an assortment of plastic bags.

'Jack, sorry I'm late. We'd better hurry. We're due at the Chichons for dinner!'

Him

It's nearly midnight by the time I reach the final two pages. I've stopped drinking whisky; I wish I'd never started. Because things are looking up. The notebook of shorthand started turning into something serious about five pages back. Okay, so, so far it's told me nothing that I don't already know. Dad's theories about the government and PharmaCare bedding together to create a positive society through medication. But then it starts to move onto his questions about side effects. He details a brief conversation he had with John Tenby – he *was* his source – over the origins of John's manufactured plant ingredient. Dad seems certain some part of *Leata* is harmful.

But then the next page steers off onto something else. 'Cloud 9' is underlined several times. The same file title from his laptop. Before he asks: *Who are Cloud 9?*

A page later: *They are the nine names behind Leata.*

I'm getting excited, working faster, when I get interrupted by a text from Hope. *Don't trust Mikey*, it says simply. Echoing what Ralph already told me.

My stomach tenses as she sends another in reply to mine. *I'm not sure. I'll see if I can find out.*

It messes with my head. Is Mikey in it with PharmaCare? Did Mikey betray Dad? I start to ring the shelter, then stop. He'll only deny it, even if it is true.

Fear's made my mouth dry. I break off to get a glass of water. Mum's asleep on the sofa downstairs, the moonlight falling on her through the lounge window. I pull the throw over her.

Back in the guest room, I continue translating the last of the shorthand. Dad looks like he was starting to make a list of these nine names. He has four filled. John Tenby is number one. The CEO of PharmaCare, Perdita Brightsmith, is number two. Oliver Wyatt-Hall, Chairman, Merkins International Bank, is number three. The fourth: a man called Professor Simeon Blythe.

Blythe? The familiarity of the name dawns on me slowly. Blythe! The house the sat nav took us to this morning! I lick my lips urgently. Dad's drawn an arrow linking Blythe's name back up to John Tenby's.

I tap onto the internet on my phone, searching for Blythe again, but this time with his first name and title. There he is! Some kind of political consultant. And a one-time Professor of Politics from Jesus College, Oxford. But I still can't find any connection with PharmaCare.

I search back through John Tenby's Wikipedia entry. Breathing out slowly as I re-read a connection. John Tenby was also a Professor at Oxford University – before he invented *Leata*.

I google the other two names next. Banging the desk with the result. Both of them attended Jesus College. 1985–1988. This *has* to mean something.

I call the number Hari gave me, leaving him a voicemail to tell him I think I might have something for OpenFreeNet. Next, I respond to that Fran girl's DM about where to meet (*How about we skive school tomorrow?*). Because this is suddenly more important than school.

I start deciphering the final two pages. My head's starting to throb from the earlier drinking. And my eyes are battling to stay open, but I've got to keep going. I'm finding answers at last. I know I am. My blood's pumping fast through my veins despite my tiredness. Was this how Dad felt when he was investigating a story? Is that why he would do anything to get to the truth?

Including sleeping with a woman who wasn't Mum?

And killing a man?

I knock my forehead as if I can dislodge those last questions. I refocus on the final page of symbols.

There are more questions about Cloud 9 and *Leata* side effects, as well as some notes on a journalist reported missing in France. I can imagine Dad scribbling, poised at the cliff edge of revelation. His script is becoming more erratic at the bottom of the page. I shake off the doubts from Ralph, that Dad was just delusional. Quickly I translate the final line.

My eyes widen as if I've never been more awake.

Someone bought a gun with my credit card. I'm being set up – someone is trying to silence me.

Jack Wright?

11

Happiness can be caught if
you don't make waves
Leata

Him

Monday. I wake up for the third time, prising tired eyes apart.
This time it's getting light. I can hear Mum moving around her
room. But that's no indicator, the time she starts work these days.

Getting up, I've not got a hangover for once, but something
else pumps my blood hard and fast through my veins, drumming
behind my eyes: Jack Wright. I'm becoming certain Dad's
right. He's behind this. That's why Mikey wanted to avoid
him that time.

I take a deep breath. The dots are connecting fast. Jack
Wright led the case against Dad five years ago. He must have
been watching Dad since. The car crash; the gun bought in
Dad's name – that must have been Jack Wright, in his position
as PharmaCare lawyer – to stop Dad going public.

Why the gun though?

I grab my notepad and make a rushed sequential list.

Dad hounds John Tenby.
Jack Wright buys gun and licence with Dad's credit card details.
John Tenby dead.
Dad dead.

The scattered pieces of the jigsaw in my mind are starting to slot together, possibilities squeezing my brain like an elastic band. Did Jack Wright shoot John Tenby to stop him talking?

Did Jack Wright shoot Dad because of what he knew?

I ball my hands up tightly. Anything to stop me going over there right now and pummelling Jack Wright's pompous face till he answers me, 'What did you do to my dad?' I've got to get more hard proof first. If the police believe Dad killed John Tenby, I need conclusive evidence to make them see differently. Right now, what I know seems torn and blurred at the edges.

I swipe my phone. I've got a Snapchat from Hari. *Send bullet points what you have so far.* I reply, then tap out a quick email from Mum's account to make my excuses to school – *sore throat.* Before checking out the latest message from Fran. She's suggesting a place to meet. Some café in Guildford.

I get showered without even needing a drink to start the day. I'm intoxicated enough already, with this new feeling taking over, firing me up, driving me forwards. Towel drying my hair, I return to the bedroom, trying to plot what I do next. I could ring Professor Blythe. Try and find out more about this Cloud 9 group. I get dressed, pulling on a jumper of Dad's that still smells of him, mint and smokes. I'm going to bring PharmaCare and Jack Wright down, Dad. I will. I must.

I grab my phone, tapping in the number I wrote down for Professor Blythe's consultancy business yesterday. There's just an answerphone, saying he's out in meetings all day. I leave my name. With a message that insists Blythe call me. I make no bones about what I'm calling about. 'It's connected to Matt Riley's murder.'

Rash maybe, but sod it, I need urgent answers. I need people to sit up and take notice of me. Downstairs, I pick up the keys to Dad's car from the hall bowl.

Her

'That last post? Have you lost your mind or what?'

Millie, Bels and Kat cast a shadow over Hope's table in the library. She'd thought she was safe in here. Millie has never liked the old part of the school, its panelled wood and stained glass. 'Gloomsville' she always calls it.

Before Hope can answer, Millie steps aside, announcing, 'Look who's back.'

Tara appears from behind them. 'Hi, Hope,' she says, blinking round eyes at Hope. Her face holds the same stunned expression as that girl Eliza Jenner whose panic attacks got cured by a Health Farm visit. A week ago Hope would have said it was a miracle; now all she sees is Tara looking lost. Like someone's snatched away her map. Not happier, just like she's forgotten what she's unhappy about.

'How was it?' Hope asks Tara. There's a faded pink mark round Tara's forehead as if she's recently been wearing a shower cap.

'Relaxing. I think. I don't remember much.'

'You don't remember?'

'Not really. The whole stay's a bit of a blur,' Tara says vacantly. 'There was lots of lying in bed and listening to sounds and messages on headphones. It helped loads.' Tara shrugs and bites her lip.

'Maybe it's time you had a spell in there too after the stuff you've just shared online,' says Millie. 'Tara's better, but she's clearly passed on her disease to you.'

Hope meets Millie's fierce gaze. The sticky-pink pout.

'I'm just speaking from the heart,' Hope replies, flushing as she realises that's what Tom said.

'So your heart is . . . ugly-miserable?'

Behind Millie, Kat giggles. 'It's like you want to be seen as a NAD yourself, Hope!'

'It's mournful! Your followers want feelgood, not feelbad,' Bels chips in, with a tut at the librarian as she shushes them.

'You might have noticed I've taken off all my links to your site,' Millie continues in a pipe-hiss of a whisper. 'But people are asking what's with you on my channel – how do you think this makes me look?' She plants manicured hands on her short, pleated skirt.

'I'm just admitting life can be swell but it can also suck,' Hope answers.

'What the . . .?' Millie rolls her green-painted eyes. She pulls the others away. 'I'll leave you to your new friend, *de*-pression. But if you choose to continue down this path, Hope, I will have to seriously consider collaborating with you again – online or in life. I have a brand as well as my happiness to consider. You might want to think about that.'

Hope stares at the four of them as they leave. Perfect hair, perfect clothes . . . even Tara's auburn bob is shiny again. *Continue down this path*. Millie's words start drawing a

171

crossroads in her mind. The desolate kind with tumbleweed and a creaky sign. *Which way?*

Hasn't she already decided on the wrong route? Since yesterday's blog post, the trolls are increasing; more followers deserting. Rats from a sinking ship. She'll admit, half of her is tugging to go back the way she came. Where she is loved and people tell her she's beautiful. Where she says what others seem to want to hear – that life is great and full of sunshine and there's no need to be anything but positive! And happy!

Except she's no longer feeling either positive, or happy. No matter how many *Leata*s she takes, happiness is seeping out of her.

She focuses back on the essay open on her laptop, as her phone buzzes. A text from Tom. He's asking her to find out more about her dad's legal brief for PharmaCare.

She holds her head as if it's suddenly heavy. She won't spy on Tom any longer. But can she deceive her dad instead? She's not seen Dad since yesterday. He came back late from dinner last night; left early for work this morning. Maybe her lie to him will reveal nothing. *Logical explanation*, she repeats in her head.

Maybe Dad does just care about her neighbour's son.

Like she does. An alien, warm feeling spreads through her. She looks back at the crossroads in her head, and starts digging around in her bag. She should still have it in here. The PAL blogger list that was handed out at the *Leata* Blogger Quarterly. She finds it – the list is sub-titled *Nasties who hate Leata*. She can hear Toby, their Social Media Manager, reciting it. She clicks onto Google on her laptop. And searches for the first site on the list.

Him

The sudden rain means no one dawdles on Guildford High Street. People are simply blurs of colour, rushing past, umbrellas up, heads down.

I find the café Fran suggested in her last message – an American diner with red leather booths and silver napkin dispensers. I take a seat, reluctantly take off Dad's army coat, now soaked. I remove my glasses to wipe them, and when I put them on again, she's there.

'Hi, Tom. It's so nice to see you again!' She's folding up a sodden umbrella. 'What's it been? Five years?'

'About that,' I say.

She moves into the opposite seat, the thin metal bracelets she's wearing colliding and rattling like a cutlery drawer. I finger my own, the inscribed bracelet Pavlin's dad gave me. *There is no beginning. There is no end.* It calms me a little.

'You look different,' I say. I remember two plaits and a pancake-round face from Year Six. Now she resembles an extra from a vampire film. Pale make-up and blood-red lips. It might be an okay look but she doesn't seem comfortable in it. 'But good different,' I add, because she's tugging self-consciously on the dyed green-blue ends of her hair.

A waitress wearing a 'Made Happy by Leata' badge, to go with her perma-grin, takes our drinks order. When she's gone, Fran says, 'I'm so glad you suggested this. I needed a day off school.' Is she nervous? Her eyes haven't yet made direct contact with mine. Her mouth stays almost ventriloquist-frozen as she talks.

I start making patterns with some spilt sugar. I've got to ask the right questions. I've got to think like my dad did, as a journalist, if I'm going to find out more about what Jack Wright does for PharmaCare. If Fran knows nothing, I'm out of here.

'I hate when people do that to little children,' Fran says, rolling her eyes at a woman across from us. Sat opposite two young kids, she's reading out a message from her *Leata* foil strip, as if it's a bedtime story. '*Get cross and you cripple yourself!*'

It makes me think of Hope, forever reciting messages. I find myself wishing I'd invited her here, picturing her sat opposite, with her smile – even the fake one – and her shiny hair and her scent of soap and something like honey.

'Do you and Hope still hang out together?' I blurt out, cursing myself for just wanting to include her somehow.

'Me and Hopeless? You have to be joking. She's a fully-paid up member of the *Leata* sorority. Yellow-brick road happy.' Fran makes a sort of grunt. 'I'm seen as the Wicked Witch at Beaton High simply for choosing to think for myself and not take the magic pill.'

'Yeah, I know the feeling. My school's not much better.' I nod to make her feel better. 'But Hope's all right you know. *Leata*-obsessed, yeah, but she's okay.' Images of younger Hope start parading through my mind as if to prove that point. I used to think she was more than okay. I used to think she was the best. She was up there with my dad.

Our drinks arrive as the woman opposite solemnly hands her little kids a screen each as if it's a copy of the Bible. I recognise the familiar tune of Head Rush. The free game app *Leata* came up with for children. Its TV strapline appears in my head like it's been planted there. '*To keep them quietly happy!*'

I tune back into Fran. 'You think Hopeless Wright's *okay*?' she's saying, her mouth drawn in a motionless line. 'My mum and her dad work together, yeah? And from the sound of Mum's conversation with Hope's dad on Friday – I picked up the phone to make a call *honest, Mum* – Hope's helping them with some seedy goings-on.'

My fingers freeze in the sugar. 'What's she doing?'

'From what they were saying she's trailing some poor boy who they're scared might cause PharmaCare a libel headache. Sounds like his dad's died and he –' Her mouth drops open at the same time as mine does. 'Shit. It's not you, is it?'

Her

Hope glances up at the clock above the library exit. She's missed almost the whole of Geography, which is possibly a shame, seeing as she desperately needs some direction. An hour's trawl of all things PAL and it's as if she's just come up for air from some underground hideout. She never realised there were that many people out there who *don't* take *Leata*. It's not what the media profess. Or *Leata*. She looks around her. How many students here don't take it, yet pretend to so they fit in?

The PAL network of blogs and channels she's been viewing carry threads with all kinds of theories about *Leata* and PharmaCare. That *Leata* might be exploiting child labour . . . or chopping down trees in the rainforest . . . funding the Progress Party and other global political parties . . . or, *yes*, lying about its long-term side-effects.

And there's worse. Some of the posts and Twitter feeds read like horror stories. A sixteen-year-old vlogger from Paris has

175

gone missing. The majority of the French press report he's just run away. His family and friends clearly think differently on the 'Find Andrei' site they've set up. They say PharmaCare was accusing his vlog of libel. Just before he disappeared.

Another blogger from Sweden is actually in hiding. She keeps changing her blog site so she can continue to post. She's one of the voices claiming there are side effects. Though there's a note on her last site that was posted yesterday from her family and friends asking her to make contact with them.

Then a group of students in New York are currently being remanded on charges of inciting terrorism. Because of their blog encouraging people to graffiti *Leata* posters and billboards.

And *Thenextbigsecretaftersmokingkills* in Australia – he's currently being sued for making claims it's addictive; that once you start taking *Leata*, you can't stop. And he states openly that he is being forcibly threatened to pull his channel.

Inside her head, it's like the light source has been changed. Why has none of this made mainstream news? She knew her dad was involved with shutting down newspapers and punishing media channels, for saying things against *Leata*. It's work she was proud of. Since she decided to be proud. But hounding young people for having a voice? And why have some disappeared?

She reaches down into her bag, pulling out the emergency box she always carries with her, unfolding the leaflet inside that she rarely examines. It holds sepia shots of attractive smiling people, interspersed between the science bit. She doesn't know half the ingredients. The main one is a long Latin name she can't pronounce. The plant source John Tenby manufactured which, mixed with a chemical concoction, creates *Leata*'s harmless magic.

But what if the magic isn't harmless? What if Matt Riley was right and there's a time bomb ticking of future side effects?

Hope chews down on the side of her mouth. In all of this, she's never thought once about *not* taking *Leata*. It seems as alien as not spraying on deodorant each morning. *Who wants to smell?*

She crumples up the leaflet and begins packing up her bag for English class. Her phone starts buzzing as she's getting up to leave. A number she doesn't recognise.

'Is that Hope?'

The voice is small and quiet; it takes Hope a while to recognise it. 'Imogen?'

'Out!' The librarian points to the exit.

Hope mouths a 'sorry', throwing her bag over her shoulder, walking away fast. 'Are you okay, Imogen?'

'No. No, I'm not. PharmaCare are still my employers – I had to admit to them that Tom visited me. But I never told them I revealed John Tenby was dead.' Her voice escalates. 'But they know. They know I talked! Was it you? Was it Tom?'

Hope stops dead outside the library doors.

'And worse,' Imogen continues, her voice becoming paper thin, 'they think I put Tom in touch with a man *masquerading* as John! What's Tom been saying?'

A knife twists in Hope's guts. She leans against the wall next to her before she falls down. Dad's failed her test.

'I don't understand what's going on,' she answers honestly. She can hear Benny in the background singing happily to himself. 'I'm just so sorry, I told –' she swallows back a confession and asks instead, 'Who are the people at PharmaCare telling you these things?'

Her stomach tenses in anticipation of her dad's name as Imogen answers quietly, 'PharmaCare's Operations Director, Nina Mitchell. She's been watching me like a hawk since John died.'

Hope's ear burns hot. She switches the phone to her other. Nina Mitchell, Fran's mother's. Dad's contact.

'I'm scared. I should never have spoken to Tom,' Imogen is saying. 'It just threw me seeing Matt's son like that.' She takes a deep breath. 'You've got to tell Tom to back off asking questions. It's dangerous . . . he can't . . .' Imogen's voice drifts off – she talks softly to Benny – then, 'Tom doesn't understand the dangers.'

'I think he does,' Hope says quietly. 'He just wants the truth about his dad.' Her voice catches in her throat. 'Please don't be scared. I'll help you,' she adds, staring hard down the corridor as if she can conjure up Tom amongst the groups of smiling girls walking towards her. *I need you, Tom.*

'Please, listen! Just tell Tom: stop asking questions.'

Benny's voice comes closer. 'Can I say hello . . . can I say hello?' and then the line goes dead.

Hope taps the phone against her chest. Her breath is coming hard and fast; a heady mix of emotions rising in her like dough. Emotions that *Leata* no longer seem able to suppress. Guilt and fear; sadness; anger. Regret.

Her route from those crossroads suddenly appears even clearer in her head.

She thinks of Slicer stalking Imogen. Of Tom burying his dad.

She has to find a way to make this right. She starts walking. But not to English. She heads straight to the main doors.

Him

I can't even close my mouth yet. I can hardly speak. My fingers are frozen in the spilt sugar on the table. My heart's pumping slowly, as if it's suddenly laden with weight.

Hope betrayed you darts through my mind, sticking out its tongue, taunting me. I stare down at the shapes I've made in the sugar.

'You're saying Hope's been spying on me?' Hope's in it with her dad? With PharmaCare? I'm torn between fear – I'm being watched? – and pit-of-my stomach hurt: Hope never really wanted to be friends again? *Stupid fool – that's you. She wanted you out of her life five years ago – why would she want you back in it now?*

'If it's you they were talking about – then yes.'

I spread my fingers out as if I'm in pain. I think of DS Miles turning up on my driveway yesterday. Was it Hope's dad who called the police on me? Because Hope told him we'd visited Imogen?

I glance back up at Fran. She's staring at me with sad eyes.

'I need to know more about what Jack Wright and your mum were discussing. Can you access your mum's emails?' I say urgently.

Fran pulls a surprised face, as much as her face muscles move. 'I dunno.' She licks her lips nervously. 'I mean, maybe. Wasn't today supposed to be about fun?' she asks uncertainly.

'Sure,' I say. I need a new tactic. 'But I need a drink for fun.' Not any more I don't. I have enough adrenalin coursing through my veins. But I need a way to get back to Fran's house. 'Do you have anything to drink at yours?'

Fran smiles coyly at the suggestion. 'Yeah, okay.' Which is when it hits me like a ball in the stomach: the nervousness; why she keeps looking at me from under her eyelids, the way Daisy at school does.

As if to prove my suspicion right, Fran adds a shy, 'I always regretted that we lost touch, Tom.'

I fix my mind against caring. Maybe it'll prove useful. All that matters is finding out the truth. *Right, Dad?*

Her

Good. Her mum's car's not on the drive. Lunch, golf, shopping. Pick one of the three and that's where she'll be. Which suits Hope – it'll be easier to search her dad's study in an empty house.

Inside, the house echoes with silence. She goes straight up there, down the landing, past black-and-white studio photos of the family taken a couple of years ago. Lily and Rose clambering over Dad like puppies. She and Mum more sedate in the background. She's never liked those photos. It's just the first time she's admitted that to herself.

Opening the study door, she inhales the scent of Dad, of hard work and seriousness. Where it usually comforts her, suddenly it seems stifling, clawing at her nostrils. Keeping little Benny and Imogen front of mind, she turns the computer screen on. She knows the password. She overheard Rose ask for it a while back when she needed to print something. It stuck in her mind – though she never let it get to her. *Happy thoughts!* Now it gets to her. *LilyRose0106.*

She sits up poker-straight as she clicks onto the folder she saw last week. The one with Matt Riley's name on it. The thumbnail photos attract her first. She enlarges them. Photos of . . . Imogen. Kissing Tom's dad.

Were these the photos that Slicer took?

Hope presses a hand against her stomach to stem the queasy feeling growing there.

She opens another file. It's untitled, but seems to be a trail of pasted emails. Between her dad and Nina Mitchell and one other: sblythe@btinternet.com. *Blythe.*

Wasn't that the name from the gated house they visited Sunday?

She rubs at her eyes before she reads the content; her insides pricking with fear at every word.

squeezing Matt Riley until he runs scared.

arrange it so Matt Riley owns a weapon?

John Tenby is at home 3pm. Thursday

She bolts up at the last one – *she has to get to Tom; warn him* – when she hears the creak of the door behind her.

Him

The house couldn't be more incongruous with Fran. Modern, mostly glass, protected by a sentry-like circle of trees. Inside, it's as minimalist as a hotel foyer, with some cloying, clinical bleach smell. The only pictures lining the walls are framed posters of *Leata* campaigns.

'You don't take *Leata* but you have to look at these every day?'

'Mum uses them like a mirror.'

'So what does that make you – Snow White?'

Fran laughs girlishly, leading me on into a sparse, shiny kitchen that looks unused. She clocks my expression. 'We mostly eat takeout.'

'What about your dad?' There's a tug in my stomach just at the word.

Fran shakes her head. 'No dad.' She collects glasses out of a cabinet, a bottle of the brown stuff, like I requested, from another, placing it all down with a clatter on a round, glass table. 'I'm adopted. I wouldn't be surprised if Mum's already filed for a refund. *It's just not doing what it SHOULD do!*'

'Sorry,' I say, unscrewing the bottle.

I pour the whisky out as Fran gets a tray of ice from the freezer cabinet. Dropping cubes into the glasses, they crack and fizz. 'Lemonade?'

'Neat,' I say. 'You should try it that way.'

'Okay.' She smiles eagerly at me and takes hers.

'So you hate your mum?' I ask. Maybe that's my way in.

Unfortunately she shakes her head. 'No – we just fight a lot. We used to get on okay – well – when I was little. When she could dress me like her mini-me and I believed she was as real as the tooth fairy.'

'My brother, Nathaniel, reckons my dad wanted us to be carbon copies of himself.' I knock my drink back, grimacing as the sweet burn scorches my throat like never before. It must be the really good stuff.

Fran copies me, coughing and spluttering but nodding as I shake the bottle for more.

'I'm sorry about your dad. It must really hurt,' she says.

I frown, looking down into the whisky; I wish she hadn't said that. I knock it back. Fran does the same. Coughs again. Her head's swaying a little. It's not even hit my sides yet. Good. I need to start snooping. I lean across and refill her glass again. 'I want to hear more about your mum.'

'What d'you want to know? That I disappoint her hugely for not popping her precious pills?' She makes a sharp cackle of a laugh, sounding half-stoned already. 'That the best thing she's done for me, is not forcing me into a Health Farm like she wants.'

I pull a sympathy face. 'What about the work she does for PharmaCare. Why would they be interested in me?'

'Oh.' Fran frowns. 'I dunno. Were you talking to the press or something? It's all Mum ever seems to do, fight people slating *Leata*.' She leans across the table towards me; her eyes glassy, she's drunk already. 'I always used to really like you, Tom. I still do.'

'Me too,' I say, because I think that's what she needs me to say. I need to give up on talk and move to a house search, now.

Fran starts moving out of her chair, slotting into another closer to me.

'Do you think you can help me?' I say, refilling her drink and encouraging her to knock it back with me.

She smiles crookedly, leaning in closer so our faces are nearly touching, before kissing me full on the lips.

I try to resist pulling back. I need to do . . . what I need to do.

Fran is slobbering over me like this is her first ever kiss after pillow-practice.

I keep my arms by my side. She's breathing heavily. A smell of incense mingling with her whisky breath.

183

I start speaking in-between kisses. 'Don't you want to get back at your mum and Hope? Find out what they're up to?' I pull away, pretending to want a drink. 'Your mum got a computer here?'

Fran knocks hers back, wipes her mouth and leans in to me again. 'Let's stop talking about my mum.' She tries to make a suggestive smile, but the drink distorts it. If I didn't fancy her before, I certainly don't now. But I let her kiss me again anyway – poking a sloppy, untethered tongue between my lips, like drunk kissers do.

'It's just. I need to find out what they know about my dad,' I murmur against her mouth. 'You understand, don't you? I just need to see your mum's computer.'

I pull back again. Her red lipstick has smeared like blood down her chin. I can feel it sticking to my mouth.

'If it means that much to you.' Fran looks uncertain but she takes the hand I'm offering to her, starts leading me into a large open-plan area; more sparse, unlived-in space. A broad glass desk with a computer is surrounded by floor-to-ceiling windows on one side, mostly empty white shelving units to the other.

'There's no one like you at school,' Fran slurs behind me as I switch on the Apple screen.

'That's cos you go to an all-girls,' I say distractedly, searching the drawers below as the computer warms up.

'I hate it there.' Fran's leaning into me, her chin resting on my shoulder. I resist the urge to flip it off. 'You have to look like an extra from a girly pop video, otherwise you're relegated to the weirdo kid pool.'

'That right?' I murmur. 'What's the Apple password?'

Fran kisses my cheek before she tells me it.

I press enter, tapping away, running a search with Dad's name first. It comes up with nothing. I'm trying John Tenby, when I catch sight of it.

Just a little behind the computer screen. A large framed picture of Fran with her mum. She's younger, eight or nine, the dark blonde curls I remember from primary. The kind of kid's smile that shows pure excitement for life. Nothing like her face shows now. I pick it up to take a closer look, something nagging at me at the back of my head. Examining her mum's face more carefully, my breath stills. The frame falls from my hands, smashing onto the dark wood floor.

'What are you – ?' Fran gasps behind me.

Hurriedly, I bend down, picking the picture out of the shattered glass. 'That's your mum?' My voice sounds faraway.

'Yeah,' Fran sways again. 'Mum's going to be mad with me. It's her favourite picture.'

'I need to borrow it,' I say absentmindedly, forgetting my computer search and starting off towards the front door.

Fran chases me, unsteady on her feet. 'What is it? Did I say something wrong? Where are you going, Tom?'

I say nothing, heading out the door, ignoring Fran's cries behind me to come back. I stare hard at the photo as I climb back into the car. It's her. I'm sure of it. The woman sat neatly, legs crossed in the backseat of DS Miles' car yesterday. A younger version, but definitely her.

They'd made me presume she was police. On purpose?

Fuck – is DS Miles even the police? Did PharmaCare themselves pass the verdict on my dad's death?

. . . Because PharmaCare killed him?

185

Her

Before she can twist round to see who it is, her hair is being pulled, and yanked painfully from her head. Her scalp burns. She lifts her hands to try and pull the stranger's grip off; scream out as she is thrust from the chair down onto the floor. A foot presses on the back of her head, pressing her face down. Her mouth and nose fill with carpet, making it impossible to breathe.

She can feel her heart pounding hard and fast against the floor. A time bomb telling her: do something, as her mind jumps between *intruder? A burglar after money?* To *is it him? Slicer?* She tries to get leverage from her knees; to move her head sideways so she can scream.

But the foot on her head grinds against her skull. Panic roars through her aching body.

Then the foot lifts. Quickly, she tries to rise up from the floor, to see her attacker, to try and reason with them, or shout out for a neighbour, readying her eyes for the possibility of a shiny tracksuit jacket.

Too late. She is being grabbed from behind again, violently yanked up as if she were some cloth doll. She belts out, 'Stop! Please, don't hurt me!' her voice catching in her throat. Behind her – the sounds of grunts and heavy breathing. Something hard whips ice cold across her cheek, stinging her skin like sunburn. Every nerve-end is now buzzing with fear. Eyes down, she catches sight of shoes, the bottom of smart trousers. Familiarity nudges at her before she is catapulted like an elastic band pinging across the room into the bookcase the opposite side. Her spine cracks against wood, the impact making her drop to her knees. Slowly she stares up; her hair covering her face.

'You made me do that.'

His face is pinched, a tight expression of detestation oozing out of every pore, his eyes alight with loathing. He might as well be a stranger attacking her. Standing there, flexing his hands as if they are itching to attack again.

'How dare you.'

'Dad . . .?' she croaks, her throat raw from screaming. 'Dad?' she says again, her words thickening with tears. 'What've I done?' The last word seeping out on a long moan.

The question must anger him. Two short strides across the room and his hands are back in her hair, coiling it round his knuckle like a boxer getting bandaged up for a fight. She shouts out, flailing at her roots as he spools it tightly back to her scalp. Her throat becomes too thick with tears to shout, to tell him: stop!

His face rounds on hers; mouth curled and folded in a snarl as if he's about to roar. 'You lied to me. You not only made a fool of me, but you put me in a dangerous position. Who do you think you are? Who?' His voice is low, vicious, but not loud. Never loud.

'Let me go.' She hears her words come out on small chokes. Her whole body is trembling.

'Do . . . you . . . have . . . any . . . idea . . . what . . . you . . . have . . . done?' He says each word as if she's hard of hearing. Or just stupid. *Stupid. And useless.*

Isn't that what he used to tell her when the teachers would call them in to complain? When she would sleep out all night in Tom's treehouse or annoy the neighbours at Halloween? *Stupid. Useless.*

Loveless.

But it never mattered. She had Tom.

Until he agreed with her dad.

That *stupid* letter she sent Tom. That *pathetic* letter.

Loveless Hope.

Him

Another message from Fran, asking again if she did something wrong. I should reply, put her mind at rest, but I haven't got the head space for her right now. I press the heels of my hands hard against my head and pace the guest room. So if Miles and that bloke the Commander are PharmaCare too, then Miles must have got authority from the police to visit after Dad died? To imitate a detective?

So where does that leave me? Where do I go for help? Who do I tell?

I decide to ring Ralph, but Molly says he's out. She must notice the urgency in my voice because she starts to ask if I'm okay. I tell her nothing. Suddenly I distrust everyone. Checking the time – Hari sent another snapchat to say he'd call in an hour – I get out my notepad and start writing it all down. Everything I know now. The bones of a story.

I title it 'Cloud 9'.

I've just finished speaking to Hari, updating him on what I know now, when I hear Mum come back in from work. 'I have pizzas, Tom,' she calls up in a voice that's straining to sound cheerful. I get up from the desk. I've got to tell her; it's too serious to keep the truth from her now. Hearing her climbing the stairs,

I head down the landing to catch her. Her bedroom door clicks shut as I reach it. I hear the usual quiet crying behind it.

I drop my head.

I need to get out of here. I pull Dad's coat on downstairs and leave out the back door; jogging through the dark to the one place that used to always help me think.

Her

Another gasp of pain, but it's not from Hope this time – 'What is it? Jack, what's going on?' Hope's mum is stood in the doorway. Her eyes squinting as if she daren't look. Palms pressed against her cheeks, mouth open, like Munch's Scream.

'Whatever it is, Jack – Hope will put it right. Won't you, Hope?'

'Put it right?' her dad spits back. 'My neck's on the line. You dance with the devil and he dictates the moves, Bryony! There is no putting right! PharmaCare think I'm double-crossing them! That I sent Hope to *help* Matt Riley's son! Right now – they don't trust me! And if they don't trust you – that's dangerous!'

Hope watches her mum make a gesture as if she doesn't know what he's talking about. She wants to ask, *what DO you know, Mum?* But her throat contracts as she gulps back a barrage of tears. They start to slide out anyway.

'Like crying will fix anything,' her dad hisses. 'You're a troublemaker. Sent to torment me,' he goes on. 'You have brought this on yourself. Forced me to treat you this way. You're still that wild dog beneath all your recent simpering and sweetness. You've been set to make my life difficult, from the moment you were bloody conceived.'

'But everything's been so nice over the last few years with you and Hope, Jack,' her mum intervenes again, 'we've been such a happy family, Jack.' She wrings her hands, making a smile as if she's the one in pain.

'*She* is *your* responsibility,' Hope hears him snarl at her mum. Not Lily. Not Rose. *Me. The Disappointment.*

'And you will book her in – ASAP – to a Teen Health Farm. It will fix her and PharmaCare will see I'm on side. Sort it out, Bryony!'

Hope can't stay any longer. She moves fast, past Dad before he can stop her, past her mum, her puffy face twisting in half-apology, half-admonishment.

Everything is hurting. Inside as well as out. She goes into her room, closing the door as something starts cracking in her head – china cup slammed on the floor smashing, as more of the past comes flooding through. The times when Dad hit her . . . in the days before *Leata*. Before she became what he wanted her to be – more like her sisters, biddable, smiling, pleasing. Those hard slaps and shoves that came every time she misbehaved or answered back, which was most of the time.

Gingerly she touches her cheek, her head. She can still feel his hands tugging at her hair, throwing her across the room. The misery is too much to bear. So what if there are side effects. She goes over to the flowery box, grabbing out the foil strip there, tearing into the first, '*Thinking troubled thoughts only leads to a troubled life.*' Swallow.

Breathing hard; shove in the next. '*Happiness can be caught if you don't make waves.*'

Another: '*Smile and you will be happy. Cry and you will be sad.*'

More: crunching, gulping; digest, digest: fast!

'There's no before or after, just the now. Live!'

More, more.

'LaughterleadstolonglifeThinktheRIGHTwayandavoid thewrongpathEnjoyeachdayasifyou'vejustbeenbornThe bestkindoflivingislivinghappily.'

More. *Damn you, WORK!*

The tray finished, she grabs another box out of her dresser drawer, spilling the foil trays out onto the carpet. She starts ignoring the messages, consuming pill after pill, challenging *Leata* to make her happy. *Now!*

Twenty-four pills. On an empty stomach. She should be dancing on the ceiling delirious.

Instead the memories keep rushing through as if the broken dam in her head can't be fixed.

Her stomach lurches; she only reaches the wastepaper bin in time. Perfectly formed yellow and blue pills surf out on a mix of lunch and bile.

Sitting back, she pants, swallowing hard. She starts to think again of the PAL bloggers who've disappeared; the anti-*Leata* voice that PharmaCare globally wants silencing. Like her dad always wanted to silence her.

She thinks of Matt Riley. And John Tenby. And what PharmaCare and her dad might have done to them.

After a while, she gets up, her head swaying with her feet. She rubs sick from her mouth. The sky outside has turned from sunset pink to inky blue. She can hear the sound of Rose and Lily watching TV below, her mum calling them for dinner.

She can almost reach out and touch the ordinariness of it all.

She has to get out of here. She walks fast, downstairs, out the front door, letting her feet lead where her mind can't.

It's not till she's walking through his back gate that she realises where it is she wants to be.

The only place she remembers real happiness and laughter and fun. And safety.

She breaks into a run as she sees the spikey silhouette of the branches it's built into. Charging fast up the creaking ladder as if wild dogs are chasing below.

Only when she reaches the wooden platform does she freeze.

Him

I jump as Hope's face suddenly cuts a ghostly shape within the square of dark sky at the treehouse entrance.

Her breath is coming fast. She looks as shocked to see me as I am to see her.

'Tom – I'm glad you're here. We need to talk.'

'No we don't,' I say, avoiding eye contact, screwing up my face, as she pulls herself up onto the platform.

'My dad took photos of your dad and Imogen. I think he set your dad up somehow.'

'How do you know that?' I snap. It's stuff I've only guessed at – but I passed it on to Hari. My stomach creases with fear. 'Are you tapping my phone too?'

Hope licks her lips, shaking her head worriedly. 'What?' She pauses. 'Tom, you're in danger. I think Imogen is in danger. And my dad is behind it.'

I make eye contact now. What game is she playing?

192

She sucks in her breath. 'Dad's employing this dog of a man and they're talking about blood money. I think they were behind John Tenby's death. Something's really wrong, Tom. It's a man Blythe – like in the house we visited – who seems to be giving the orders!'

I tighten my fists. I feel so alone right now. 'Get out! Why would I believe anything you say – when you've been spying on me for your dad?'

'You know?' she moves closer. I back away. 'You don't understand. I didn't realise. I thought I was helping you.'

'Helping me? Reporting back to your dad where I went, who I saw? If Imogen is in danger, it's because you told your dad we met her.'

'I didn't mention Imogen . . . but,' she bites on her lip, 'I told them about the shelter . . . you're right, I started it, and I'm sorry, I didn't –'

I shake my head furiously. 'Stop talking,' I say. 'Just go.' I turn my face away. 'Get lost. Get away from me. I never want to see you again.' When she doesn't move, I repeat it. Angrier. More forceful.

Her own words, from five years ago. The words that put an end to us – Hope and Tom.

They chase her back down the ladder.

TRUTHS

I hold a beast, an angel and a madman in me, and my enquiry is as to their working, and my problem is their subjugation and victory, downthrow and upheaval, and my effort is their self-expression.

Dylan Thomas

12

If you don't stoke a fire,
it will simply burn out
Leata

Her

Livelifewithope

Thursday 14th September

If our happiness is manufactured – forced from self-medication – what sort of happiness is that?

I know this will lose me more of you, followers. But I'm going cold turkey. The pill on my last message said, 'If you don't stoke a fire, it will simply burn out.' But the thing is, I think I want to keep the fire going. Like this slogan on my old friend's T-shirt said, I want to burn, burn, burn. I want to know what's it like to really feel alive.

Look up from your screens for a moment, check out the world you live in, and ask yourself: is your life truthful? Or just the version of truth you're being forced to swallow?

I lift my hands from the keyboard. I don't bother wiping the tear trickling down the side of my nose. I let it pool on my top lip; there'll be more where that came from. *Tom never wants to see me again.*

I press publish on my dashboard. *Nor should he.*

Tom's better off without me. *Because you? You're stupid, useless. Loveless.*

I flick onto my blog. Trolls are still stalking there, vultures soaring in to join the afterkill.

'*Live life with hope? More like with misery.*'

'*Pull yourself together you stupid cow.*'

'*Just go jump off a bridge if that's what you want. The rest of us want FUN!*'

The last is from a fangirl who started every day telling me how beautiful I was.

On Facebook, I find Millie, Bels and Kat making it clear through coded conversations that they have to distance from 'hopeless' negativity. In my emails, Toby, *Leata*'s Social Media Manager is announcing I've contravened my sponsorship contract. That accounts for the gap on my blog where their panel advertising used to run.

I've been sent into the wilderness. Or rather, I've taken myself there.

I refresh my blog page. People have started posting comments already on what I just published. I pull my head back, surprised that the incoming isn't all bad. *Jay99* is saying he knows how I feel; he's stopped taking *Leata* too. He's campaigning his local GP for proper help with his anxiety. *Daisychix* says she's joining me on my *Leata* diet because she's watched her sister sinking under agrophobia 'and no one will help except to prescribe a PharmaCare

Health Farm'. Others are querying whether *Leata*'s even safe to take.

I glance over at my numbers in the box at the bottom of the screen. My total – it's starting to climb again. There are retweets and shares happening. I take a breath, sharing it myself, as, 'Hope!' Mum appears at my door. Her puffy face filled with a forced smile, she's dressed in her tan and pink uniform for a day playing golf. 'Great news! The Health Farm in Watford has a space for you from tomorrow. '

'I'm not going.'

'Dad says you have no choice,' she says, the words at odds with the beam she gives me.

My stomach clenches. I say nothing as Mum fidgets by the door. 'We're leaving for school in a minute. Why not go in for today. It'll distract you.'

I sniff, reluctantly nodding. She's right. I can't just stay here. Doing nothing, except checking for comments. I get up and grab my bag, chucking stuff inside it as she adds, 'It's all for the best.'

Out on the landing, there's drilling noises. Dad's got the odd-job man in, fixing a lock to his study door. His tinny radio finishes the song it's playing and a *Leata* advert kicks in. Reminding me, in case I've forgotten. '*Life's short. Enjoy it!*'

For once, Rose trots solemnly alongside me as we walk into school. Her eyes seem to be asking me silent questions. I don't know how to answer, except to tell her: our dad's a monster. But I don't even say that. Instead I shake her off and head to the toilets, closing the door on the last cubicle as I wait for a gaggle of chatty Year Ten girls to leave. Once it goes quiet, I make the call.

'It's Hope. I need to warn you,' I say when Imogen answers with a hesitant 'hello?'

'Hope? You shouldn't be calling me,' Imogen replies, her voice terse, tense. 'It's not safe. I'll text you, okay?'

'Imogen?' The phone goes dead. My blood runs colder. I scratch absently at one of the many *Leata* messages graffitied on the back of the toilet door, '*Play the game of positivity. Everyone's a winner,*' jumping as my phone buzzes.

Warn Tom 2be careful. I'm being watched at work. I'm making a run for it. I'll be in touch again. Tell Tom I'm sorry.

Him

I meet Pavlin a few roads from school. His kind, dark eyes hang heavy as I fill him in on everything I've told his cousin Hari.

'You'd better call Hari, this time, in case they are tapping my calls. Remind him – if the police are letting PharmaCare impersonate them . . . if they've got coroners fabricating verdicts . . . then he's got to be really careful.'

Pavlin nods his head soberly. 'Don't worry. Hari will know what to do. OpenFreeNet can release things in ways that don't look like it's come from them. Let me talk to him.'

Pavlin makes the call. I tug Dad's jacket tighter against a fierce wind that wants to disable our walk. Across the road a man in overalls is up-high, cleaning PAL graffiti from a *Leata* billboard.

'Okay,' Pavlin breathes out as he comes off. 'Hari says you need to try and get the other five names that make up this group, Cloud 9. OpenFreeNet are one more story away from

200

shutdown. His counterparts across the world are getting threatened. One has gone missing in Australia. So they need as much concrete proof as you can give them.' Pavlin nods his head encouragingly, as if he believes I can get that. 'Other than that, he's talking about a hacktavist strategy and how we have to plan for maximum exposure so it doesn't get instantly dismissed as hate press by all the *Leata* lovers.'

Pavlin puts an arm around my shoulders as we battle on through the wall of cold wind. I put mine round him too and keep it there till we get to our study room. We must look like a couple of kids coming off the football pitch. I don't care; he's on my side. I dump my bag and head off to Economics.

Mr Jones' class is a double, so I use the time to plan how I find these five other names. In the end I decide I need to convince Ralph somehow to help me. Looking up, Mr Jones has his eyes closed. He does that whenever he talks. Around me, students are taking the opportunity of a long sermon to stare down at their phones. I get mine out, to text Ralph, sitting up straighter when I see Hari has messaged me with a time and new number to call him. Another text pings through as I hear 'Tom Riley?'

Mrs Mayhew, from the school office, is peering round the door. 'Headmaster wants him,' she clips primly at Mr Jones, who stops talking and opens his eyes. He nods at me to go.

Blowing out through my cheeks, I collect my stuff – it'll be another visit to check on my emotional progress. Whether I've seen the light and turned to *Leata* to get me through yet. Or whether I've read that PharmaCare leaflet on grief. *Have I thought about a Teen Health Farm?*

I follow behind Mrs Mayhew's tightly curled head. It's a short walk to the headmaster's office. We're outside his door, when I remember to check the last text.

I freeze. Blood pumping fast, thudding into my ears. It's Dad's number.

Get out. They're coming for you.

Mrs Mayhew pushes me forward.

Her

The English class has been plastered with replacement posters of the new curriculum texts. The picture of the Brontë parsonage has been swapped for Jane Austen's Hampshire home. *Crime and Punishment* has been replaced with *Barchester Chronicles*, *Macbeth* with *Midsummer's Night Dream*.

It feels like the same has happened to me. The propaganda in my head telling me how to live, and behave, and feel, has been defaced, torn down. My stomach boils with the need to act. To stop Dad from hounding Tom. To protect Imogen somehow, so she doesn't need to run.

I zone out of Ms Shone talking about themes of bad parenting in *Persuasion*, until I hear the bell go for break. Leaving, I see Fran collecting a pile of books off Ms Shone. I hear her whisper, 'Don't tell your mum,' to Fran.

It jolts my mind – Nina Mitchell. I wait outside for Fran to catch up before I say, 'Did Tom ever get in touch with you?' as students flood the corridor.

'Tom?' Fran breathes back as if I've uttered some evil name that shan't be spoken. 'Was it you?' Her expression suddenly hangs somewhere between panicked and pissed off. 'Did you make Tom ask me out? For a laugh?' she continues before I can answer.

My mouth gapes. I don't know how to answer her, except, 'I'm sorry. I thought you'd be good for each other.'

Fran shakes her head dismissively in short, sharp movements. Jolting away fast, she knocks into a group of girls. They elbow her back, giggling, 'Watch it, Frigid!' and the pile of books in Fran's arms scatter across the corridor.

I rush over to her, bending down to help pick them up. *Jude the Obscure. Anna Karenina. Madame Bovary.* 'I should borrow these after you,' I say, handing them back to her. There are tears welling up in Fran's eyes. I take a breath, asking as gently as I can. 'Have you seen Tom then?'

'*Seen* Tom?' Fran stares at me, eyes hostile as she chokes the words out. 'He came to my house. Acting like he was interested in me. Some game of yours? Like spying on him?'

'You told him I was spying on him?' My stomach is sinking lower by the second, churning and tightening. 'I'm sorry. I didn't know he'd gone to your house, honestly.'

Fran swipes at her eyes. 'Forget it,' she says. 'Mum says all men suck. Something we're bonding on at last.'

I stare down at the books piled in her arms. 'Your mum won't bond over your reading those.' I put a hand out to her as she turns away. 'Please. I need your help, Fran. I think your mum, my dad are doing bad things. Dangerous things. And Tom's in trouble.' My face pleads. It stops her pulling away more. 'Look – I'm sorry if Tom was an idiot with you. He can't be thinking straight,' I continue. 'But he's finding out some home truths about *Leata*, and PharmaCare don't like that.'

203

Fran exhales heavily, coming closer to me, screwing up her mouth as if she wants to hurt me. 'Is that why your dad's sending you to a Health Farm?' she says, eyeing me suspiciously.

My breath quickens. 'How do you know about that? Fran, please,' I add as she stays silent.

Fran shifts the pile of books in her arms, steering me back into the now empty classroom behind us. She shuts the door behind her.

'I don't want to get my mum in trouble,' she says, nodding her head until I say, 'I get it.'

'She came home, she was furious, her whisky half-drunk and Tom had smashed and stolen her favourite photograph of us.' Fran blinks rapidly. The tears start to escape all the same. She brushes them away roughly. 'I told her Tom had wanted to get on her computer, and she lost it, big time. Threatened me with a Health Farm too!

'Then your dad came round.'

I feel the hairs on the back of my neck prick up. 'What did he want?'

Fran puts her books down, pulling on the green-blue ends of her hair. 'I was sent upstairs, but I could hear him pleading with Mum. He said he had *you* under control, that you were getting treated. And he was blaming Tom's behaviour on some Mikey bloke. "All Mikey's fault for planting ideas in Tom's head," he said. That he'll "sort them both".'

'He'll sort them?'

Fran's stiffly held face collapses. She looks suddenly younger. 'What's going on?'

'The stark truth: I think our parents are involved in murder to protect some sinister secret about *Leata*.'

'*Murder?*' she balks. Her eyes fill with water again. 'What secret?'

'That it might be harmful,' I say back, before I add, 'I'm really sorry if Tom upset you. If I've ever upset you.'

She opens her mouth to say something and stops, as if she's just realised who she's talking to. Her eyes hardening, she gathers up her books and walks away from me. I watch her turning out down the corridor, her head bowed amidst the hordes of wide-beaming girls, tossing their shining hair.

Him

Three pairs of eyes turn to me. One belongs to the headmaster; the others to police.

My heart starts beating an erratic rhythm. Sitting there – in the centre of the headmaster's desk, as if it's some poor animal on a vet's table – is my Puma bag. And beside it – three transparent bags set in an ordered line. I recognise them enough to know they're no washing powder granules.

I hardly hear the headmaster begin to talk. The drumming of my heart is so loud now I can hear nothing else, except the voice in my head. *I'm being set up. I'm being set up like Dad was.*

I am tuning back in as the policewoman to my right takes over from the headmaster. 'An anonymous call told us to search your belongings . . . you understand, Tom, we have to take this kind of thing very seriously. Immediate expulsion is the least of your worries.'

'It's a prank,' I hear my voice finally croak. 'That's not mine.' My limbs are starting to go numb.

The policewoman steps closer to me. She's using official words, familiar only from TV, 'arresting you . . .', 'right to remain . . .', 'anything you do say . . .' I can hear my breath rapidly leaving my nose. PharmaCare are the police. The police are PharmaCare. I'm in a Kafka nightmare – saying anything is pointless. Because this is payback. They can do what they want to me. They got Dad in the end. They're going to get me.

Her

All I can do is breathe in and out all the way to Vauxhall, one foot in front of the other. It's the only plan I can think of: start with Mikey; find out why Dad's after him; if Mikey's on Tom's side or not. I can only pray that he is.

It starts to rain. Drizzly, spitting rain from sagging grey clouds overhead as I approach the entrance to the shelter under the train arches. I spot Mikey stood on the step outside, sucking on the stub of a cigarette between nicotine-stained fingers like it's his last chance at oxygen. Next to him – a man with a Father Christmas beard and a thinning fur hat. Recognising me, Mikey plucks out the cigarette, stamping on it with a grim-faced smile. 'You here for me, darlin'?'

I nod, tightening my voice so I don't start blubbing or something. 'I've got to speak to you about Tom.' I try and soften the suspicion in my tone.

But Mikey doesn't hide his. He makes a curt nod of his head at me and turns to say a slow goodbye to Bearded-man. 'Make sure you come back tonight, Barney. I'll make good on a bed for you.

'Poor Barney.' Mikey cocks his head backwards as he waves his pass at the security pad and we enter into the shelter. 'Would you believe five years ago 'e was a banker in the city with a beautiful wife and twin daughters? We're all a few bad decisions away from destitution. Right?'

I nod. Right now – I couldn't agree more.

I follow his limping gait into the canteen, finding myself calmed by the serenity of the apple-green seats and the blue sky walls. Even the residents seem different. Unless it's me that's different. Some are finishing lunch. Others are chatting, or reading. A couple are playing a card game.

'Is Aggie still with you?' I ask Mikey, searching the canteen for the girl with the blonde dreadlocks from last time. Maybe I can properly chat to her this time.

Mikey pulls a face. 'Aggie? No, Aggie's no longer with us.'

'She got her own place?' I ask, expectantly.

'You could call it that.' Mikey crosses his chest. 'Went to one of them PharmaCare 'Ealth Farms – only way the doc'd agree to renewin 'er meths' prescription, right? I don't see many of my guys again after they 'ad treatment there. An' I didn't see Aggie either. But I heard about 'er. Found dead. And guess what? Coroner just ruled it 'eart failure. Lots of weak 'earts in London town at present, you ask me.' He kisses the silver pendant around his neck. ''Oping she's some better place now.'

I'm staring hard at Mikey's wizened face. My own heart pumping double time. 'Why couldn't someone have helped her?'

'Someone? Oo's someone then? That you? Or government wiv their quick fix solutions that are all about makin' money outta happiness?'

He relaxes his face when he sees the expression on mine. His voice softens too. 'Listen, girly. Everyone keeps poppin' them happy pills so they can pretend life's pretty; blame ugliness on those who look ugly to their eyes. But life ain't pretty.' He makes a dry laugh. 'Like those Georgian ladies that used to wear wigs an' perfume to cover the smells of their unwashed bodies . . . we spray out scent to 'ide the dirt beneath. But don't mean the smells aren't still there . . . does it?' He continues walking into the kitchen.

I smile a hello back to purple-haired Tammy, her arms deep in washing-up suds, and follow Mikey into the stock room, like Tom did when we were last here. Inside, Mikey turns on me swiftly, 'Is Tom okay? Not 'erd from 'im.'

I'm breathing fitfully. I'm still reeling from the news about that girl Aggie. I feel somehow responsible. Like I'm no better than Dad. 'Tell me first – whose side you're on. Tom's? Or PharmaCare's? My dad's a lawyer for PharmaCare and – '

'Oh, I know oo yer dad is, sweet'art.'

'And I heard him talking about some information they wanted from you – I thought you were Matt Riley's friend? – yet you've been selling PharmaCare something?'

Mikey scratches his temple, looking thrown. 'Yeah, all right.' He sucks in breath through his teeth. 'PharmaCare were sniffin' round me after young Tom brought them to my door, weren't they. I was gonna sell Matt's last bit of research for his story to make 'em bugger off. Earn some money for St Paddy's at the same time. Cos that's my priority, always 'as been, them boys an' girls who are invisible to the rest of you lot. Right?'

'Isn't Tom your priority too?'

'Yeah, well.' Mikey bites down on his lip. 'I 'ad Tom in mind as well. I weren't gonna give it to 'im, cos I wanted 'im to back off and stay right out of it.'

'He hasn't.'

Mikey nods slowly. 'Yeah. I was startin' to get that impression. That's why I 'eld onto what I 'ave. Sold off summit else. Some bullshit information. Stuff Matt wrote ages ago. Bought my guys a week's worth of food, it did.'

I take a deep inhale, trying to slow my heart rate. I can't think properly with my blood surging into my ears.

'Can I see what it is you have of Matt's?'

Mikey draws in breath. 'Told yer – that's summit I'm keeping as collateral for me – or Tom if 'e needs it.'

'He needs collateral right now,' I say urgently.

Mikey examines me, breathing out the smell of stale smoke. He gets out a packet of tobacco from his shirt pocket. Unfolding it he shows me a small memory stick nestling inside. 'Carry it on me all the time. Safest place.'

He folds the packet back up. 'All the same with you, I'd rather put it in Tom's hands meself, if – ' His mouth freezes on the last word.

I follow his gaze. Back to the door.

13

Life's short. Enjoy it!
Leata

Her

I stare at my dad standing there. Flanked by two others. One's that good-looking detective who was waiting for Tom on his drive on Sunday. The other . . . Slicer.

'Hope! What are you doing here?' Dad hisses through gritted teeth. Knee-jerk, I step back, half-cowering behind Mikey. Except it's soon apparent. They've not come for me.

'We have some more questions for you.' The detective steps forward towards Mikey as I step even further behind.

I feel Mikey fumbling for my hand, discreetly pressing the tobacco pouch into mine. I push it quickly into my jacket pocket.

'Brought the pitbull with you?' Mikey nods his head at Slicer, who's started wandering through the stockroom. 'Know why 'e's called Slicer?' Mikey twists round to ask me. 'Cos he used to be known for getting what he wanted outta people . . . with a cheese slicer. That's the kinda company yer dad keeps.'

'Get over here, now,' Dad snarls at me.

I stay put. Mikey's saying calmly, 'I told you all I know last time you visited. Transaction complete.'

'Like to talk to you all the same,' the detective replies, tilting his head in a way that seems to say, *you've no choice in the matter*. 'The *pitbull* here will help you if you won't come.'

Slicer comes back towards us, cracking his neck one way then the other, as my dad steps forward. 'Or how about DS Miles here arrests you for taking young girls into your store room? We can make her say whatever we need her to say.' Dad reaches for my arm, yanking me over to him.

'As if I will corroborate any of that!' I shout at him, trying to pull back towards Mikey, standing in front of him as if I might protect him somehow.

'You'll do as you're told,' Dad spits out, dragging me away again. 'You'll say what I tell you to say. You'll think what I tell you to think.'

'It's all right.' Mikey turns to me. 'Let's not get nasty. I'll come with you.'

DS Miles smiles 'good man' and starts leading him out, Slicer trailing behind them, a salacious sneer all for me drawn on his face.

Dad makes a vice-like grip on my arm. 'I'm not coming home with you,' I say.

Tammy's purple head appears round the door. 'You all right, love? Need any help there?' as Dad pushes his face into mine. His familiar aftershave makes me feel sick.

'You come with me now,' he whispers tightly into my ear, 'or I will get my contacts at the council to shut this godforsaken place down – pronto.'

I draw a sharp breath. I think of Aggie, and the others out there. Of Barney with the Father Christmas beard promised a bed for tonight.

Forcing a smile back at Tammy, I answer, 'I'm fine, just fine.'

Him

Students and teachers stare, half-horrified, half-curious, as I'm paraded out the school's front doors towards a police car.

I managed to excuse myself for the loo before we left. I cleared my phone's call log and all its messages. Not before time – the policewoman searches me and confiscates my mobile before we drive away.

Glancing out at the view, we're soon crossing over the M25.

'Why aren't we going to a station near school?' I ask as we pass signs to London.

'We have instructions to take you somewhere else,' the policewoman replies curtly. Both fix their eyes out front as if they don't want to look at me. As if it's them who're the guilty ones.

My mind's already filling with scenarios of what's going to happen to me. At least I've passed what I know to Hari and Pavlin already. OpenFreeNet can still release that. Now, I've just got to protect them all. Admit nothing, whatever they do to me. My heart speeds up another gear.

A while later we're crossing Lambeth Bridge. Dropping down from the street into an underground car park.

As the car pulls up, and they lead me out of the back seat, I see him, across a line of parked cars.

'Mikey?' I shout out. He's being directed into a lift. By Ethan bloody Miles. I gulp air. Trying to reconcile both Ralph and

Hope's warnings about Mikey – with the fact he's here now with Miles. So he is betraying me? He betrayed Dad?

'Mikey?' I say again as the lift doors shut out his face, and a Suit fills my vision.

'I'll take over from here,' he says to the policewoman holding my arm.

Her

I sit in the back of Dad's car, staring out of the window at the darkening sky. Stars are forming, pricking alight the further we drive out of London's smog. I never liked travelling in Dad's car; its ever-present new car smell always makes me feel sick. There's a box of *Leata* in the seat pouch in front of me, its slogan facing out, '*Life's short. Enjoy it!*'

Dad wears gloves to drive; the only noise filling the silence is the sound of their leather moving against the steering wheel. He's refused to talk since he pushed me roughly into the backseat. He won't answer my questions about what's going to happen to Mikey.

Even when I threw out the accusation that Dad hired Slicer to kill John Tenby and added, 'Did you kill Matt Riley too?' he refused to answer me.

By the time the car pulls smoothly into the drive, I'm half-faint with frustration. Dad pushes me inside. I hear the feet of my sisters scuttling away upstairs. Mum is standing all agitated by the table in the kitchen. A large glass of white wine beside her. 'Jack! Rose and Lily are in their rooms like you asked,' she tells Dad, her eyes flitting between me and him; nervous, as if she knows that Dad's going to blow. My whole body's tensing for that moment too.

It comes as he closes the door.

The slap on the side of my head sends me half-flying across the room. A sound storms my left ear, as if water's rushing in. I lift my hand to it as he comes in at me again, slapping my cheek this time.

'Not her face, Jack,' I hear Mum pleading. 'People will ask questions . . . not her face!'

Dad backs away, hissing at me. 'Not only are you openly slagging off *Leata*, but you're plotting behind my back with people who want to see PharmaCare brought down! Do you want to kill me? *Do you?*' He comes in again, coiling my top in his hand so my face is forced close to his. I can smell his last meal on his breath; see right into his bloodshot eyes. Spittle pools at the corners of his tight mouth.

He shoves me backwards so I fall into the handle of a drawer, spiking my back. I yelp out in pain as he continues, 'You're to blame! Defied me, disobeyed me as a child, constantly.' I watch his fists flex. They have Mikey. Tom hates me. Imogen is leaving. Helplessness grows mould-like inside of me.

Him

The Suit blandly pushes me forward to the same thin silver lift doors Mikey disappeared through. He scans a pass card, before the doors open. Together, anger and panic are brewing a storm in my stomach, as the Suit leads me into the lift – it descends – then out again, into some kind of concrete basement. We walk down a corridor of low ceilings, and eventually into a windowless room with just a table and four chairs. The Suit shuts the door as he leaves. I take a seat, staring round at grey walls and a concrete floor. There's a camera up high in one corner, a red light on it.

I sit there and start having stupid thoughts, from will Mum bury me next to Dad? to wanting to know what will happen to Dad's Puma bag they confiscated, when the door opens again. DS Miles walks in slowly, chewing gum.

'Tenacious little sod, aren't you? What the hell were you doing at Nina Mitchell's house?'

My heart answers for me, thumping maniacally against my ribcage as he takes a seat opposite me, throwing Dad's notebook onto the table. 'Makes for interesting reading.'

'How d'you get that?' I say, rubbing a hand over my mouth.

'We had to search your stuff at home too. Check there were no other drugs there.' He pulls my phone out of his pocket and slides it back to me. 'You cleaned that up like your dad deleted his emails.'

My jaw clenches at the mention of Dad. 'I want to go home.'

'Oh and you will. Your mother is distraught, naturally. The plan was to keep you in a Health Farm till your trial, but your mum's refusing. Kicking up a right stink actually. Didn't know she had it in her.'

I raise my chin higher, feeling a rare rush of pride for Mum, and notice the video camera light has turned to green. Miles stares round at it too.

'Who's watching us?' I ask.

'Why do you care? You're a teenager, you're always being watched – why else does the internet know what you want to buy before you do!' He re-adjusts himself in his seat.

'I know you're not police,' I say. 'You work for PharmaCare.'

'What?' The U-bend smile comes out. 'I'm kosher mate, the real deal.' Miles flips his jacket open to show a gun holster strapped to his chest I never even knew he carried.

'As in mafia kosher? And I'm still not your mate.'

Miles tips his head and taps the side of his nose. 'No – as in your mum's taxes pay for me. My job – is to take care of secrets that threaten national security.' He widens his eyes as I narrow mine. 'Like the death of one *Leata* inventor.'

My mind flashes with the river outside. 'Where am I?' I say, my voice thin.

'Thames House. Secret Service.'

'You're MI6?' I almost stutter.

'MI5. Why do people always get that wrong,' Miles smiles broadly.

My heart speeds up.

'So the Secret Service plant drugs on me to stop me asking questions about PharmaCare?'

'Tom, Tom.' Miles shakes his head slowly. 'You're jeopardising a serious investigation. We had to take steps to silence you. Fairy steps,' he adds, as if this is nothing. Nothing compared to what they could do.

'You're working for PharmaCare,' I say again, as if I'm not getting through.

Miles places a hand beneath his chin in thinking pose. 'MI5's remit is to protect the safety of society. Not to allow mind terrorism to hijack people's quality of life,' he says as if he's quoting from some textbook.

'You're bullshitting me.' I point a finger, jerking it at him as if it were a weapon.

He breathes in deeply, snapping both hands out from his sleeves. 'We simply require some cooperation from you. Cooperate – and everything will return to normal. Because we want to help you, Tom.' He slants his head sympathetically. 'We can arrange for Health Farm treatment to get you over your dad's death, you know. We *are* the good guys here.'

I pull my hands into tight fists. I'm an inch away from smashing them into his smug face. 'And what are you doing with Mikey Jones?'

'Mikey? He's helping us with our enquiries. Very helpful,' Miles winks.

My whole body tightens as I interpret his meaning. Mikey *is* with them. I join my fists, knocking them against my forehead.

'Don't press self-destruct,' Miles says clearly, calmly, looking at me from under raised brows. The vertical smile has totally dissolved; his eyes turn serious as he leans forward. 'How do you know your dad wasn't on the wrong side? How can you know for sure?' He pulls back, examining me. I can't read his expression.

'I won't stop till I find out the truth,' I hiss back.

'The truth's only what we want it to be. Choose to wash in your dad's dirty water, and you won't come out clean. Nor,' he adds, 'will your family. How about if your mum loses her job? She's cliff-edge close to it – did you not know that? Her job, Tom? All she has left to keep her going?' He ticks his head. 'And let's see.' He taps his fingers against his mouth. 'We understand your brother's involved in a spate of plagiarism – hard worker right? Ambitious? What a shame if he doesn't get his degree. Or how about that little Indian friend of yours? Sikh, isn't he?

What would his community say if they find out it was he who supplied you the drugs?'

I jolt up from the table, sending my chair flying behind me. My body overheating from anger and frustration. 'I'm going to expose you all,' I spit out.

Miles leans back, linking his hands behind his neck casually, as if we're just two blokes enjoying a pint in a bar. 'Expose what? Like I said. The truth is what we all want it to be.'

I'm breathing hard and fast. All I want to do is scream. An animal roar of a scream. 'You can't do this.'

'We can, and we have. Miles clocks an eye at the camera; back at me. 'You're being put under house arrest. We have you by the balls, mate.'

Her

'I should have expected this from the way you started life,' he says, cold eyes moving over me.

'What do you mean by that, Jack?' I hear Mum ask faintly.

'You,' he snaps back at her. 'You tricked me into marriage.'

'No, Jack! I just forgot to take my contraceptive pill! That's all.' Mum takes a large swig from her wine glass.

'Just forgot? Oh yeah, of course you did.' Dad rounds on her, a fist held high now. 'You saw the gravy train rock into your station is what you did. She might not even be mine. I wouldn't put that past you. Looks nothing like me, or her sisters.'

'That's not nice, Jack,' Mum's voice quakes, 'of course she's yours. You're his,' she says, trying to pass me some kind of reassuring smile, before her hands go shaking back towards her wine glass.

Dad's face whips round, staring long and hard at me. 'Right now I wish she wasn't.'

I try and stand taller, holding my hands up in case he comes at me again. Instead he goes to the door. He draws a long breath, glaring back at Mum. 'I have to go out again. I have an urgent meeting near Windsor to rectify this mess.'

Near Windsor? My muddled mind makes a connection – Blythe's house was near there. Is that where he's going?

His last words are for me – he reminds me what he'll do to the shelter if I try and leave the house, 'turfing the residents onto the streets just as the weather's turning cruelly colder.' Adding, 'Tomorrow morning, your mum will drive you to the Health Farm. I don't want to set eyes on you again until you're treated for this . . . this *mental* illness.' He emphasises the word as if it's something that disgusts him. 'You will get cured, Hope. And your Tom Riley will be muzzled. For good.'

Him

I can see Mum, standing under the porch light as the Suit drops me off. He drives off again before Mum gets to the car.

'Oh, Tom.' She hugs me to her. The kind of hug Dad used to give, squeezing the air out of me.

'Thanks for standing up for me,' I mumble into her hair.

She pulls me inside, shutting the door behind us. 'As if I wouldn't! How dare they keep me from you! Whatever you're up to – it's a first offence, they can't go holding you in prison, or insisting you go to some crackpot Health Farm. And house arrest is extreme!' Her thin face turns woeful. 'They say they found cocaine – cocaine, Tom?'

'It wasn't mine, Mum,' I reply plainly, but she doesn't hear. She's moved onto blaming herself now.

'I haven't been present. I've failed to help you,' she's saying. 'But I'm going to be different from now, I promise, Tom.'

I'm trying to tell her, it's not her fault, as she starts in on Dad. '. . . It's his influence; keeping dope around the house; drinking all the time. Then leaving us to this . . . if he hadn't, hadn't . . .' Her voice trails off. She's clutching at her mouth as if she's suppressing something from coming out.

I bring my arms back around her for another Dad-style hug.

'It'll all be okay,' she says, stroking my hair. 'It'll all be all right,' she continues, as if she's trying to convince herself.

I pull my face back. 'Is everything all right at work, Mum?'

She clears her throat. 'Work? Don't you worry about stuff like that.' But I can already see it – the way her eyes stretch and strain. There's a lot wrong with work. They're already doing what *Agent* Miles threatened they would. I breathe out. 'I need to call Nathaniel.'

Mum makes a face of relief, as if she's off the hook from discussing it further. 'Good idea. He's been worried.' She picks up the landline, dialling the number for me. 'Here, I'll make us some dinner.'

'Drugs, Tom?' Nathaniel says straightway. 'Mum's hanging on by a thread, she doesn't need this. You –'

'It didn't happen, all right?' My voice twists like his. 'It's a load of bollocks. I've been investigating Dad's story. PharmaCare want to keep a lid on what I've found so far. MI5 is where I've just come from, not some poxy police station. They've been spouting national security at me.' There's silence at the other end of the line. 'You still there?' I say.

'Yeah,' Nathaniel says quietly. 'Someone's been messing with my stuff. A copied essay I never submitted . . . '

My heart pumps harder. I've no way out of this. I either do what they say, stay silent, or else they'll hijack all our lives. 'It'll be them,' I exhale, rubbing my head.

'What's this about, Tom?' he asks, his voice sounding scared.

'The police and MI5 are in it with PharmaCare. Jack Wright set Dad up; now they're doing the same to me. Dad must have found out something really bad on PharmaCare – or he was about to.' I take a breath. It feels strangely good to be telling my big brother everything at last.

Until he says, 'So back off!'

'What?' I reply, pulling my head back from the phone.

I hear him hissing out words, his tone barbed. I move the receiver back to my ear. 'Back off from this. Now. This is your life. My life.'

I shake my head slowly, my stomach shrinking. 'How can you say that? PharmaCare most likely killed Dad! And –'

'It won't bring Dad back,' Nathaniel breaks in. 'I don't want my life ruined by the fact Dad ruined his.' His voice turns desperate. 'What future will you have if you get thrown in prison? Or if I get done for cheating?'

My stomach is kneading itself like putty from frustration. I have to stop myself punching a fist hole into the front door. Because he's right, isn't he? I might not value my life much since Dad left – but Nathaniel's? Mum's? I'm supposed to protect them. And what about Hari, and Pavlin?

'But doesn't it matter more what happened to Dad, than what they'll do to us?' I say, losing strength from my voice. I already know how he's going to answer.

'No! Dad no longer has a life and we do!' His voice deepens as if he's squaring up to me. 'Dad made the choices that messed up his life – not us.'

Tears start to leak out of my eyes. As if he can hear them, Nathaniel's voice turns softer. 'The person who was most important to Dad: was Dad.'

My phone is vibrating in my pocket. It's Pavlin calling.

I switch it to off.

Her

I unwrap the memory stick from Mikey's tobacco pouch. The smell reminds me instantly of him and more guilt wraps itself like sticky tape to my insides. It was me who took Dad and Slicer to the shelter in the first place. And now St Patrick's is without him.

I look out the window to check that Dad's car isn't on the drive before I slot the stick into my laptop. I click on its only file.

It looks like a draft article. Its title: 'Cloud 9'. But it reads as if it's a personal letter to someone.

*I've found every one of the nine names. Nine members
of the elite club, Cloud 9, who conceived, funded and
built Leata into what it is today. Nine members who*

were all at Oxford University together between 1985 and 1988. Two tutors. Seven students.

> *Professor Simeon Blythe*
> *Professor John Tenby*
> *Damian Price, Prime Minister*
> *Maurice Read, Chancellor*
> *Sarah Day, Home Secretary*
> *Perdita Brightsmith, CEO, PharmaCare*
> *Commander Philip Menton, Director of*
>   *Internal Security, MI5*
> *Bea Tyler, MD, Star Media*
> *Oliver Wyatt-Hall, Chairman, Merkins*
>   *International Bank*

I am stuck, repeatedly scanning the same three names on the list, as if somehow I've imagined the Prime Minister, the Chancellor, the Home Secretary there. The Progress Party aren't just in bed with PharmaCare . . . the Progress Party created the very drug they endorse? My head's spinning with what this means, as my eyes move on, my mouth moving soundlessly over the postscript at the bottom.

> *Cloud 9 protects a big secret, I'm sure of it, from what I've heard so far. Bear with me, will you? I just need to press my source to reveal it. She's got all the other information for me so far. I know Tenby will tell her the big one if she keeps on asking him. She's keen to help me, because she cares for me. I will get to it. I will uncover the final secret.*

I hear Mum coming back upstairs. Quickly, I take a photo of the file on my phone. Unplugging the memory stick, I hide it under my mattress. I lie down on my bed, pressing my fingers hard against my head.

She?

14

Dig a hole for the bad stuff and
good things will grow
Leata

Her

'Great! You're packed already! Happy seventeenth birthday,
darling! Into the kitchen, see what we've got for you! Lily and
I spent all Sunday afternoon shopping!' Her voice is pitched,
glossing over anything real.

'I have to go, Mum.'

She checks her watch. A beam drawn on her plump face
like the fifth Teletubbie. 'We have time! The Health Farm isn't
expecting us till eleven! Birthday breakfast, Hope! You can
eat as much as you want on your special day!'

'I'm not going to the Health Farm,' I say eventually. My
voice sounds dry and monotone next to hers.

'Why?' Her puffy eyes widen.

Why? The answer became clear in my mind overnight, like
scraping a patch of ice from a frosted windscreen. I've got to
risk St Patrick's being closed, for something greater. 'Because

I won't be the daughter Dad wants.'

'But the Health Farm is expecting you!' Her voice cracks. 'They will make you better! Your father insists you go!'

'No – I've seen what they did to Tara.'

'You can't leave.' Mum moves to stand squarely in front of me. I can smell last night's wine on her breath, mingling with strong coffee.

'Happy birthday, Hope.' Rose slinks into the hallway. Her serious face wearing a pained expression.

'Open your presents!' Lily dances out behind her.

'Back into the kitchen.' Mum swings round at them. Her voice unusually stern. Her face reddening.

Rose stays put. 'You can't force Hope to go to a Health Farm.' Her face starts to crumple as if she's about to cry.

'Quiet, Rose, I can't think!' Mum goes over to her handbag on the hall table. Rummaging inside she pulls out a box of *Leata*. Ripping out two, she shoves them into her mouth, pressing a palm against her lips as she jerks her neck to force them down without water. She turns back to me, fingers pinching at her temples, pulling the skin there taut so her puffy eyes become stretched. 'You must try and see it from Dad's point of view. You were always such a difficult child. Not compliant and obedient like the other two. Forever answering back; so strong-willed.'

'But for five years I have played compliant, obedient!' My ex-followers can testify to that.

'But darling – five years isn't that long in an adult life!' Mum's perpetual-chirpy voice is straining at the seams. 'And to go supporting Tom Riley in his hateful campaign against PharmaCare . . .'

'Is that what Dad calls it?' My words come out strangled. 'Have you met Slicer yet?'

'Who?'

I make a groan for 'I give up'. What is the point? She won't hear it. 'I'm going.' I push on past her plump frame, throwing a semi-smile of goodbye at Rose. Her mouth trembles back a reply of some kind.

'You can't just leave.' Mum's heels click after me to the front door. 'Stop this silliness! Dad says, you're . . . you're *mentally ill* . . . you don't know your own mind.'

I blink, fixing my mouth in a straight line to stop the scream bubbling up inside me. 'You let him hit me,' I say neutrally.

Mum makes goldfish gulps of breath. 'No – I – I talked to him. He'll stop that. Go to the Health Farm like he wants and we can go back to being a happy family!'

'We never were one. We're all just good at pretending at it.' I make a face at Rose – it falls somewhere between 'sorry' and 'see?'

'Hope: "*Dig a hole for the bad stuff and good things will grow*" and then you can be happy!' Mum beseeches.

I don't even bother answering that one. I dive out the door.

'But what will the neighbours say! They'll think . . . they'll think it's all my fault,' Mum calls out after me. 'What will I tell the school? Your father?'

'The truth,' I say, striding faster down the drive. 'The truth,' I shout again, without looking back.

Him

She's standing there, sort of hopping from foot to foot as if she's in a hurry. A large rucksack on her back.

Her hand springs out when I make to slam the door back on her.

'Hear me out first.' She looks anxiously behind her. I glance too. The police car that was here for most of last night must have left. I have no doubt it will be back.

Hope takes a gulp of air before pouring out words like she's doing some school presentation she's practised and just wants to get it over. 'I'm sorry I spied on you, okay? I genuinely thought I was helping you. Helping Dad.' She shrugs despairingly. 'Helping myself.' She looks behind her again.

'You going somewhere?' I gesture at the bag.

She nods. 'I don't blame you for hating me, Tom. But I'm seriously out of my depth and I just need to give you something.' She looks behind her hurriedly again. 'I don't have long. Mum will be calling my dad.'

'What's the problem, Hope? The happy pills not helping you deal with life any more?' I say stonily.

'I'm not taking them.' She looks intensely at me. I'm inclined to believe her. Unbrushed hair. Missing smile. Eyes stern, minus their usual strip of kohl.

'This is me. Without medication. Okay? Just listen to me.' She brings a memory stick out of her jacket pocket, forcing it into my hand. Her phone next, swiping it and pushing it in front of my face. 'Your dad's notes for his story.'

I read down the list on the screen. 'The Prime Minister?' I say aloud. I shouldn't be shocked by now, but 'Government *created Leata*?' . . . and . . . 'Commander Menton, MI5?' I think of the Commander in his straining suit. I can feel my whole body tensing with renewed fear. MI5 are controlling it, right from the top?

'Where did you get this?' I say, my voice tight.

'From Mikey at the shelter, and now he's in trouble.' She takes a quick breath. 'And I know Imogen swore she wasn't your dad's source, but I think she was. She's scared, about to run,' she spills out hurriedly. 'That's where I'm going now.'

I peer closer at Hope, suddenly noticing that the pink stripe on one side of her cheek isn't because she's been heavy-handed with the blusher. 'What happened to you?'

'My dad's what's happened.'

I don't say anything. I don't know what to say. My mind's finding it hard to digest everything she's telling me.

She starts walking away then suddenly turns and comes back again. 'But how could you treat Fran like that?' Her mouth strains as if she can't find the right words. 'You took advantage of her!'

I open my mouth to defend myself – my face burning – shut it again.

'You shouldn't use people like that. Whatever you're going through.' She screws up her face. I can't tell if she's just angry or fighting tears. 'It's no different to what your dad did to Imogen.'

The last sentence slams into my guts. I bite down on my lip; something close to shame rips through me at the comparison. *Am I behaving like Dad?* 'I'm not cheating on anyone. I'm not married!' I say back, bruised.

She shakes her head at me. 'You don't get it, do you?'

I make a face back, *get what?* I mean, who's she talking about now? Fran? Or her?

She turns to leave again. 'Watch yourself, Tom. I'll let you know if I find anything from Imogen.'

I stare after her, walking away from me down the drive.

'Wait,' I shout, 'I'm coming with you.'

Her

It only takes a few minutes for Tom to come rushing out of his front door, a similarly large rucksack hanging off his shoulder.

We dart straight to his garage, instantly reading each other's mind – his dad's car again, it's the safest way to travel. We chuck our bags in the back seat. Tom starts the engine, glancing at me, 'happy birthday by the way,' he half-smiles, before reversing the car out onto the driveway.

I notice the noise first, screeching to a stop on the road behind, before I see it. The familiar navy BMW.

I draw a sharp breath as I watch Slicer getting out of the passenger seat. Dad stays put; he stares fixedly ahead, like he doesn't want to look.

'Keep driving,' I say urgently to Tom who's asking, 'Who is that?'

'Keep driving!' I scream out. Slicer is walking down the driveway. I catch the glint of a blade by his side.

'I can't, I'll run him over.'

I swing my leg forward, pressing my foot down over Tom's on the accelerator. We shoot out of the drive. Slicer jumps out of the way at the last minute, tumbling down onto the front lawn.

Tom is breathing hard as I remove my foot and he changes gear. Not in time. Slicer is up, darting across to us. His hands slam onto the bonnet, the knife pointing upwards. His features snarl at us through the window.

'Go!' I urge Tom. He swerves the car round one hundred and eighty degrees, sending Slicer flying again. Shooting us straight through the prickly hedge that divides our homes, dragging half of it behind us before skidding us out onto the road towards its only exit. I glance Dad's furious expression as Slicer limps back to his car.

'Faster, Tom. He can't catch us.' Please, no.

Tom takes a right swerve into the next street, speeds us bumping across a wasteland waiting for new builds, down another. Left, right, out onto the main road.

'They're still behind,' I gasp, twisting my neck, watching as they swerve round another car to get closer to us.

Tom speeds up towards the crossroads. The traffic lights are turning amber. Now they're red. 'Keep going!' I shout out.

Tom's foot presses harder on the pedal, careering round the oncoming traffic either side.

I breathe hard as I watch Dad doing the same behind. As I look out front again, I hear it. A crash of metal. I twist round. A car has smashed into them. The BMW's side is dented. Another car swerves and blocks them in.

Tom drives faster.

I take a long breath, pressing my head against the back of my seat, as Tom's phone buzzes. He chucks it over for me to read.

'Your *dad*,' I tell him urgently, and read out the message. '*Ditch your phone or else you'll be traced. Get a new one. Text me a number.*'

'My anonymous Samaritan knows I'm on the move already?' Tom says, pushing a nervous hand through his hair. He glances at me. 'What you waiting for? Do it,' he says.

I wind the window down, chucking out first his phone, then mine. My tablet too. I tense as I hear them smash and shatter on the asphalt.

'This is a first – out from instant communication,' I murmur, winding the window back up.

'Back to where we were five years again then.' Tom looks at me fleetingly.

15

Give the gift of a smile!
Leata

Him

We're both breathing a little calmer as we join the A3. Hope fills me in on her visit to Mikey; tells me about this Slicer. I update her on Miles working as an MI5 agent and what I know about Cloud 9. We both share information on her dad, and John Tenby's murder, as well as mystery man, Professor Blythe. Until we're on the same page. But then we always did used to read the same books.

A silence drifts down over us as we get into London and start retracing the route we drove a few days ago. 'Last Sunday,' Hope says, reading my mind. 'It feels a lifetime away.'

We make the decision to abandon the car at Finsbury Park, in case Hope's dad already has the police searching for our registration. We buy two pay as you go phones from some stack 'em high electrical shop near the Tube. Hope raises neat brows as she tries to navigate the non-swipe, no-internet technology, as we wait for a bus to take us to Muswell Hill.

'Who've we got to communicate with anyway? Now we're fugitives?' I say, trying to make her laugh. Because she looks like she's going to cry.

At Muswell Hill, we have to ask someone for the way to Imogen's road. It's further than we thought. There's a chill in the air. As if autumn's finally realised it's no longer summer. It makes us walk faster, down the main street.

As if to taunt us, nearly every shopfront advertises *Leata* in some form or other. A poster in the charity shop promotes an event *Leata* is sponsoring: *'Give the gift of a smile!'* The pharmacy announces *Leata* Happiness Week starts end of November, *'banish those winter blues'*. Even the bookshop has a big window display with a bestseller from some *Leata* blogger – *Be Like Me!* by *Happyaslarry*.

I share Hope's relief when we turn the corner into Imogen's road and see she's there – packing the car outside her house. Benny, wrapped up in a scarf and bobble hat, is swinging on their metal gate.

'Imogen.' Hope darts forward. 'Benny!' she adds as he rushes, shiny-faced, towards her. She gives him a hug. I stand back a little, watching the Hope I remember. The Hope who cares, and cares deeply.

'Hope, Hope, why do cowboys ride 'orses not cows?' Benny's asking Hope as Imogen looks both ways down the street, before beckoning us impatiently inside.

'What are you playing at?' Imogen says as she closes the door behind us.

I scratch my head, unsure about being here, inside her house. Was this where Dad came when they . . . ? I shake it out of my mind.

'You'll get in trouble.' Imogen's face hangs heavy with worry before she adds, 'Who's done that to you?' She gently moves Hope's cheek to the side.

'We're already in trouble,' Hope replies. 'We found Matt Riley's draft article with the names of the nine who created *Leata*. Matt wrote his source is a woman. Did the list come from you, Imogen? Are *you* the source?' Hope finishes, appealing with those big browns of hers. It'd be enough to make me confess.

Benny is still bouncing up and down around us all. 'Hope, why can't dogs drive cars?'

Hope pats his bobble hat, staring earnestly at Imogen. 'Please. We're desperate.'

Imogen moves her head, as if she's trying to dislodge something painful. Eventually she lets out a long sigh. She looks at me as she says, 'Hope, if you can take Benny to get the rest of his bags. They're in his room.' She waits until they're upstairs before she turns to me again.

'Yes.' She fixes her lips tightly as if she's trying not to cry. 'I was your dad's source.' She bends down to zip up a bag by her feet. 'I'm sorry I lied to you.' Looking up, tears are in her eyes. 'I think John let PharmaCare believe that it was him who was Matt's source, because John guessed it was in fact me. Because I was the only person he confided in about Cloud 9. PharmaCare aren't even aware I know anything!' Her eyes blink fast. 'John was protecting me.'

I stand and wait for her to continue. Benny's squeals and questions fill the air from upstairs.

'And instead he gets killed by Matt – for not revealing to me the final secret!'

'My dad didn't kill John Tenby.'

'He did. PharmaCare told me – it was Matt.'

'They lied,' I say. 'Hope's dad is Jack Wright, the lead lawyer for PharmaCare. He organised John Tenby's death. And probably Dad's too.'

Imogen lets out a strangled gasp.

'I need to know,' I continue. 'The big secret?'

Imogen seems to slump. I push out an arm to keep her upright. She almost laughs. 'I don't know what it is.'

I'm bowing my head – the nine names alone aren't going to be enough – when I hear her add, 'But I think I know where you can find it.'

Her

I walk downstairs with Benny, dragging his Thomas the Tank Engine suitcase behind him.

'John left me a letter when he died,' Imogen is saying. 'I think he recorded the secret. I suppose he wanted me to have it.'

She looks between me and Tom.

'Can we see the letter?' I say, lightly, for Benny's benefit.

Imogen shakes her head. Benny speeds off down the hallway pretending to be Superman. 'I burnt it. It was too dangerous to keep. It mentioned the title of a book he'd left for me in his office. *The Fundamentals of Existence.* "It will answer the big question you asked me, keep it safe in case you need it," he wrote.'

'And you think this book holds the secret?' Tom asks.

'I'm sure it does. That was the *big* question I asked. That Matt pushed me to ask: if there *are* side effects. Though I suppose I wanted to know it for myself too.'

'So where's the book now?' I say, my eyes darting round.

'I never picked it up. How could I?' she adds when I shake my head in disbelief. 'It's in John's office. I told you, Nina Mitchell and her cronies watch me at work constantly. They would know instantly I'm up to something if I'd gone into John's office. And they're probably waiting for me to do that to see if I do know anything. They'll be ringing soon just to check why I called in sick today. Which is why I really must get going.' She calls out for Benny.

I'm inclined to agree. She has to get Benny somewhere safe. 'Where will you go?' I say as I trail them to the car.

'We'll be okay. John left me some money along with the letter.' Imogen gets Benny into his seat, strapping him in. 'Maybe I'll come back if this is ever over.' She turns, staring strangely at Tom behind me.

'We'll get the truth out there,' I whisper, so I might believe it myself. We have to. Imogen and Benny can't stay on the run for life. Nor can we.

'You'll need this,' Imogen is saying, leaning over the driver's seat to rummage in the glovebox. She straightens up, handing me a blue and yellow security pass on a loop. PharmaCare's silver logo glints next to a faded picture of Imogen with longer hair. 'The photo is so old, from a distance they won't know you're not me. This is for John's door.' She taps a key card attached to the pass. 'I don't know where the book will be in John's office,' she says, with a sad undertone, 'he loved reading, so there are many.'

I thank her and help her take the rest of the bags to the boot after I've told Tom to wait inside. It's more likely the

237

police will be searching for him than me.

'Stay here tonight if you want,' Imogen says when we're finished, giving me a brief hug. 'But I wouldn't hang around much longer than that. There's a spare key on the hall table.' She gets into the car, starting the engine.

Benny knocks on his window, excitedly calling out, 'Hope? Why do the leaf fall off trees, Hope?'

I try to match his grin, blowing a kiss through the glass. 'Because everything has to start again,' I answer him, as the car pulls away.

Him

We start plotting the minute Hope's back in the house. I agree with her, we'll stay here, just tonight. 'We have to get that book,' Hope is adamant. I'm less sure. Even with Imogen's security pass, it's dangerous. And we have no idea if we'll even find it.

I call Hari on the dinosaur phone, leaving a message for him to call. By the time we hear the sounds of children outside coming back from school, he rings me back on a borrowed number. I update him on all that we have now. That the nine names include the Prime Minister and MI5. Then I put him on speaker so Hope can hear too.

'We'll need to choose a channel not connected to OpenFreeNet to release the story first,' Hari's saying, 'to stop us getting shut down.'

Hope is pointing at herself vigorously.

'Are you sure?' I mouth at her and she nods, eyes wide. So I suggest it.

'Okay, that sounds good,' Hari replies. 'Especially as Hope's already a name in the vlogosphere,' he says. His voice climbs excitedly as he starts to lay out how it will work.

'It's important we do it right. We release three names each over three days,' Hari continues. 'That way we build up a drama. People like to tune in for a climax – especially if we get the big secret too. It will ensure a bigger swell of an audience, worldwide.'

Hope agrees eagerly like she knows what Hari's talking about, even if I don't. He starts sounding like Pavlin as he excitedly runs through some hacktavists' plan they're preparing with the PAL network, to get the information running through all kinds of feeds and sites and threads. 'We've got two major platforms on board too,' Hari goes on. 'One's an underground movement that hacks into all kinds of political sites. The other's the Big Pharma Watch-out – they specialise in stories on *Leata*. Now, we just need a campaign name. Something to make sure it trends.'

'Cloud 9,' I bite back fast. 'We call it Cloud 9.'

'I was thinking more on the lines of STOP*Leata* . . . you know.'

'It will make sense. Cloud 9's the secret club who started *Leata*.' And it's Dad's story, I add to myself.

'Okay. Hashtag #Cloud 9.'

#*Cloud* 9. I can feel excitement stirring within me. Is this how Dad felt? Is this what made him lose sight of what was right and proper?

Lastly, Hari tells us, '. . . meet us in Bristol, day after tomorrow? We should be ready by then.'

Hope nods; I say, 'We'll be there.' It's best we leave London soon anyway. Before we end the call, I ask him to run a search on Mikey, to somehow broadcast the fact he's been wrongfully arrested. I need to do something to help him. Who knows what they could be doing to him right now.

By seven we're both shattered. Hope's using Imogen's computer to make contact with the PAL bloggers she's in touch with. While she puts social media to rights, I make us a meal of whatever is left in Imogen's cupboards: baked beans, some green potatoes; scrambled egg with the last of the milk. I was up for going shopping, but Hope's anxious we don't leave the house, not until we go for good tomorrow.

We daren't put the lights on either, so the lounge goes steadily darker as we eat on the coffee table. I shuffle closer to Hope to see her as we chat quietly. Closer up, her face is drawn, her features pinched and strained. Like mine, her eyes are bloodshot. Unbroken sleep is a long ago memory.

It's virtually all we talk about – how with OpenFreeNet's support maybe we can pull this off. Maybe we can blow the lid on PharmaCare wide. Even bring them down. If we can prove *Leata* is harmful.

We don't touch on anything else. The past, recent and long gone. Her spying, my being an idiot with Fran, our old friendship. It all feels out of bounds.

'What if it's wrecked my body, my mind already?' Hope wipes her mouth with the back of her hand, pushing her empty plate away. 'What if it's a planned plague, some mad way to dramatically reduce the population?'

'Or more likely: reduce emotion in the world – and they don't give a toss about any long-term side effects.'

'What does a world look like with no emotion?' Hope says.

'No more wars.' I screw my eyes up, contemplating that one.

'No more love, just the "happy face" variety. Feelings courtesy of emoticons.'

'Shit no – then we have to bring them down,' I say. Hope laughs.

I wash up as Hope grabs some duvets and pillows from upstairs. We decide to sleep on a sofa each in the lounge. Dressed, in case we need to make a quick exit.

I shuffle down under Benny's Toy Story duvet. Apart from an orange strip of light coming from the streetlamp outside, it's completely dark in the room. Maybe that's what makes me say it.

'Sorry.'

Hope's voice across the room asks faintly, 'For what?'

I inhale, exhale; rub at my face. Sit up. 'For getting you into this. For falling out.'

'Which time?'

I laugh briefly. 'Both times.'

She's quiet for so long I think she must have fallen asleep. Till her voice floats back across to me. 'Why *did* you never talk to me again when we were younger?' There's a pause. 'After we kissed?'

'Because you told me you didn't want to be my friend any more. What was I supposed to do?' I answer rhetorically, maybe a little too bluntly. I didn't realise till right this minute I was still so pissed off about it.

I hear her shuffling into a sitting position. A grey shadowy figure across the room.

'What were you supposed to do?' she repeats.

I think I hear tears in her voice.

'You were supposed to come grovelling,' she continues. 'You were supposed to say sorry for upsetting me. You were supposed to try and understand why I was mad with you!'

A burst of anger travels across with each word. She's going on before I have chance to butt in.

'How could you have thrown our friendship away like that?'

'*You* did,' I say back. Well, she did.

She takes wheezy gulps of air as if she's exasperated with me. 'I was upset! Scared! All kinds of nervous, about starting a new school without you. And then you, my best friend in the whole world, you reject me! What I wrote meant nothing to you!'

I lean forward, getting angrier myself now. 'Hope – I didn't *reject* you! I was an eleven-year-old boy – marriage wasn't high on my agenda.'

She's gone quiet again. I bite down on my lip. Throwing the duvet off, I get out and root through my rucksack in the dark until I find my wallet.

I take it over to her sofa, perching on the edge. My voice comes out with a long exhale. 'I've kept it all this time. Because it did mean something.'

Her

I unfold the small piece of paper he's pushing towards me, turning on my phone to shine a light on it. Instantly, I recognise the foil star stickers and the pictures of dragons and dolphins I liked to draw.

Tom,

Wow, that was weird. Did you know you were going to kiss me at the same time I was going to kiss you? Great minds think alike? Oh, I'm sorry, only I have the great mind. Ha, only joking. It was nice. I liked it a lot. And I really needed it.

Cos I'm petrified about starting school next week. I can't imagine going to school without you. Mum keeps saying I'll make new friends. But I don't want any other friends. I only want you Tom.

So here's the slushy bit. BEWARE these words might make your squirm. Will you marry me? Don't laugh. I mean, it makes sense, yeah? You and me? Kermit and Piggy. Together always!

Okay – reasons I want to marry you.

You kiss nice. You really do!

Sometimes you make me cross, but mostly you make me laugh.

Yeeess, you can be really, really like mega-annoying (especially when you insist Luke Skywalker is a better fighter than Han Solo, just cos he has the Force) but you are also the KINDEST person I know.

I think of us being best friends forever and I feel so so so safe.

Can we make a promise? A promise forever? Here it is – in four years, one month, two or nine days (depending on whose birthday!), we turn sixteen. Let's run away and get married! We can come back *and live in the treehouse together like Tarzan and Jane!*

Okay, in case you've not got the question I'm asking (you can be dim sometimes. Only joking again) – I suppose what I'm saying is: Tom, will you be mine forever?

Love, Hope

P.S. Answer straightaway

P.P.S. Treehouse after dinner?

P.P.P.S. I promise to take ALL the blame for messing with Mr Austwick's gnomes. Even though YOU broke Fishergnome.

P.P.P.P.S. I just got given a phone (we can text!). Oh and Mum's still banging on about getting my first Leata prescription. Since when did I do anything that made Mum and Dad happy? Me and you Tom – that's all I need.

I look at Tom. 'You've kept it all this time?'

Him

'You were really waiting for me just to come grovelling? That's all?'

Her

'You don't know what it took to write that letter; how I felt. Dad was on and on at me to have nothing more to do with you – because of your dad's libel trial. And I chose you. Because you were more important.'

Him

'My dad saw your letter and took the piss out of it. That's why I emailed back the way I did. I was embarrassed.'

Her

'It really hurt – your email. I got enough mocking, enough of being made to feel stupid at home, from Dad. That's why I reacted so badly. I didn't mean for you to take my words seriously.'

Him

I strain to see in the dark; her lips are trembling; the whites of her eyes watery.

Her

'It was my first ever real kiss, Tom.'

Him

'Mine was Suzi Teller behind the bike sheds,' I say, trying to bring some levity to the situation. It doesn't work. 'I'm sorry. I am.' Something heavy is dragging through the pit of my stomach. Regret? Yeah, regret. A big huge dollop of it. I put a hand forward, gingerly trying to touch her cheek, except Hope moves and I just get her ear instead.

I take a breath. 'The reason I never talked to you after you said we weren't friends any more . . . it was because Dad convinced me you thought you were too good for me, off to your swanky school. "Like father like daughter," he said.'

I pull hard on my neck. As it hits me.

'It was about them. Not about us.' I pinch my eyes.

'They messed with us,' Hope is saying. She folds the letter up and hands it back to me. Shifting down the sofa, she says quietly, 'We'd better try and get some sleep.'

I cross back to my own sofa. Even though something's tugging at me to stay at hers. To say something else. To make up somehow for five years of not knowing each other. I pull the Toy Story duvet back over me. It doesn't reach my feet. 'Hope?' I say softly across the room. 'It might not have been my first. But it was my best. If you'd have turned up at my door any time after we fell out, I'd have made it up with you.

'You just never came. Till now.'

16

The world shines brighter
when you smile harder
Leata

Her

I bolt awake from a light and fitful sleep as I hear it; a violent banging on the front door. Immediately I imagine: Dad. He's hunted me down, come to get me! To incarcerate me in a Health Farm. Slam Tom into prison. I fumble for the kitchen knife I placed under the sofa last night.

The banging stops, then comes again, harder this time, rattling the glass in the front door. Tom is up, scrambling for his glasses. His hair all over the shop. The bell's pressed next. Continuously.

'We have to get out. Now,' Tom is saying, shoving his feet into his Converses.

I grip the knife as we urgently stuff items into our rucksacks, grab our coats.

More banging, this time with a voice: 'Imogen, open up. Now.' It's not Dad's. 'Imogen, I must speak to you.'

'It's Nina Mitchell,' I hiss at Tom. His eyes stare back at me, a panicked white amidst the fuzzy grey early light.

'Come on.' He pushes me down the hall, into the kitchen. I watch him fumble with the key in the back door until we are out, the chill of early morning hitting my face like a wall of glass.

Diligently, I insist on locking it behind us, then we run to the end of the garden, clambering over the back fence, jumping down into another garden. We creep up its path, out the side gate and into another suburban road – breaking into a run, rushing past the first commuters and the rattle of a milk van.

We keep running. The knife still held tightly in my hand.

Him

I watch her putting on make-up on the Northern Line. Smearing gloss over her lips. Stretching them into that plastic smile I've not witnessed for a while. Raking her hair sleek and neat. Fake Hope again.

We get off at King's Cross station, and go into the first greasy spoon we see, wasting time until normal office opening hours. We share a full English with two teas, counting the cash between us. Thirty-two pounds, eighty-five pence will have to last us. We daren't use our bank cards.

Stepping outside forty minutes later, the sky casts a gloomy grey over the concrete skyline. Yet still, the tall PharmaCare building cuts a proud figure. Its wide glass windows twinkling, as if even the weather can't dent its happy mood.

I follow Hope towards it – she's the one leading this mission; she always was the Holmes to my Watson – on through revolving doors and into a sparkling bright foyer.

I try not to stare around like I'm in another world. But I am in another world. It's like the setting for some futuristic film, complete with robot-women at reception, dressed in air hostess blue and yellow. Fixed above their heads is a large screen showcasing the latest *Leata* advertising campaign.

New and shiny; walls of white painted glass. I can almost see my reflection in the polished white floor. *Leata* brand colours are splashed everywhere. Even the table football we pass has men in tiny yellow and blue strips.

Hope is talking all bright and breezy nonsense by my side. Hyper-happy-Hope again. Pretending to be showing me around. Only I can recognise the anxiety showing in her eyes, the slight tremor in her jawline. She has tucked her hair behind her ears, like Imogen's on the security pass looped round her neck, but if anyone glances long enough at the photo to recognise it as Imogen, we're done for.

I trail Hope, her head held high up to the security gate. The man there's smiling like you never see security guards smiling. *Leata* happy.

'Can I just take my friend into the canteen for a coffee? Really quickly, I promise,' Hope asks, batting eyelids; cute smile; her hand spreading casually across her chest to cover the security pass.

I hold my breath.

'As long as you sign him in,' the guard replies cheerfully.

We all smile. 'You know, maybe I'll just get us takeout,' she beams at me. We pull back. 'Change of plan. I go in alone,' she whispers to me. I can hear the nerves escalating in her voice.

'No. You need a lookout,' I say under my breath. 'We can't split up.'

'And I can't risk signing in as Imogen. We're sticking out too much anyway with our bags, the way you're dressed,' she says, looking at my clothes – another of Dad's T-shirts, Dad's jacket and my dirty black Converse –'Wait outside.'

Her

I follow three others into the lift, beaming all the way. It hurts my cheeks. I'm out of practice.

'My message this morning was *"Everyone votes for happiness".*' A woman slides in next to me, a Starbucks in one hand, shiny briefcase in the other.

'Mine was *"The world shines brighter when you smile harder,"* I lie.

'Oh, I sooo love that one. I've had it twice now. I got a coffee mug with it printed on for my husband.'

'Lucky husband.' I force a laugh as fake as hers.

We both smile some more into the mirror, the messages printed there appearing scrawled over our reflection. I want to scratch them off.

The lift doors open. 'Sixteenth floor. Executive suite,' the recorded 'happy' voice trills.

I step out, holding the directions Imogen gave me like a personal sat nav in my head. Take a right, down through the open-plan secretary pool, another corridor; next right. The first double doors . . . I'm there.

I swallow back the panic rising tidally in my chest as I lift the key card, stopping as a group of smartly dressed people walk past. I smile away – the one easy thing about pretending you work here – and get out my new crappy phone. Pretending to speak into it, I jig excitedly on the spot; my free hand trying to discreetly slot the stiff card into the door behind my back.

'You!'

I jump. A middle-aged woman, brown hair pulled into a tight bun, is coming towards me. She points at me with the pen in her hand.

I freeze, my heart pounding so loud the whole floor must hear it.

Him

I'm pacing back and forth outside with our bags. I can't keep the nerves from my face, my feet. I stride further away from the front entrance in case I'm starting to look suspicious. Pulling Dad's old flatcap out of my jacket pocket, I put it on.

I look back towards the glass front of PharmaCare, more fear hijacking my body. Is she in Tenby's office yet? What if she gets caught? What will I do then, carry on? Or surrender? I can't do this without Hope.

I need to do something constructive. I think of Ralph. I've not spoken to him yet. We still need his help.

My mobile doesn't have enough top-up for a long call and I need to keep what's left in case Hope rings. I look around for a telephone box. I've never had to use one before. I walk away a little, obsessively staring back at the revolving doors, till I spot one beyond the water fountains, back towards the station. It stinks of piss and mildew inside; stubs of cigarettes carpet the floor. I'm half-surprised to find the phone actually has a tone.

'Tom!' Ralph exclaims when his wife Molly passes the phone to him. 'I've tried calling you. Your mum's going out of her head with worry. What the heck are you playing at! Drugs! Escaping house arrest!'

'I've been set up.' I lean my head against the glass, fixing my mind against the image of Mum alone at home. 'Tell her sorry, will you? That I'm trying to sort it.'

'Tom – you've got to tell me what's going on.'

I take a breath. 'We've got information that will damage PharmaCare. And we're just about to find out *Leata*'s big secret – the one Dad was after when he died.' My eyes stay fixed on the front of PharmaCare. *Please, Hope, be all right in there*. 'I can't tell you over the phone.' I slot in more coins as the beeps go. 'It's serious shit, Ralph. But you can be part of announcing it, if you can convince the *Daily Herald*. In memory of Dad,' I add.

'You've really discovered the big secret Matt was banging on about?'

'You should have believed in him, Ralph.'

I hear him sigh long and hard down the phone. 'All right. All right, Tom. I can hear you're serious. Let's meet then – tell me where.'

I try to think on my feet. 'Can you head to . . . I dunno, Trafalgar Square, like now? I'll text you where I am once I'm there. But . . . Ralph – don't tell Molly, don't tell anyone.'

Her

'Are you up here for the nine thirty meeting? It's been delayed by ten minutes, okay?' Tight-bun lady says.

'Okay!' I beam back, pulling my phone back to my ear, for a faked '*Really? But that's fantastic!*' Until the woman leaves and the corridor goes momentarily quiet. Hurriedly I turn, slotting

252

the key in, my ears pricked for more incoming. I try the handle. It's still locked. My breath's coming out in short bursts, the key card slipping in my clammy fingers as I try again, slower this time.

Yes. The door clicks open. I slip through it, locking it behind me.

I make a long exhale, before staring hurriedly around. Imogen wasn't joking – John Tenby loved books. This is going to take ages. There are shelves and shelves of them; old, new, thick, slim. The only wall not covered is the one made out of glass. A floor-to-ceiling window framing a perfect view of London.

I start searching to the right of the desk, its weighty, dark wood incongruous with the corporate PharmaCare furnishings. *The Fundamentals of Existence* . . . where are you? I've made it halfway around the room when I finally see it. Red and leather-bound, like an old-fashioned encyclopaedia. Pulling it from the shelf, hands trembling, I start flicking through text on the *fundamentals of existence*, not knowing what I'm looking for. Then, in the middle, the font suddenly changes: a smaller typeface. I find where it starts, my heart whirring. I need to know what five years of taking *Leata* has done to me.

My body rocks as I read it. I can't believe my eyes. I slam a hand across my mouth as I almost shriek out loud.

Leata, the smaller typeface reads . . . *it's a placebo.*

. . . *The components of my manufactured plant source: a special hybrid of lemon balm and chamomile, mixed with water and the prescribed list of innocuous chemicals. Harmless, ineffective ingredients all of them, making a wonder drug that casts the spell to send us all happy.*

My eyes skim over more words, before: . . . *the plant source I created in the lab might have a mild calming effect, but no more* than, say, peppermint tea. My challenge was ensuring the formula was complex enough to remain undecipherable, so that none of my science colleagues might identify its components. The few who did, PharmaCare paid off handsomely.

I keep reading as Tenby lists the precise route to making *Leata*, and ends with an outline of the strategy he was presented with.

Professor Simeon Blythe is the mastermind behind Cloud 9 . . . he set out to use clever marketing and media, product messaging and advertising campaigns, for Leata to brainwash the nation into believing themselves happy. Like it says in Hamlet, 'There is nothing either good or bad, but thinking makes it so.'

Him

My whole body jolts against the phonebooth as they walk right by me. Their backs straight. His bent nose, the suit straining over the familiar barrel stomach. The Commander. Miles' boss, who I now know to be MI5. And a member of Cloud 9. Walking alongside is Nina Mitchell, Fran's mum.

My chest tight, I exit the booth, following behind them. I watch them walk in through the revolving door of PharmaCare.

Grabbing my phone out again, I punch till Hope's new number comes up. Through the glass, their heads are disappearing towards where Hope caught a lift. My heart bangs in my chest, constricting my throat.

Come on, come on, pick up. I start pacing, grinding my phone against my ear till my skin burns.

'Hope!' I say as finally she answers.

And the line goes dead. I stare at the phone. I'm out of top-up.

Her

'Tom? You okay?' I listen to silence the other end. I try calling him back but it goes straight to voicemail. He must be warning me of something. I close the book and start moving towards the door. My hand's reaching out to unlock it, one ear pressed to hear into the corridor beyond – when I catch it. Voices coming towards me. Getting louder. I jump back at the sound of a key card being slotted into the lock. *Oh, god*. I look around frantically. The only way out is the glass window. Sixteen floors above ground level.

Him

I keep making to dive through the revolving doors, before I stop again. I need to rescue Hope. Get her out of there. But how? I'm almost crying. I clutch at my hair. My heart is ramming so loud against my ribcage, I swear I can hear it over the thrum of Kings Cross traffic.

I can't bear the idea of losing Hope.

Not after Dad.

Not now.

Her

I try hard to hold my breath; the book pressing tight against my chest to stop it even rising. If they look carefully at the reflection in the window they'll see me curled up, under the desk, a faded part of the composition of St Paul's grey dome, the Grater and the Shard.

'And you said someone checked thoroughly in here?' A gruff male voice asks.

'We looked in-between the books; lifted up the carpet. We found nothing.' I know that voice – it's Fran's mum, Nina Mitchell, again. 'Just like there was nothing in his house when we searched it.'

'I have my people trying to locate Imogen Poole.'

'Good.' She sniffs. 'What is it you believe she has?'

The desk above me creaks as a body weighs it down. The male voice exhales heavily. 'John Tenby's solicitor finally admitted last night – under severe pressure – that he passed on a letter to Imogen at John's bequest. He says he has no idea of its contents. I think he's telling the truth. Blythe insists we find this letter. He also wants you to employ your rat to get rid of that boy once and for all. The girl too if you have to.'

'Slicer? Get rid?'

'Don't get sentimental on me, Nina. You said Jack Wright's washed his hands of the girl.'

'He has . . . but he wouldn't want us to . . . she's in the same year as . . . '

I squeeze my eyes shut to stop the moan escaping from me. *He washed his hands of you ages ago.*

'If you want to keep your job there's no room for sentimentality.'

I hear the door open again, followed by a different female voice. 'Menton, there you are. My secretary said you'd arrived.'

'Morning, Perdita,' this Menton says, lifting his weight off the desk.

Names are already flashing in my head from Tom's dad's list. *Perdita Brightsmith, CEO, PharmaCare. Commander Menton . . . Shit*, MI5.

'Nina, go and wait in my office,' Brightsmith says.

The door shuts again.

'Well?' the woman barks.

'I have the situation under control. Blythe isn't overly worried.'

'Blythe believes we're invincible! History records the fall of power – and he's naive if he thinks nothing can break us. Has he moved his documents into Merkins Bank vaults like the rest of us?'

'He still doesn't believe everything should be in one place.'

'But he has the Magna Carta of documents stored at his house, for god's sake! We have massive leaks springing up everywhere! Imogen Poole disappearing with god knows what information. And this Riley boy – what are we doing about him?'

'We're going to remove all our problems, Perdita.'

Brightsmith sucks in her breath. They come closer to the window. My muscles tense as I see their faces reflected in the glass above mine. His is round and over-fed. I recognise the woman's polished Scandinavian features instantly from the media. 'First, dress the problem appropriately. I have given Bea the green light – Star Media will be releasing news of John Tenby's death tomorrow morning. Blythe approved it. I called an urgent meeting of our Positive Press members last night to update them. Fight fear with fear, yes?'

I hear feet padding out again. The door shutting – this time it locks. I breathe out like I've just shot up from underwater. Stumbling out from the desk, I return to the door, listening until it goes quiet.

Quickly, I unlock and move back into the corridor; walk fast, head down to the lift. Praying desperately that no one sees me.

My throat swelling with fear, my mouth dry, I wait for the lift to reach my floor, hugging the book tightly to me. Once the doors open, I rush in, relieved it's empty – until it stops at the tenth floor.

My eyes dart to the ground as he gets in, chatting with a colleague – the beard, the low-hanging jeans: Toby – *Leata*'s Social Media Manager.

'What are you doing here?' I glance up to see him staring me down in the lift doors' reflection. 'We cut you off. You're causing us big problems.' His eyes turn to me.

'Yeah,' I say brightly, counting the levels. *Five, four*. 'How stupid have I been?' *Three, two*. 'So I just met with your boss, didn't she tell you?' *One*. 'To see how I can turn it around, come back on board.' *Zero*. I rush out.

My arm gets yanked back.

'OMG! My boss is CURRENTLY at the New York office!' Toby raises a 'got you' sneer on his face. He looks over at the security guard, the one I was trying to charm earlier, clicking his fingers. 'Hey, over here!'

I wrench my arm away. I have no time to think. I dart forward, pushing in behind a woman through the gates; they snap shut against my back. I weave fast through the waiting area to cries of 'stop!' A group of Japanese businessmen inadvertently save me as they enter, filling the foyer. I spin through the revolving door, the sound of a scuffle behind me.

My eyes manically search for Tom.

'Run!' I scream as he almost slams into me. 'Run!'

17

Not all questions bring
the answers we need
Leata

Him

Even by Charing Cross, we're both still panting hard like we've just run a marathon.

As we reach the Strand I come to a sudden standstill, bending over like I'm winded, as it hits me. My eyes blink back hot tears. 'Shit, Hope. I thought I'd lost you too.'

She crouches down, so her head is close to mine. Her breath fast. 'I'm here. I'm okay.'

'No, you don't understand,' I stare down at the ground, pitted with rounds of dirty gum. 'People go. They leave you.'

'I'm not going anywhere.'

My breath rattles in my chest. 'You just said, you heard they're going to hunt us down, get rid of us. Like they got rid of John Tenby, and Dad!'

'But right now we're here still,' she says, pulling my chin up to see her. 'We're alive.'

Gradually, I nod; I rub my eyes and straighten up. 'So now we know their dirty secret,' I say, thinking back over what Hope whispered to me as the Tube rocked southward. *Fucking placebo?* 'People are getting prescribed to inhale air, to make them feel good about themselves.'

Hope's eyes dart left, right. 'We should get off the streets.' She starts pulling me across the road.

'Maybe we shouldn't meet Ralph,' I say lamely. My legs feel weak, as if my body's giving up. Hope tugs me harder.

'No, come on, let's do it. Like you said, we need someone in the press on the inside, a paper *not* owned by Star Media.' She glances around. 'The café in St Martin's crypt.' She pulls a wry smile. 'If anyone's following us, we can claim sanctuary in the church.'

Once I've topped up my phone and texted Ralph, I let her drag me underground, down a narrow staircase into a serene space, far away from the traffic chaos just outside. Subdued honey lighting glows on a brick-vaulted ceiling. Tombstones cover the floor. Epitaphs engraved on stone amongst the civilised clink and clatter of afternoon tea.

'Sit,' Hope commands me, claiming a table in the furthest corner behind a stone pillar. She leaves to get us drinks. I raise my eyes to the curved ceiling, imagining an altar above us. Surely the church can't be in bed with PharmaCare too.

Eventually Hope returns with a tray. 'I bought us coffees, double shots. Cake too. Sugar for shock, that's what we both need.' I can tell by the tone of her voice she's trying to act like everything's okay, for my behalf.

I reach my hand forward and clutch at hers. It's trembling like mine is. 'I'm so sorry I got you into this, Hope.' I can feel the tears threatening to return. I clench my mouth to halt them.

'I got myself into it,' she says, grabbing one of the cake slices and taking a big bite. 'I'm okay. I feel sort of delirious with fear to the point I can't feel frightened any more – you know, how people say pain can get so bad you don't actually feel it?' She talks with her mouth full, like she used to.

It makes me smile. I gesture at my own mouth to show her she might want to wipe hers.

She laughs; takes a slurp of coffee. 'We've got to get access to Blythe's house somehow. He's the one behind it all. Find out what they say he's hiding there before they remove it. It'll be the final proof we – '

'He's here,' I interrupt her, waving a discreet hand round the pillar as I glance Ralph's red head cutting through the room.

'Hell, Tom,' he says as he reaches our table. He looks as tense as I feel, bags under his eyes; his hair is sticking up in places. 'What we going to do with you?' he asks, passing a tired 'hello' Hope's way.

I introduce them as he passes over an envelope with a sigh. 'I really don't want to fund this, but I made your mum a promise to give you some money. She says she'd rather you ate than not.' Another sigh. 'I wish you'd stop this and go home.'

I thank him for the envelope, pushing it into the top of my rucksack. 'We *know* PharmaCare's big dirty secret, Ralph. We know it.'

Ralph taps the table, looking from me to Hope, back to me again. 'Are you for real?'

His response makes me impatient. 'Ralph! Dad was telling the truth; he wasn't deranged, delusional! There are nine powerful people at the helm of creating and driving *Leata*. We know who they are. And the secret they protect.'

Ralph shakes his head; pinching both eyes with finger and thumb. 'I've heard these stories before. Rumours, conjecture. No one ever has any proof. Do you have proof?'

I tighten my hands round my coffee mug. 'Dad listed the nine names and –'

'Tom, people won't believe your dad! People love their *Leata*. Like people love their cars, their TVs, their tablets. The public won't let you damn *Leata*! "*So what?*" the man on the street will say, and carry on taking it . . . because it makes him happy!'

'We have proof about their big secret,' I say, annoyed at his tone. 'We have it in print. We're going to get our message out there.' I stab at my chest. 'Internet, international media; a bloody plinth in Trafalgar Square and a loudspeaker down Oxford Street if we have to! Whatever it takes. We will expose PharmaCare and people will see what they've been swallowing!'

Hope passes me a sharp look. I shake my head briefly, to let her know I won't. We agreed, we won't say anything until we film the vlogs. *Don't trust anyone*, Mikey said. Shit, I hope he's all right.

Ralph is pushing out a hand at me, frowning. 'So tell me: *is* it side effects? Is *Leata* bad for you?

'I can't tell you yet.'

'Hell, Tom: my kids take it.' He raises his hands in the air when I don't answer. We stare each other out. 'Okay. So what do you need from me?'

'Get me a promise from the *Daily Herald* that you will run the story and I will hook you up with the release just before it comes out online.'

Ralph bites down on his lower lip. Eventually, he pushes himself away from the table with a long sigh. 'All right. Okay . . . give me a minute, let me talk to my editor, yeah?'

Hope's eyes follow him as he walks away. 'Sod him if he's not keen. The *Daily Herald*'s just one paper in a mass of global media.'

'He's my godfather. My dad's best friend. I have to give him heads up, even if he doesn't fully believe us.'

I jump up to help a woman with a pram navigate the small space beside our table. The pram bangs against Ralph's chair as she passes, knocking his satchel onto the floor.

I bend down, shoving loose items back in, when the colours catch my eye. The distinctive shades of blue and yellow.

I tug it out. A security badge, not dissimilar to the one Imogen gave Hope, except this one, above Ralph's name and mugshot, is titled *Leata Positive Press Member*.

I glance up. Ralph is still over on the far side of the room, his phone pressed against his ear; one hand gesticulating as if he's arguing over something.

I flick the badge Hope's way.

'Shit, Tom,' her mouth gapes open. 'The Positive Press network. I read rumours about it on a PAL blog. And Perdita Brightsmith mentioned meeting members from it yesterday.'

I rub at my face, thinking about what the Commander said in the car that time, how they bury bad news.

'We have to get out. Now.' Hope starts tugging me upwards.

We're making our way to the exit as Ralph reaches us. 'What are you doing?' He looks down at the badge still in my hand.

'Tom.' He licks his lips nervously. 'Come back to the table. Please. Let me explain.'

'Show me your phone first. Show us who you just called,' Hope interjects.

'So many press are doing it now. Why should I be left behind!' Ralph reaches out to me. 'Molly and I desperately needed the extra money. For a bigger house . . . good schools for the boys . . . you can't comprehend the pressures being a parent puts on you, Tom, not till you have a family of your own.'

I bare my teeth, resisting Hope pulling on me to leave. 'My dad had a family too, Ralph. What about my dad and *his* family?' I throw the words out as new ones form in my head. 'It was you, wasn't it?' I stare into his familiar grey eyes. We're both breathing hard, two bulls in a field. 'The nine names – he sent them to you. Dad wrote up those notes for his story – for you!'

Hope's grip on me loosens. She steps closer towards Ralph, her brow creasing.

Ralph wipes a palm over his mouth.

'And you called him in. You told PharmaCare that Dad had something on them,' I say my voice thin.

'I thought your dad was taking the piss at first . . .' Ralph breathes out, 'but he was adamant – about the Progress Party having created *Leata* – *Leata* creating the Progress Party. And then this big secret, that he reckoned was about side effects. I asked PharmaCare, because I wanted to know the truth. How was I to know they'd mess with him – if I'd known . . . I would never have . . .' He collapses his face into both hands, lifting it again. 'They promised me they didn't kill Matt!'

Slowly, I shake my head at him.

'You don't understand how they operate,' Ralph appeals to me, his eyes panicking. He lifts his fringe. 'They did this when

I asked questions about what happened to Matt.' The bruise there has paled to a bluey yellow.

'Almost *Leata* colours,' I say, slamming the security pass into his chest. 'You traitor,' I hiss. 'You might as well have killed him yourself.'

'Tom. I had to look out for my family. Your dad was –'

I don't hear what Dad was. My arm swings up, my fist making contact with the side of Ralph's pale skin. 'That's for Dad.'

Ralph stumbles backwards, a hand clasped to his jaw; his eyes registering shock.

I shake my knuckles; already they throb and sting.

'Consider yourself officially relieved from godfatherly duties.' This time I let Hope guide me away.

Her

We move fast, back up to street level – the distant sound of sirens mixes with other traffic. 'Ralph must have alerted them,' Tom breathes out.

My heart is racing. Something tells me we're running out of time, out of luck.

'We've got to hide. Quick.' I grab Tom's hand, pointing over the road at the National Gallery. 'It should be packed with people.'

We take the stairs two at a time, diving inside the main doors, as the sirens become louder. From the foyer, we hear the screech of tyres out in Trafalgar Square.

'Try and look normal,' I hiss at Tom. His mouth is wide open; his forehead glistening with sweat.

I tie my hair up into a ponytail, stabbing it into a bun with a pen from my bag. Reaching across, I pull off Tom's glasses. 'Can you see still?'

He stares back at me dazed, but nods.

I pull the flatcap from his pocket, pushing it onto his head. 'Here's what we're going to do,' I say, trying to get him to focus. 'We split up, just for fifteen minutes or so. They're looking for us together,' I add when Tom shakes his head briskly. I grab a map from the nearby leaflet stand. Despite the *Leata*-sponsored audio guide 'touring paintings with positive depictions of the human condition', the National Gallery's not yet been wholly sanitised of 'negative' pictures. 'Meet me by *Samson and Delilah*. Level Two. Fifteen minutes.' I push him off in the opposite direction, watching him hesitantly slope away, before I go on.

I keep walking, past a panel advert for a new Monet exhibition: '*His happy period*'. Naturally it's sponsored by *Leata*. I could almost tear it down.

Eyes averted from the guards, I stay to the most densely populated galleries. If I enter a room that's quiet I turn round again.

Ten minutes later, my skin's prickling with regret. I'd rather know Tom's safe and risk being spotted together. My phone has no signal, I've no way of reaching him. Looking down, I realise I still have his glasses clutched in my hand.

I begin making my way to Level Two. As I get closer, I start to rush. A feeling of foreboding is washing through me; the same I got when I wrote that childish letter of a marriage proposal. A fear that everything is going to dissolve, that I'm going to lose Tom. Our friendship. My safety net.

I walk faster still. *Please be there. Please be okay.* Down corridors, through swing doors, past rooms of seventeenth-century art with portraits of fine ladies and gentlemen that the audio guide includes on its 'happy' tour.

Something tugs and pulls inside of me, when I spot Tom amidst the crowd of people admiring *Samson and Delilah*. A feeling floods me, like sand mixing with sea water . . . all the adoration I held for him as a kid, washing over the way I've viewed him distantly these past years.

He's pretending to concentrate on Samson; but his lips move as if he's talking to himself; his eyes darting nervously. I push gently past people till I'm standing right behind him. I lightly flick the back of his head like I used to as children. 'Are you scared you'll lose *your* strength if you cut your hair?' I say, my voice low into the side of his neck.

'If it's a weakness to look neat and ordered – and I consider it to be – then yes,' he says back, under his breath. He turns, breathing hard. His face close to mine.

Instinctively our heads slant and tip at the same time. I'm not even thinking as my mouth moves – to meet his.

It's as if we never left the treehouse.

The first kiss, continuing into the now.

Tom and Hope. Against the rest of the world. His lips soft. His skin smelling of Tom.

Shockwaves ripple through me as he puts an arm tightly around my waist. We kiss harder, until the crowd sways and someone jerks into us. Our mouths pull away. 'We'd better go,' he says softly.

He takes my hand, staring intently at me with his newly naked eyes.

We head together, hands clasped, down to the ground floor, on into the packed café, both freezing as two policemen sprint past the far window.

We stay put. I pass Tom his glasses as he swears under his breath. We wait, until more crowds of moving tourists swarm in front of the glass. Slipping out of the café exit quickly, back into the cold, we walk fast, staying hidden amidst crowds of people, until we reach Leicester Square. It's satisfyingly crammed with tourists, all nationalities, all ages, like some global melting pot. We keep walking full pelt, zig-zagging through the crowds and out the other side. It starts to rain as we approach Piccadilly Circus. It offers a welcome shield, the number of umbrellas that spring open.

We join a sprawling queue at the top of the steps into the Tube. Above us, the Circus signs glow. The largest one, which not so long ago belonged to the red and white of Coca-Cola, now sports the blue and yellow of *Leata*. It flashes with its daily message as if it's mocking us. '*We all win the race when we're happy!*'

We keep moving with the crowds further down the stairs when Tom suddenly stops, checking his phone from his pocket. He meets my eyes, gripping my hand tighter. 'My Samaritan caller. They want to meet me. Now.'

Him

'It's saying head down Piccadilly towards the Ritz.'

I hold the phone out in front of me like it's a diviner leading us to water. By the time the Ritz comes into view another text bleeps through.

Cross the road and keep walking down. Pass a chocolate shop on the corner. Turn right. A building at the end. Go through the black door.

We do as it says, though Hope's more hesitant. 'What if it's a trap? Look what just happened with Ralph.'

I take a breath. 'This person has only ever helped me the whole time. I need to find out who it is.' I mean, it *can't* be Dad – that's stupid. Isn't it?

We find the building, stuck at the end of a cul-de-sac directly off Piccadilly, a road I've never noticed before. Entering through a grand door, an elderly security man is sat in a room just off the black and white chequered hall. His aged voice croaks, 'Can I help?' as another text comes through. I repeat its message. 'We're here to see Dr Talbot. Number thirty-three.'

'Go on up then.'

We walk further in; it's like a building turned inside out – old-fashioned galleries above host black doors to flats, with Victorian lamp posts spaced between them. We start climbing the main stairs. My mouth is clamped dry as we knock on flat thirty-three.

The door opens without revealing who's behind it. I go first, with a stop hand out telling Hope to wait.

Her

'You!' I hear Tom say.

His tone gets me ready to run. I twist my arm to feel for the shape of John Tenby's book in my rucksack. All the truth about *Leata* concealed within it. We can't risk losing it now.

'I'm on your side,' I hear a man's voice saying smoothly.

A little more curious than fearful now, I slide past the door, next to Tom.

The handsome detective from the other day – who Tom revealed works for MI5 – he's standing in the shadows of a narrow unlit hall.

'Hi, Hope? I'm Agent Ethan Miles,' he says, facing me squarely. 'Your dad's going pretty mental about you.'

'My dad is pretty mental,' I reply dryly. The agent laughs.

'How do you have Dad's phone?' Tom suddenly launches himself forward, clutching a fistful of Agent Miles' suit. I don't know whether to haul him off or help pin Miles down.

In turn, Miles stays passive, swatting his hands in a placating motion. 'The phone was in the evidence bag. Commander Menton sent that first text. He wanted to spook you into backing off. When you did the opposite, I used it to try and help you.'

Tom keeps hold, but loosens his grip. 'Why help me? When you work for PharmaCare?'

'Hey, no. I work for Her Majesty's Service. I'm James Bond, not Darth Vader.'

Tom sniffs, takes his hand away, leaving a crumpled shape on Agent Miles' shirt.

'I had to act that way; toe the party line. But I'm a normal guy.' Miles pats himself down. 'I'm not that complicated. I didn't like what they were doing to you is all.'

Tom places a hand on my arm as if we're leaving.

'What is this place?' I ask, staring round into the gloom.

'Don't worry – it's safe. It's one of the flats we use to house defectors. Strange place though, isn't it? No space to swing a cat and all that.'

'We're not here to buy it.' Tom edges closer to the door, his hand poised to push me out first.

'I get it. You want to know you can trust me.' Miles makes a smile, his eyes shining. 'Listen – I'm on what you might call a secondment to PharmaCare,' he explains, his strong aftershave sending wafts into the small corridor every time he moves. 'I take the stuff, *Leata*, it keeps me happy – so I reckoned it'd be a good gig when they promoted me last year. It's quickly turned sour. John Tenby wasn't a threat to national security as far as I can tell. And to put some kid against the wall, just for wanting to know what happened to his dad – you're the same age as my baby brother.' He joins his hands and points his forefingers at Tom. The gesture reminds me of some cheesy newly qualified teacher. For some reason that also makes me start to trust him.

'Shall we?' Miles indicates the door closest to us off the corridor.

Tom's edgy still. I gesture with my eyes for 'give him a chance,' and follow, tugging Tom after me into a small box of a lounge, filled with furniture that looks like it came from communist Russia. A cream net curtain covers the window.

'I want to make money, get on in my career, yeah? But this is too much to stomach,' Miles continues, running a hand over his short hair. 'You know, I'm not the type of person to question things.' The smile grows a little. 'Like *Leata* says, "*Not all questions bring the answers we need.*" Right?' He pulls a serious face. 'But right now: all I do is question. They've put a kill order over your head, Tom. This isn't what I signed up for. And no one else in MI5 knows what we're up to. Commander

Menton – he has a licence to kill without any kind of approval. He can do what the hell he wants.'

'Because he's part of a group who run the country, manipulate the world,' I say, noting Tom's cautionary gesture with his hand. 'We can't say,' I add when Miles asks what I mean.

'So did Menton . . .' Tom asks, swallowing forcefully, '*approve* Dad's murder?' He shoves his glasses back on, fiddling with them.

Agent Miles looks uncomfortable. 'You really want that information, mate?' He draws a deep breath.

Him

'All right, okay.' Miles licks his lips. 'The person who shot your dad . . .' He pauses, staring between me and Hope. 'It was the woman who worked for John Tenby. Imogen Poole.'

A sharp gasp leaves Hope's mouth. I feel her hand tighten round my arm. I'm struggling to catch my breath. 'Imogen?' I whisper back hoarsely, thinking I only spoke to her yesterday.

'Yeah.' Miles slants his eyes at me apologetically. 'Crime of passion, mate, it would seem. Or a set-up, if you want to look at it that way.'

'She killed Dad?' I say.

Hope goes and sits down on one of the small brown sofas. 'Why?' I ask.

'Your dad was going to get arrested for John Tenby's murder, Tom.' Miles swings round to look back at Hope. 'PharmaCare's Jack Wright had arranged for a gun to be bought on Matt's behalf. Arranged for his lapdog, Slicer, to use it – on Matt's behalf. They employed Slicer to shoot John Tenby, to keep

MI5 "officially" out of it. Next, Menton uses Imogen Poole as the honeytrap to get Matt Riley to meet her in Richmond Park. For her to hand Matt the murder weapon. The plan was to pick him up soon after, as if he were on the run.'

'But Imogen used the gun on him?' My words come out tight and fierce.

'Commander Menton knew there was a chance she might do it.' Miles lifts and drops his shoulders. 'I was there – Menton pumped her up, telling her Matt killed John Tenby. And that she might be next if Matt saw her as a threat.'

'No wonder she was a wreck,' I hear Hope say. 'Poor Imogen.'

I round on her. 'Imogen Poole shot my dad, Hope!'

Hope looks startled. 'I know. I'm sorry, I –' She shakes her head, mouth gaping.

Miles breaks in between us. 'Tom, your dad's days were numbered regardless. He was already a dead man walking. He was going to be shut away for life for murder, if he wasn't taken out before that.'

I stay silent. So does Hope. The only sound is our heavy breathing.

'Imogen's since run. My unit has been ordered to kill her. So far, I've diverted the tracking team from her.'

'Then stop diverting,' I hear myself say.

'No!' Hope shoots back.

I turn on her again. 'She killed Dad!'

'You heard Agent Miles. Imogen was set up! Benny is just three! He needs his mum. We can't let them find her! You have to understand it from her perspective.' Hope cuts a hand fiercely through the air. 'She'd been used by your dad, she thought

273

he'd killed John, the man who was like a father to her! That your dad might threaten her and Benny next?' She stands up, moving closer to me. I stare into her eyes. They used to be my favourite eyes in the whole world. How can they not see what I see? Imogen deserves to be punished!

'How would you act – if you came face to face with the person who killed your dad, Tom? The day after he had died? And you held the murder weapon in your hand?'

I pull back, my body held rigidly from hers. I suddenly find I can't even look at her. 'It's about the truth, isn't it?' I hear myself mutter. 'It's always been about the truth.'

It's my turn to sit down. I say nothing as I hear Hope impeach Miles, 'Don't let them kill Imogen.'

I stay quiet as they move on and Miles starts asking, 'So what help do you need from me?'

I hear Hope explaining that we need to gain access to Professor Blythe's house. I catch Miles saying Blythe is the man Menton reports to. But I don't hear any more. There's a noise in my brain. It's telling me to leave this mission and go and find Imogen, slam her face into a wall, trample on her heart like she's ravaged mine.

Her

Agent Miles leaves to get us a car and other stuff to help us with what we need to do next. Tom is still sat on the sofa, his hands clasped in front, starting fixedly at the brown and orange patterned carpet.

I don't bother to say anything else. I know I should console him. But he wants me to join him in his anger for Imogen.

274

When I can't. I feel sorry for her. And am fiercely protective of Benny. I see them running from danger, his little curly head bobbing alongside his mum. I can't condemn them. I don't understand how Tom can. But I get that he wants to.

I stand by the window, constantly lifting the net curtain. This Agent Miles seems okay, but we shouldn't trust anyone. We've got to be ready to run any moment.

I'm starting to get nervous – it's been two hours – before Miles bounds back through the door, brandishing burger boxes and bags of fries. 'Who's hungry?'

'Starving,' I answer. I pass some food to Tom, telling him he has to eat. I'm glad when he does.

Agent Miles drops a long bag from his shoulder to the floor, swinging a set of keys round his finger that he chucks at me. 'I got you a car. And I have a man I trust checking out Blythe's house. It'll be a Fort Knox. But I've brought you an MI5 lock-pick and I'll try and get you a passcode for his alarm.' He unzips the bag. Tom looks over as I peer in – it's like life-sized loot from a game of Cluedo. Rope, a piece of lead piping . . . a revolver.

'You're joking aren't you? We don't know how to use one of those.' I point at the black metal gun as Miles lifts it out.

'Before you go, I'll give you a crash course. I don't usually go round giving guns to teenagers. But whether you want it or not, you're probably going to need it if you want to stay alive.'

He pulls a small box out gently. 'If Blythe has anything it'll be in a safe. In here are silent explosives. I'll explain how to use them too. Just be careful with them unless you want to end up as bomb victims before you even get started.'

I suck in my breath. I try and catch Tom's eyes, to share my anxiety, but he's back looking intently at the carpet.

'Also I've got a couple of wigs, some hats, sunglasses. Best to keep disguised. Just make sure you don't end up looking like extras from the Muppets.'

Him

I don't say much, but I let Miles show me how the gun works. I think of Imogen and Commander Menton and suddenly I want to know – how to kill. I find myself bristling as I watch him teach Hope – standing behind her, Miles' hands clasping hers, his cheek next to her cheek, to show her how to aim. He didn't do that with me.

Lesson over, we get our bags and Miles goes out ahead, to give us the all clear, before he leads us downstairs and out through a twilight-lit garden at the back. I ask him about Mikey as he points us over to the car. 'They're still interrogating Mikey,' Miles says, grimacing. 'But I'll keep an eye on him. And you do me a favour,' he continues. 'You get caught, you don't mention my name, yeah?' The smile creeps up again. 'I'm skilled at covering my arse so don't you go uncovering it for me, however an attractive arse it might be.'

He leans in through the car window once we're inside. 'I'll do my best to keep the team off your scent. But do what you're going to do and do it quick.' Miles sniffs, straightening up. 'My old dad always says there are only two kind of men: the ones who want power and the ones who are powerful – and it's always the former who end up at the top.' He smiles. 'I hope what you're going to do changes that.'

I tick my head at him. 'We'll try,' I say, gazing over the dashboard to work out where all the controls are.

He bends down again as I start up the engine. 'Hey. Just tell me will you, what it is, yeah? This big secret about *Leata*?'

'Just stop taking it,' I say, winding the window back up. 'Something tells me you're happy as you are, *Ethan*.'

18

Learn the ways to live happily
Leata

Her

I don't know where Agent Miles found this car, but it looks like it's had a lifetime on the rally circuit, all dents and scrapes and a layer of dust over its black bodywork. The inside's not much better either. My seat feels sticky; toffee wrappers and drink cans litter the floor and back seat. The heating doesn't work. I pull my coat tighter round me. And Tom's not great with the controls; it keeps grating every time he changes gear. I wish I knew how to take over. Suddenly I don't like being in the passenger seat. But having never driven anything but a dodgem car I've no choice.

It's getting late by the time we join the motorway. Tom keeps rubbing at his eyes and he's driving more erratically, even for a car he doesn't know.

'I think we should stop at the next service station. Bed down there. We'd only have to do the same in Bristol until we meet Hari tomorrow.'

Tom's eyes stay fixed ahead.

'Talk to me,' I say, a little crossly. I'm getting a bit sick of the silent treatment. That kiss is fast becoming something I must have dreamt up.

'I'm too tired to talk,' he says, copping out. But after we pass Swindon, he starts indicating for the next service station.

We discreetly put on disguises: a blonde wig for me, a beret over it, to conceal the otherwise obvious-wig look. Tom's wearing his dad's flatcap again. A pair of aviator sunglasses have already replaced his spectacles, despite the black sky. We book into a room under false names, using the cash Ralph gave Tom.

It's basic – a desk. A TV. Tom turns it on straightaway, flicking to a news channel, anything but Star Media. I go to use the loo, and when I come out, Tom is muttering, 'Holy shit,' at the screen.

My body tingles with new fear. '*According to a statement from MI5, Matt Riley shot John Tenby causing a fatal heart attack,*' a news reporter is saying, '*Matt Riley later killed himself.*'

'Commander Menton,' Tom says under his breath as a large man fills the screen. His title: Director of Internal Security, MI5.

I make a sharp intake of breath as he starts speaking. 'John Tenby's death was undisclosed due to a covert operation. We've been forced to go public because Matt Riley's son, Tom Riley, has taken up his father's mantle. He has brainwashed a vulnerable seventeen-year-old, Hope Wright.'

Both our photos suddenly flash up on screen. Mine's a school shot taken last year when I was still in uniform. I look like a kid. Whereas Tom's some CCTV close-up – the grainy image makes him look like a threat all right.

'This is what they meant in the office, *fighting fear with fear, dressing the problem*,' I say to Tom.

'Tom Riley poses a serious threat to national security,' Commander Menton continues. 'He is also wanted on class-A drug charges, as well as the suspected abduction of Hope Wright.'

'They're painting you as the monster, me the victim,' I tell him.

Tom's face crumples as he stays staring at the screen. 'Bastards,' he says simply.

Him

We act all polite around each other as we get ready for bed. I don't see any point in discussing what we've just seen, I tell Hope when she tries to talk about it. I think of the kiss and I just want to hold her. I think of Imogen killing my dad, and the fact Hope sides with her, and I can't even look at her. I just need silence. I lie rigidly in our shared bed, clinging to the very edge, so not one bit of me touches her. A mix of fury and frustration rocks my body, fuels my breathing. I just want a few hours to turn off the lights in my head and still my heart. To try not to think about how Dad needn't have died. That if Imogen hadn't shot him, he might be imprisoned for a murder verdict I could have proved unlawful. I could have saved him!

Natural light's filling the room as I blink awake. Looking at my phone, we've overslept massively. Ten a.m. I stare over at Hope. Our legs have got entangled, like they used to when we lay or sat together as kids. Mum used to say we were like a couple of puppies, that it was hard to know where Hope began and I ended.

Asleep, her face falls into the shape and fullness of eleven-year-old Hope. I can almost forget the anger I feel towards her for backing Imogen. I nudge her gently. She wakes up suddenly as if she's under attack. As she takes me in with those wide eyes, my anger steadily trickles back in. 'Come on, we're late,' I say.

Her

It's gone midday by the time we arrive at Bristol.

It's another hour before we find our way to the location Hari texted Tom this morning – in the middle of some half-built business estate, a mid-rise that looks as if it's still a shell. A girl with a dyed red high ponytail and jeans tucked into cowboy boots is loitering by the front doors. She starts towards us as we get closer. 'Tom? Hope?' she says in a high voice. 'I'm Adele. Everyone's upstairs. No lift. The building's not in use yet.'

I'm relieved to finally remove the wig – it itches, makes my scalp hot. We follow Adele through a fire exit and up a concrete staircase. 'One of our lot knows the architect,' she explains. 'Eighteen floors I'm afraid. Take a deep breath.'

We're all three panting as we reach the top floor. Open plan, a series of anglepoise lights are rigged up across an otherwise deserted floor. Adele walks us through small groups of college-age girls and boys, all of them sprawled across the carpet, in groups or alone, some lying on their stomachs the way small children do, staring intently into the blue glow from their laptops.

'Hari – they're here,' Adele calls across the room before she sits down cross-legged next to a boy with a Mohawk and a stud through his bottom lip.

It must be Hari who comes sauntering over. Through the shafts of golden light, his hair thick and flowing, he appears more like some mystical god sent to save us.

Him

I've met Hari a few times in the past, at random family events of Pavlin's. He doesn't wear a patka any more. I can still remember Mr Balil's shock and disappointment when his nephew cut his hair. But now it's grown long again, wavy, jet black with copper highlights. He's more broad-chested than I remember. Maybe that's why Hope seems to gasp as she says, 'Is that *Hari*?'

I make a purposeful tut at her gawping, then I spot them, following behind him.

'Pavlin, Daisy!' I rush to meet them, throwing my arms around Pavlin, almost crying with the joy of seeing his kind face. We pull away, slapping each other's backs.

'Yeah – surprise,' Pavlin says. 'Couldn't have you getting all the excitement.'

Hari's introducing himself to Hope, kissing her on both cheeks like adults or the French do. I thrust myself towards Daisy to do the same, albeit awkwardly. Her cheeks burn as she says shyly, 'Great to see you're okay, Tom.'

'Let's get to work, we're on a deadline,' Hari says, slamming his palms together.

He finds us both laptops. 'Ironically, they're the ones the university get free from *Leata*,' he smiles, tapping the engraving on the front. '*Learn the ways to live happily.*'

Hope must be feeling the freeze from me as she sits a little apart to write the post she's going to publish in tandem with her YouTube vlog.

It's fine by me.

I hear her announce eagerly to Hari. 'I've just hit four million followers!'

'People love you again,' I say under my breath, adjusting my glasses as I watch her listening intently to whatever Hari's saying back.

The whole floor is busy, 'making contact with other groups across the UK and globally, linking in with the PAL network and other platforms,' Pavlin says. He and Daisy are part of the hacktivist-group. Feeling out of it, I start checking the latest news on us (I'm still a terrorist. And Hope's still my victim). I can't find anything on Mikey, but there are some tweets doing the rounds from St Patrick's shelter saying he's missing. My stomach screws with itself. Three days, till the whole truth is out there. *Stay alive for three more days, Mikey.*

Her

'Ready?' The girl who let us in, Adele, stands in front of us with a video camera. 'Everyone's ready for an evening of posting and hacking. We just need a film now,' she says.

'I've never done a vlog before,' Tom says to her in a nervous voice, as Adele adjusts the backlight.

'That's the least of your problems,' I smile, but he's still hell-bent on cold-shouldering me.

Adele steps forward. 'Just let them see your eyes. That you're honest,' she says.

I clear my throat, staring ahead, as Adele pushes Tom's fringe back from his face.

Tom flushes, pushing his glasses up his nose.

'I'll do most of the talking if you like,' I say once Adele's back behind the camera.

'Nothing's changed there then,' he says.

I'm about to turn and ask him what his problem is, when Adele starts counting down.

In the end Tom talks as much if not more than me. Once we get going it's like he forgets the camera's there, that he's pissed off with me. Passion takes over. He talks about his dad and Mikey. And how 'they'd better not hurt Mikey'.

I take over to pull us back to the agreed script. 'Over the next three days, starting today, we will tell you the story behind Cloud 9, behind PharmaCare – and what their drug *Leata* is doing to you. On the third day: their big secret that will blow your mind.'

'Nine powerful people are involved in an elite club called "Cloud 9",' Tom breaks in. 'It's a conspiracy that launched *Leata* twelve years ago . . . you will want to know their big secret. Because it affects everyone, whether you take the pill or not. The big secret Cloud 9 kill for.'

Adele cuts. I remind Tom we can't mention murder. Not till vlog number three, Hari briefed us, so the courts can't automatically shut all content down.

Starting again, I look straight down the camera. 'So, the first name,' I say, as if I'm announcing the lottery numbers, but on *Crimewatch*, 'is . . . '

'You're a natural,' I smile teasingly at Tom once we've done all three vlogs. Changing our tops so it looks like three different days.

'Thanks,' he mutters, and walks away.

Him

I start heading back to Pavlin and Daisy. I don't mean to be acting like a shit. But my skin prickles with frustration when I see Hope acting like that conversation with Miles never happened.

When I hear Hope protecting Imogen over again in my head, it feels like we're back there . . . when she broke us up . . . when she left me anchorless all those years, without her.

So yeah, I'm pissed off with Hope. She should be on my side.

I hang around the hacking team, while Hope helps Adele edit the videos.

Before the first vlog is posted, Hari stands on an upturned plastic box. It's late now; the sky's darkened outside and the anglepoise lights reflects us all in the glass as if we're double our numbers.

Hope comes and stands the other side of Pavlin. I give a shrug to her 'okay, Tom?'

'Tonight,' Hari says, looking round, 'in approximately fifteen minutes – war will commence.'

I watch everyone whooping, punching their fists in the air. I suppose it does have a feel of going into battle. The virtual kind.

'Remember, they will fight back nasty,' Hari continues, 'make sure you keep changing laptops and tablets. We publish, we share, we hack, then you switch IP addresses pronto. It's the only way to ensure we don't get traced. We'll have to get cleverer over the next two days, so we can post without getting caught.'

'Your cousin's a great spokesperson,' I hear Hope tell Pavlin. I pretend I've not heard, purposefully smiling at Daisy along from me.

Once Hari's done speaking, there's another frenzy of fingers flying over keyboards; eyes fixed on screens.

The vlog is posted on Hope's *Lifelife* YouTube channel, before being shared on OpenFreeNet globally. Then onto the other partnership platforms, and leaked onto the sites and channels and walls the hacktavists have gained entry to.

A sense of silent excitement fills the air as Hari walks through the hunched and spread-out bodies, announcing, 'Okay, we're done. Five minutes to clear out of here, lights, computers, everything out.'

He stops by me. 'Don't look so worried, Tom,' he says, smiling. 'We dump the laptops, we pick up others. We have sources to help us with that. Never own anything and stay free, right?'

I nod. It reminds me of something Dad would say. 'Stay free.'

Once we've finished clearing up, some of us head down to a bar by Bristol harbourside. The water laps angrily outside, but the bar is warm with a low light and we find free tables in a far corner. Hari and some others take the borrowed laptops back to the university. They bring new ones back with them. Everyone's in high spirits as we check online. 'We've gone viral,'

286

Hari snaps his fingers in the air. 'Views are already well into the millions. #Cloud9 is trending, big time. It's happening!'

I take a sip from my beer and stare round at them all as they holler and slam each other's backs, and clash beer bottles. It's a mix of all kinds of students, geek guys, goth girls; some with piercings and tattoos and coloured hair; others dressed more conservatively, eyes lowered. But all have real smiles. Their own messages. It makes me wonder if there is somewhere to belong once I'm done with A levels. Dad said there was. 'Just stay intact through school, and come out yourself.'

But how do I know anything Dad said is right any more?

I take a gulp of beer. He's become like some hero whose flaws are revealed as the film progresses. But you still root for anyway. I feel my eyes filling. *I miss you, Dad, you bastard. I miss you.* I take a longer drink from the bottle. Ignoring my own warning, *take it easy*. It's not like it's the hard stuff.

I hear someone teasing Hope to reveal 'the big secret'.

'Leave her alone,' Hari says. So far only he and Adele know the truth. I watch him put his chiselled, manly arm around Hope; his long hair mingling with hers.

For some reason it makes my anger towards her swell.

I drain my beer back and reach for another.

Enjoy life's journey
Leata

Her

I shake Tom awake. He's sleeping head to toe on the sofa with Pavlin. I shared a bed with Daisy upstairs, at Hari and his friends' student digs.

I shake him again. There's no rush to leave. We can't reach Blythe's house any sooner than nightfall. We can't risk a break-in till its occupants are fast asleep. But something about the fact Tom's still fast asleep after the way he acted last night annoys me. I poke him this time. Hard on the shoulder.

'What?' he answers groggily, hand to his head.

I want to tell him he drank too much. I want to tell him he was an idiot on the walk (or rather sway) home, pestering me about whether I fancied Hari. Before putting his arm round Daisy, keeping it there, embarrassing her I could tell, with his slurred praise. And after how he treated Fran!

I poke him harder even though he's awake now. 'We've got twenty-four hours to find more proof, remember? We have to plan what we do if we can't get into Blythe's house,' I snap.

He rubs his face and groans.

'And don't get drunk again. Not while we're doing this,' I continue, annoyed at myself for letting it get to me.

He mutters something that might be an apology before he stretches. Putting his glasses on, he makes a surprised face as if I've just come into focus. So now he jokes? After ignoring me for two days!

I stiffen. 'We're running for our lives. Take it seriously.'

'I'm going to get a shower,' he says, getting up and shuffling out of the room as Hari and some others start traipsing in, with tired faces. The TV gets turned on. We steer clear of Star Media, but even the BBC hasn't reported our story yet. Clearly PharmaCare's firing on all barrels to stifle it, whilst escalating the terrorism charges. Commander Menton makes another appearance; this time a studio interview. He sits explaining what a danger teenagers like Tom Riley pose to positivity. 'We must stop youths like him terrorising society.'

Hari and some of the others are already busy on computers, posting the second vlog on my *Lifelife* channel to share. Within seconds it's causing more of a stir than the first. Partly because it shames the MD of Star Media, as a Cloud 9 member, for broadcasting and printing *Leata*-biased news stories . . . for her own profit.

Hari quickly becomes excited. '#Cloud 9 – it's taking over the internet. It's alive with PAL bloggers and tweets joining in.'

'The non-conformists are revolting,' I hear Pavlin say to Daisy. 'How did we suddenly become cool?'

'The Prime Minister's turn tomorrow,' Hari says, then swirls his fist in the air. 'Man! Retweets are in the millions already. And hey, look – we're even getting some offline media at last.'

We crowd round him. The press in developing countries who don't yet endorse *Leata* prescriptions are using their free rein to launch an attack at PharmaCare. To shame them.

But then Hari clicks onto another page and there's a chorus of curses, as we read about OpenFreeNet's main contact in the USA – he was arrested last night their time.

'War is raging,' Hari concludes, staring round at us all. 'We'd better armour up.'

Tom is stumbling back into the room, his hair wet from the shower. 'Look,' he says, holding out his phone to me.

Him
We wait until early evening, abandoning the car as Agent Miles' text instructed ('*Security cameras snapped you at a motorway station*'), to make our way via public transport to Temple Meads station, joining the commuters leaving Bristol. I'm wearing Pavlin's leather jacket. I've swapped Converses too. His are pale green and much cleaner. I know who got the better deal. It feels sort of liberating to be wearing someone else's clothes rather than Dad's. As if it's connected, I don't feel so mad at Hope any more. Walking alongside me, she's dressed all in black, care of Adele. She's still got on the blonde wig, but under a low beanie hat that I saw on Hari last night. I'd ask how she came by it, but it seems like it's her turn to be pissed off with me.

We left our bags at Hari's. We have only a smaller rucksack I borrowed from Pavlin, carrying just the gun and some of the equipment from Miles. We left John Tenby's book with Hari for safekeeping.

A giant screen hangs next to the destination board as we enter the station. It films people live as they come in, the words above it written in *Leata* script and colours: 'You're on camera – so smile!' Hordes of people pause, like daffodils at the sun, to watch themselves above the messages streaming beneath. *'Enjoy life's journey, with Leata!' 'Just look out the window and enjoy the ride!'*

My hangover getting worse, I go and buy some soluble aspirin, swilling it in a bottle of water while Hope gets us tickets at the kiosk. The plan is to return to Bristol by first thing tomorrow to film any extras for the last video. If we don't make it in time, I have Pavlin's iPad packed so we can film and post it ourselves.

'Did I say or do anything last night to annoy you?' I finally ask as Hope re-joins me with tickets.

'Forget it,' she says.

I knock the cloudy water back, gagging at the taste. 'Is that forget it for real, or "come grovelling" forget it?' I can see my words sting her.

'Let's just do what we have to do,' she answers finally. 'Forget everything else.'

I shrug. If she wants to keep the chill from thawing between us, I'm not going to challenge it. Besides, from what I remember, she was the one making a fool of herself last night, giggling around Hari like everything he said was funny.

Hope's phone buzzes in her pocket. 'A text from Hari,' she says. *Talk of the devil.*

'How come he's contacting you now?'

Her forehead creases as she reads it. It must be the beer still in my system that makes me want to push out a finger and smooth it down.

'Hari says PharmaCare are threatening to serve a writ on OpenFreeNet. My channel's been blocked. He doesn't think they have a leg to stand on yet. And the video's already gone viral. But it means we need further proof more than ever, Hari says.'

Hari this, Hari that. 'Is Hari our manager now or something?' I mumble, pressing a hand against the part of my head that hurts most.

She doesn't say anything. Just gives me that fierce look again.

We're both silent on the train. The screen in front of my seat has the app for playing *Leata*'s children's game, *Head Rush*. Adults get the *Leata Countdown to Happiness* app. I stare out of the window as the view exchanges Bristol's candy-coloured terraces for green rolling hills and patchwork fields.

Next to me Hope stares fixedly out of the opposite window.

I puff out my cheeks. 'I can't even remember how I acted last night. But I'm sorry if I was an idiot,' I say suddenly.

'You should apologise to Daisy, not me,' Hope says stiffly.

'Okay, I will,' I say.

She stares at me. 'We're being hunted,' she says quietly. 'It doesn't matter.'

'It matters to me,' I say honestly. I won't be like my dad. 'I'm not going to drink like that again.'

Hope draws a deep breath, and whispers, 'I'm scared.' She bites her lip as a tear slowly drops from her eye.

My insides slump. I do it instinctively – like I used to when she came over to the treehouse, upset over the grief her dad

292

was giving her. I pull my arm out from between us and I put it round her shoulders.

I never told her it was going to be all right then. And I don't now. Who knows what's going to happen next.

I never thought we'd ever stop being friends.

I never thought I'd lose my dad before he reached old age.

I dip my head in towards hers and she presses hers against mine.

And that's how we stay for the rest of the train journey.

Her

An hour and a change of trains later, we arrive at a small village station. It's just gone nine. Despite the rain, or maybe because of it, it's the picture of middle England. A prettily painted platform with well-dressed passengers sitting as neatly as the station's boxes of winter plants. Though even here, posters and benches advertise *Leata*.

We head out into the grey air, into quiet, leafy streets lit by the orange glow of streetlights, and start searching for the road we recognise from the drive here last time. Despite the fact Tom and I have made up, my stomach is filling to the brim with fear, like the swollen rain clouds above. I hardly notice we've stepped from the train holding hands, until Tom squeezes mine harder.

'We stay alive, that's all,' Tom says. 'Hari knows what he's doing. People are listening. They can't hurt us now we've gone public. There'll be too many questions.'

I try and tell myself he's right. But I know from first hand how fickle internet followers can be. It's all about the truths people want at the time they want it. 'They believe us today,' I say, then point ahead. I remember passing that pub. 'But what if they believe the likes of *Realboystuff* and *Positiveandperky* tomorrow?'

Him

It doesn't take us too long to find the house and its large gated entrance. There's no way we're getting over that without being seen, even in the dark. We move round to the adjacent street, and find there's only a small wood spread out at the back of Professor Blythe's extensive grounds. Beyond that a high red-brick wall.

Jumping up intermittently, we see when the ground floor lights go out around ten thirty. By eleven the upstairs is in darkness too. We decide to wait another hour to give them the chance to fall fast asleep, pacing the small wood to keep warm, blowing on our hands so they don't seize up.

'Okay, let's go,' I say when the hour's up.

The wall's old, so some bricks jut out to give a bit of leverage. I climb over, jumping down the other side, tumbling down a grass slope. Trying to keep the yelp of agony to my throat as my ankle twists over.

I hobble up, making use of Ethan's rope – throwing it over the wall and holding it as Hope makes her way to the top. As she hangs off the edge, I tell her, 'Jump. I'll catch you.' Which I kind of do. I cushion her fall anyway.

'You're hurt?' she whispers as I limp up.

'It's nothing, come on.'

Her

My hands and knees sting where I scraped them on the wall. And Tom doesn't look okay. He's hobbling as he walks and even in the dark I can see his face pulling into a grimace of pain.

We creep through the shadows of a manicured lawn and tidy shrubbery, keeping close to the wall in case we trigger a security light. Our torches out ready but not turned on.

Locating a back door, we use the high-tech lock-pick Miles gave us. Credit card slim, Tom inserts it down the line between the door and the wall and presses to activate. Both the Yale and the Chubb locks open automatically.

As we step inside, the alarm starts its warning beeping. I make my way fast to the front of the house, torch on, to find it. Spying a white box by the front door, I frantically enter the code Miles texted before we left Bristol. Only breathing again when it works.

We keep our torches low, quickly examining the rooms until we find one resembling a study. Going in, we close the door gently, sweeping our torches around it.

Him

The desk drawers are filled with papers and files. Hope starts to sift through them as I circle round. My torch illuminates a black-and-white framed photograph on the wall. *Jesus College 1987–1990*. At least five of Cloud 9 are there, including Damian Price, the Prime Minister. Lined up proudly; their poses reflecting the arrogance of the privileged. Eyes shining confidently, as if the world is built only for them.

The man in the middle, the list below tells me, is Professor Simeon Blythe. A haughty face and slicked back hair. A self-satisfied smile.

I'm lifting the frame off the wall to show Hope when my

eyes widen at what's behind. A small silver safe door is built into the wall.

'Eureka,' I hear Hope hiss over my shoulder.

'We don't know the combination.'

'Fuck combinations,' Hope says. 'That's why Miles gave us these, remember.' She fumbles a box into my hand. '*Silent* explosives.'

I set one up following the instructions Miles gave us – a small black cylinder, stuck to the metal box with purple putty. I pull the ring out and we both stand back. It makes a tiny pop and crackles like an indoor firework.

There's a hole in the door, but it's still locked.

'Stand back,' Hope says. Her arms are stretched out; she has the black gun already in her hands, aiming it at the safe.

'Shit, Hope, which are you, Thelma or Louise?'

'It's okay, it has a silencer,' she says as I make a panicked sound. She pulls her face back. And fires.

It takes two muffled shots for the hinges to snap.

Hurriedly, I reach in, grabbing what's there – a heavy pile of papers and files, with a roll of paper on top.

Hope starts unravelling the scroll.

'Shouldn't we just take it all and run?' I say nervously.

'Video it first,' she says. 'Let's send it to Hari now. Just in case we never get back.'

I don't want to entertain that thought, but I dutifully pull Pavlin's pad out and press record on the video function. I pass it over the paper she's now flattened out onto the desk.

'Their *Magna Carta*,' Hope explains for the camera. 'A declaration with nine signatures under a summary of what *Leata* will do for society.'

I pan its heading. '*Cloud 9's Utopia*'.

Hope starts flicking through the top folders beneath. 'A collection of contracts. It doesn't stop with nine names.' She fingers through paper after paper inside. 'Tom. It's more like Cloud 99. This is un- . . . shit, Lord Richard Mills, isn't he a cousin of the royal family? It looks like he was at Eton with the Prime Minister. And, my god, there's an Archbishop signed up too. And the Head of the Metropolitan Police, Tom. Wait.' She makes a noise of pain from the back of her throat as she rifles through further papers. 'The American President's signature . . . the German Chancellor . . . Spain. France. Sweden. Australia. It goes on . . . There are signed contracts here from leaders worldwide . . . they are on the PharmaCare payroll. It looks like profit from sales goes to their political parties . . . to keep them in power . . .' She keeps reading. 'As long as they ratify Cloud 9's political practice: *Positivity yields prosperity*'.

Her

Tom is breathing hard. 'This is big. Grab it all, we've got to go,' he says as he emails the film to Hari.

'It's worse,' I say, my voice straining with my stomach. 'Video this too.'

He does as I ask, directing the tablet over the first page of a thick document I've opened. Tears prick my eyes as I explain for the camera. 'It's their policy plan. A three-stage attack at cleansing society of 'negativity'.

Tom curses under his breath as he moves the video over a summary of its contents.

1. *Completion of sale of NHS Mental Trusts
   to PharmaCare*
2. *Fast-track Health Farm treatment of emotional
   disorders, mentally ill, addicts and disaffected*
3. *Intensify treatment and commence 'removal'
   of untreatables*

*Medicating and servicing mental illness is a
drain on the economy and detrimental to the general
positivity of the nation. Ultimately, the Progress
Party's aim is to rid society of a certain, mentally ill,
'strata' of the population.*

I flick deeper into the document. 'It charts current methods
being used,' I whisper hoarsely, slapping a hand to my mouth
when I see what the video now sees. Images of young people
strapped to beds. A copper band round their heads. It flashes
up in my mind – the pink mark around Tara's forehead when
she returned from the Health Farm.

'Shocked, are you?' a voice says politely behind us, as light
floods the room.

Him

We both whip our eyes round. In the doorway – an older version
of the man in the photograph flanked by students – stands
proudly in a burgundy dressing gown. A gun directed at us both.

'Well, aren't you clever little children. Persistent too. Now
back away from the desk. Over there. Towards the window.
Go!' he adds in a bark, flicking his gun when we don't move.

Hope moves, dragging me with her; I'm still videoing. 'You're a monster,' she says. 'Those photos. That's treatment you're administering – NOW. They were taken at a PharmaCare Health Farm!'

'Indeed. Turn that thing off and I'll tell you more,' he says coolly. I lower the pad and pretend to switch it off. 'We might as well enjoy a little storytime before the adults arrive to take you home from the party.'

Her

Adrenalin pumps through my body; Blythe has called someone already? I glance at Tom, dragging my hat and wig off. Do we run? Ram into him before he has chance to shoot? I suddenly feel like a complete novice. Stupid child soldiers who've gone into battle without proper training. Why did we think we could pull this off? My only hope is Hari's got the video.

'So you've been looking at the photograph of Cloud 9 at Oxford, I see? Happy days,' Blythe continues. 'Yes, Damian Price was my best student.' He makes a face as if he's a proud father. 'He and our current Chancellor had been at school together. They arrived burning with political ideas. We spent wonderful afternoons debating how utopia was possible. A utopia that would build a happy, prosperous society . . . It was Damian who got on board the cream of his friends. Perdita Brightsmith was going to inherit her small family firm PharmaCare and Bea Tyler would be taking over her father as MD of Star Media. And Philip Menton was already on a scholarship with MI5. It was as if it was fated really.'

'And Professor Tenby?' I ask.

'Oh, I recruited John. He was the best scientist at the university. I knew he could do it. Create a harmless drug that makes people happy.' He looks into the air to his right as if he's reminiscing. Tom pulls a face at me, nodding curtly at the pad in his hand. He must have left it on record.

'A formula that no other scientist could decipher and dispel,' Blythe continues. 'Few did. We silenced those who mastered its formula. People can always be silenced if the price is high enough. And if it's not,' he dances his gun through the air, 'there are other ways.'

I take a sidestep to hide Tom completely from view, saying angrily. 'Your story's not going to have a happy ending, Professor Blythe.'

Him

Temporarily concealed behind Hope, I quickly swipe onto Hari's email. Attaching the last video. I press send.

'We have nine names,' Hope is saying, fixing her eyes on Blythe so they stay with her. 'We have a motive. We have a dead body. And we have a big secret. They'll perform this in the West End once the truth is out.'

Blythe's gun rocks through the air as he starts to laugh. Big, bellowing laughter. 'The public won't believe *you*, my dear,' he says. 'People want a happy ever after. That's why Disney died a billionaire.' He smiles thinly at us. 'You think society will let you take their *Leata* off them!' he continues, echoing Ralph. 'They won't let go of their cigarettes and nuclear weapons, so, why an innocuous drug that hurts no one?'

'You've been playing games of power with the public, people

won't like *that*!' I pitch in – Hari has visual proof, as well as John Tenby's book – now we just need to get out of here. 'This is corruption at its highest level! The government should exist for the people!'

'No – no.' Blythe shakes his head enthusiastically, as if I'm one of his students and he truly believes I'm wrong. 'The people should exist for the government. Unless you're the game-players, you're no one. One of the crowd.' He starts to get excited. He really believes this shit. 'The masses need to be told what to do, what to eat, how long to sleep, what to buy . . . because in their next purchase . . . lies happiness!

'Why else do people want to stare at screens all day rather than communicate properly? The internet's a giant global field for all the sheep to parade into, following the sheepdog, *doing as, saying as* . . . pouring ice water over their heads if everyone else does it; liking what everyone else likes, so they blend in and everyone *likes* them back.'

'No! You're wrong!' Hope is shouting. 'Right now, social media is filled with angry people who are going to take you down! For every blogger you have manipulated there are another dozen seeing you for what you are. And they are fighting back, spreading the truth over your manure of lies!'

'Well, I'd say there are a few less of your PAL bloggers, since we started an operation to rid ourselves of the most anarchic. It won't be long before we manage all internet content.' Blythe pulls a sycophantic smile. 'We've made people happy, and society prosperous at the same time. And it's not just us! Every slogan you read on every product you buy has a message for you . . . brainwashes you.

We're a happy nation as a consequence of *Leata* – why on earth would you want to pull that down?'

'Because you are murderers as well as manipulators. You were instrumental in my dad's death. You ordered the execution of John Tenby!' My blood's at boiling point.

Blythe reacts just as angrily. 'Pah! John Tenby was one of us – Cloud 9. We all agreed to live by the sword, or die by the sword. John fell on his.'

'He wasn't my dad's source.'

The Professor's eyes narrow a little. 'No? Well, he soon would have been . . . his soul always was too poetic. And your dad? He was a pumped-up little man seeking a sense of worth. But *we* didn't kill him, so if you've done all this out of revenge then you're sorely mistaken.'

'This isn't revenge,' Hope interjects, grabbing my arm, pulling it as if she wants us to leave, now. Even though it's impossible. 'We simply believe people have the right to know the truth. Always.'

'The truth?' The Professor's small smile grows. 'How wrong you are, my dear. What we've created – is the only truth people want. Same as heaven is full of fluffy pink clouds with angels playing harps, and death won't happen to you. Why else do you think religion was created?'

Her

I pull on Tom's sleeve again. We're running out of time. We have to find a way out of this. 'Okay, fine, carry on with your brainwashing with harps. You'll never hear from us again if you let us leave,' I lie.

'You're going nowhere.' Blythe raises his gun higher, training it between my eyes. 'I will shoot. I have no sentimentality about life. We're just cockroaches scampering around. That's why we need organising to live comfortably.' He clears his throat. 'Besides, don't you want to hear how the story ends?'

'We've already read about your happy ending,' I say, tightening a hold around Tom's arm. 'The vulnerable, the disaffected, the plain depressed – you get rid of them, or subject them to nineteenth-century methods of dealing with mental illness.'

'Ah, yes, electric shock treatment was a success back in the day. Lobotomies are on our agenda next. But only for those we must treat, because their families would cause a stink if we don't keep them alive.'

I think of Aggie. It all makes sense. 'You're murdering vulnerable people who don't have families to fight for them?' I hiss, my throat tightening at the thought of the extent of what's been going on while I've been blithely promoting *Leata*.

Blythe shrugs. 'Only those who are a pestilence, a plague on society. You squash a cockroach if he attacks your food source.' He turns his head as I hear it. 'Ah, now there's a sound that's music to my ears.'

The sirens become louder, tyres skidding and engines whirring to an abrupt stop on the road beyond.

He backs away, the gun held out still. 'Let me open the gates so our guests can come in.'

'Out! Now!' Tom says as Blythe drifts into the darkness of the hall.

I wait for a shot to the back as we bolt out of the study, back the way we came, towards the door we broke through.

Him

We make it.

We both skid to a halt, breathing fast.

They are already waiting there.

Three, four of them in uniform blue.

'You took your time. I thought you were patrolling the area?'

Blythe saunters in behind us.

20

Close your eyes to ugliness
Leata

Him

They hold us back in the study. Blythe has retreated upstairs to get dressed.

'We're waiting for officials to come to take you away,' a policeman finally explains when Hope asks again. Another hour, and the *officials* arrive. Flanked by more uniforms: Commander Menton. Nina Mitchell . . . and Agent Miles, a gun by his side.

I see Hope shake her head angrily at him. Miles pulls a face back as if he's saying 'so what?'

'You bastard,' I hiss at him. Soon after, Blythe enters the room, launching a diatribe at Menton. 'You clear this mess up. Start doing the job you're paid to do.'

'Sorry, folks, you've got to come with us,' Miles is saying tonelessly. 'You're terrorists and we're arresting you under the Prevention of Terrorism Act 2011. You're not the ones in control here,' he adds as Menton calls him over. 'Face that fact and come nicely.'

Her

I stare around at their faces. All the police were dismissed when the others arrived, except for one uniform who still has his gun trained on us while Miles and Nina Mitchell get briefed by Blythe and Menton. Terse, whispered words hum in the background. It already feels like I'm in some film noir scene – I have to think darkly.

This is war, Hari said.

And I'm not going without a fight. I know that. *Burn, burn, burn,* one of Tom's T-shirts said.

Hari has enough proof to bring PharmaCare and Cloud 9 down. There are plenty of PAL supporters and bloggers to keep the truth out there.

Before the policeman can act, I take a leap sideways, slamming into the desk where I think I remember putting the gun down. Grabbing it from under the pile of papers, I lift it up, swinging it around, unsure where to place it. Commander Menton and Blythe stare over at me, their faces: one shocked, the other bemused. I move it onto Agent Miles, as he lifts his own gun. He's the one who betrayed us.

'Now, now. Don't get excited, little missy. Put your gun down,' Blythe is saying. He starts to make steps towards me, his thick hand outstretched.

I think of my father, his large hand wrapped in my hair. I see a future being shut in a cell, following a lobotomy. Tom, shot dead.

The bullet leaves the gun in my hand, ricocheting me sideways and stumbling into Tom. He catches me as I see Blythe fall to the ground, as another shot sounds out. I drop down myself as if someone has taken the ground away.

Tom's face fills with horror. 'Hope?'

Him

Arms are pulling me away from her.

I am screaming all kinds of words. But mostly, over and again: 'Hope!'

I keep my eyes on hers. I need her to stay awake. I need her to be all right.

Her eyes remain open, but the sleeve of her black jacket is turning darker. It looks wet – blood. She's bleeding.

I struggle like a wild animal to get away from the policeman and Miles.

Menton is stooped over Blythe. 'We're losing him. Quick, get an ambulance here.'

I hear Nina Mitchell saying, 'Get them both out of here before anyone else arrives.'

Hope is being lifted by Miles. Her face has turned almost white, but she is moaning. I let the policeman drag me outside only to stay close to her.

On the driveway, there's a white van. Hope is bundled inside first. Me next. As the doors slam shut, I charge over to her.

Someone's already crouched there, holding Hope up in the pitch black.

'Bloody hell, Mikey?' I say, then to Hope, 'Are you okay – where did they shoot you?'

'It's my arm, I think,' she murmurs, her throat rasping. 'It hurts a lot.' She takes a sharp breath as Mikey helps me take off her coat. I rip off the sleeve of her top, using the torn piece to dab at the wound.

Mikey tries to examine it in the dark as Hope winces. 'I think it's just a flesh wound. The bullet must 'ave just grazed you.'

I throw off my own T-shirt – Mikey rips it to use it as a bandage.

'How come you're here?' I ask him. 'What did they do to you?'

Mikey sucks in his breath. 'Beat me around a bit, nothing I couldn't 'andle – kept me 'oled up, 'oping I'd talk, I guess. Then got chucked in 'ere just over an hour ago. It don't look good this, Tom.'

'No,' I say, as the van's engine starts and we start driving away. I grip tighter to Hope as we're bounced around. Burying my face into her hair, I kiss her there over and again.

'I'm bloody sorry,' I say. Not for the first time.

'We're together,' she murmurs back through teeth gritted with pain. 'We're together. In the treehouse.'

Her

I'm in agony. My arm burns and stings and sends pain like an alarm round the rest of my body. Yet I'm glad to see Mikey here. Even gladder to be held tightly in Tom's arms. We did what we could. Life will end like it started more or less, with Tom.

He keeps kissing my head. I want to turn my face. I want to meet his lips like we did in the National Gallery. But the pain's too much to move. I press my whole body into his instead and I try and imagine we're in the treehouse; safe. I think of our shared past spent playing at Star Wars; summer days squirting each other with water pistols . . . hours lying together simply watching clouds drift by. I won't think about what's about to happen.

* * *

It's probably a couple of hours before the van starts to slow and then comes to a stop.

'I'll try'n distract 'em. You carry Hope an' run,' Mikey is saying fast.

I shake my head for 'no' but Mikey insists.

I hear Tom deliberating. He's looking at me in the dark like he just wants to save me. I like the fact they're both hopeful, but I know there's no way out of this now, for any of us. It won't be hard for PharmaCare to pin mine and Mikey's deaths on Tom. And his – on a pointless act of terrorism.

The van doors open. Shadowy bodies are outlined against the dark denim sky.

I watch the silver glint of Miles' gun beckon us out. The uniform is next to him. Armed too.

Tom spits in Miles' face as we climb out. He just smiles, takes out a tissue from his suit jacket and wipes it off.

I'm propped up between Tom and Mikey. I blink, looking around at where they've brought us. The full moon in the sky gradually lights up dilapidated farm buildings around us. An old caravan that looks burnt out.

My body's shaking with pain as I glance Nina Mitchell is standing by the front of the van too. Her hands are trembling. 'Do it in one of those buildings,' she says to Agent Miles, hardly daring to glance at us. '*Close your eyes to ugliness,*' I hear her mutter to herself. She looks like she's about to be sick.

Miles is holding his gun out as the policeman steps towards us.

'Let them go,' I hear Miles say. I whip my head round, momentarily forgetting the pain. Agent Miles' gun is no longer aimed at us. It's on Nina.

The uniform swings his weapon at Miles, looking perplexed, whose orders he should follow. Nina shouts out a command to 'Fire!' and he makes his decision.

But Miles makes his quicker. The policeman drops to the ground, writhing and moaning on the floor. Mikey quickly limps over and picks up his gun.

Nina is screaming, as Agent Miles turns his gun to her; she starts pleading 'I have a daughter!'

Tom wraps his arms tighter around me, as the moonlight illuminates the panic in Nina Mitchell's face. I think of Fran. Her mum's all she has. I want to tell Miles not to kill her. All I can do is shout out a weak, 'No!'

Him

Together Ethan Miles and Mikey tie her hands together, gagging her mouth, agreeing with Hope, to keep Fran's mum alive. Dragging Nina Mitchell in her smart power suit to the burnt-out caravan, they leave her legs only loosely tied so she can still take tiny steps.

'It'll take her into tomorrow night to reach the main road again,' Miles says as they walk back towards us. 'The policeman will live. We'd better get going. I've got a safe house sorted for you. We'll be good there. You can release your final vlog or whatever it is you kids call it. What?' he adds as I look at him half-shocked, half-grateful. 'You really thought I was on the bad side?

'Like I told you the other day – the truth's what you want it to be.'

ONE YEAR LATER

21

Happiness is the sum of the lies you
accept and the truths you reject
Livelifewithhope

Her

It's a sunny autumn morning after weeks of heavy rainfall.
Stepping out of the thin terraced house, Hope exhales a breath
of relief to be out of there – holed up with maudlin Grandma
Lizzie, who Mum swore she'd never live with again. She sets
off towards the station, consoling herself: university is just
under a year away.

At the Tube platform she notices a couple of girls nudging
one another and pointing. She's still getting spotted for being
the girl who exposed *Leata*. If her YouTube channel being
the first to broadcast the scandal wasn't exposure enough,
the media circus that followed, as she and Tom gave evidence
at the subsequent Cloud 9 trials, secured her face in minor
celebrity pages.

It was only a few months ago that the police called off the
twenty-four-hour guard that shadowed her. The death threats

are few and far between now. She's grown a thick skin over the past year to the many trolls on her blog.

She slips onto the first Tube to arrive, avoiding the carriage with those girls who are now making their comments more vocal. Taking the last free seat, her fellow passengers are fortunately too busy looking down at screens or staring blankly at the framed advertisements to notice her. Hope gets out her book to stop herself doing either. But not before she's clocked the adverts above the window opposite. She still finds it strange, the absence of *Leata* and PharmaCare everywhere. Not that their replacements are that different. There's an advert for a plastic surgery clinic, featuring a girl who only looks a few years older than her. Hope taps self-consciously at her face as her eyes skim over, *'Did you know your skin loses elasticity by age thirty?'* Either side is a pharmacy chain boasting the best natural herbal remedies for stress, and an insurance company telling passengers death lurks around every corner: *'Prepare Yourself!'*

She opens her book, trying to concentrate on Jude and his dream to reach Oxford, but next gets distracted by the familiar snap and crackle of foil.

Glancing up, the man at the end of the carriage is popping a pill out of the familiar blue and yellow box. She's heard that a number of people still buy it on the black market; that some private doctors prescribe it even though it's now been unequivocally proven a placebo – they say it's the comfort of taking it, like a cigarette with no nicotine.

Hope closes her book along with her eyes. And goes back there. It's a trick she's learnt – to calm herself. Imagining herself in the small cottage with its grey slate roof.

Sometimes it can seem like a memory of a holiday in her mind. Not a fugitives' lair. Nearly three months they lived there, Hope, Tom, Mikey and Ethan Miles. Holed up in a remote forest in Wales. Cut off from the outside world; their only visitor an insider contact of Ethan's, who delivered weekly supplies and news about how the scandal was taking shape. Telling them about the arrests of Hari and many other hacktivists, including Pavlin, and their eventual release without charge.

While the media stormed, she and Tom lay in front of real fires, eating food cooked by Mikey. Listening to Ethan's animated stories from his life to date (he had many). Mostly they slept, limbs entwined. Holding tightly onto one another as if they were freefalling through the sky.

Living day to day, simply, without any communication or television or distraction. While outside, the truth spread in both the virtual and real worlds, like fire through the Australian bush, lighting up news platforms and walls and posts and media networks globally.

Gradually, people near the top began to rock those at the peak. The point of power toppled, in countries worldwide.

Hope could feel only a strange feeling of regret when Ethan's contact declared them safe; that Hope wouldn't be prosecuted for the death of Professor Simeon Blythe. They had to open the arched door to the little cottage and come out blinking into the noise and the chaos again.

Him
His mum briefly strokes his back as he bends down to unload the dishwasher. He straightens up and grabs her into a bear-hug.

The ones Dad used to make. He realised months ago, his mum's just not good at making the first moves. But she likes a hug. Like anyone.

Tom's the first to pull away. 'What you up to this weekend?'

'Right now, I'm going to tackle those weeds on the front lawn. The new neighbours are worse than the Wrights for their neat borders. How do they find the time to do it?'

'They don't. They pay someone else.'

His mum laughs, 'I'd rather do it myself,' and walks away. Soon after, he hears her talking at the front door. Before, 'Tom! Ethan's here to see you.'

He appears soon after. The U-bend smile at full throttle on his handsome face; his suit jacket slung casually over his shoulder. Shirt crisp white and shoes polished.

Ethan makes his usual cheerful small talk as Tom finishes putting the dishes away. The way he's dressed, it won't be a social call, though Ethan has been known to make them. He's taken on something like fatherly duties since their three months in the cottage. Tom hasn't the heart to tell him he doesn't see him that way.

'Do you have some news for me?' Tom cuts to the chase, slamming the dishwasher door shut.

While he and Hope were giving evidence at the public trials of Cloud 9 and their associates, Ethan was attending a private version, hoisting out the corrupt members of the Secret Service. It ended with his promotion – to track Cloud 9 conspirators still out there.

'I followed up that latest hate feed on Twitter,' Ethan says, pouring himself a coffee from the cafetière on the kitchen table. 'Three men are being questioned. But generally I'd say it's simmering down out there. People are starting to forget what *Leata* did for them. They're moving on to the next big thing. The hit reality programme on TV!' He pulls a wide beam.

Tom breathes out a puff of relief. That last hate trail was making him nervous; only because it was Hope they were primarily stalking. She's the one who insists on keeping a profile on social media. Unlike him; he's cancelled every bit of himself on the internet. He prefers to skulk in the shadows even more since what happened. But then Hope always was the more sociable one. 'I feel safe in my blogging community. They root for me,' she says when he frets.

'But,' Ethan continues, taking a quick sip of coffee, 'I did want to inform you about a development.' His convivial face turns serious.

Tom stops what he's doing.

'We got another call in about Imogen. Our man in Italy has his sights on her.'

'You're still looking to me to make that decision for you?'

Ethan scratches his head. 'My new boss wants your dad's story buried. Move on. Close the door. I'm under no obligation to haul her in. But I think it should be your call, Tom. You tell me what you and your mum would like done to your dad's murderer.' He pauses before asking, 'Have you told Hope we're still tracking Imogen?'

Tom shakes his head. He knows he should. Like he should tell her he doesn't want to go to university. Secrets and lies; already, he can feel them rising up between them like the wall his dad built from his mum. *He won't be like his dad.*

'It's your call, mate. You tell me to arrest her and I will.'

Tom crosses his arms, trying to think. 'I'm still not sure Mum could take a trial. Raking up Dad's death again. She's just got life back to some kind of normal.' But he knows his mum's only half the excuse. What would it do to Hope? If he was the one instrumental in bringing Imogen to justice. In robbing Benny of his mother?

It would fracture them.

'Well, maybe have one last think.' Ethan waves a hand through the air, a strong waft of lemony aftershave blowing around with it. 'About the right thing to do.'

Tom makes a faint nod. *The right thing to do*. He's no longer sure he knows what that means.

Her

She gets off at Vauxhall for St Patrick's shelter. MI6's green glass looms over her – it's a familiar place after she and Tom had interviews in there as well as MI5's HQ on Millbank. Those first few months after they came out of hiding were filled with interrogations. They both stayed at Tom's house under police guard. There were many people out for their blood. Not everyone was pleased to see *Leata* exposed and PharmaCare brought down. Hope and Tom – they were the ones to tear down the curtain surrounding the wizard, and reveal that Oz wasn't magical after all.

Clearly many people wished they'd left the curtain drawn.

Gradually other news overtook. A new government, for one. Another royal baby. Escalating terrorist attacks that were nothing to do with a drug that has no effect.

Hope went home when the threat to them started dwindling and her face wasn't so frequently published in the press for murdering Professor Blythe. She'd have preferred to have stayed living with Tom, going to his school, but since Dad was imprisoned, Rose seemed to need her, and Lily had started suffering from these panic attacks that her mother couldn't cope with. Mum's perfect baby behaving anything but perkily.

And her new sixth-form college is okay. Next year, a university far away, even a new name if she can. Just her and Tom.

She passes under an empty billboard. The economy has experienced a slump since the Progress Party was kicked out. Consumerism took a dip along with 'positivity'. Though the new government still makes promises about its own brand of happiness.

Hope heads into the shelter, throwing out friendly exchanges with the residents she knows. Into the kitchen, she starts chatting with purple-haired Tammy, who's furiously peeling potatoes. Mikey limps in soon after, as Hope puts on her crew apron, ready to open the shutters, to start serving food with a natural smile. People still need smiles. People still need hope.

Him

'Before I go I think you should take a look at the latest list,' Ethan is saying as Tom makes fresh coffee.

'More names?'

Ethan makes a helpless gesture. He reaches down into the

319

attaché case he's brought with him, showing Tom a long list of doctors, dignitaries, journalists, politicians, even a handful of celebrities. The rolling list Ethan's unit keep an eye on.

Tom read an article by Ralph the other day. '*Cloud999*', Ralph titled it, alluding to the number of high-profiles still existing who've never been revealed. Ralph emailed him the link, probably hoping it would be a prompt to making up. But Tom won't respond. In his mind Ralph's still as guilty of his dad's death as Jack Wright. At least Jack Wright is having to serve twenty years for his part, along with Slicer, Commander Menton, Nina Mitchell and some of the others. Even the ex-PM, Damian Price, was proved accountable.

'You really think a footballer can incite bad feeling against us?' Tom balks, pointing at one of the names.

'Don't you remember how it all happened?' Ethan says.

Tom shrugs. Like he can forget. He just needs to read *Livelifewithhope* to remind himself what happened every day of the past year. A big part of him wishes Hope wouldn't reveal their story to the world like that. It's not his way. He prefers to keep his life to himself, guard his secrets. He's more like his mum like that, he realises now. But he knows Hope finds it cathartic. So he tries to keep it to himself when it bothers him.

'Corruption can snowball if you get enough people backing one bad person, yeah?' Ethan slaps Tom on the back. 'We have to keep a close eye on anyone heard talking favourably about *Leata* and Cloud 9, online or offline.'

Tom nods, though he's still not sure – it smacks of another version of police-stating.

Her

She gets off the train and walks the familiar roads until she spies Mrs Riley kneeling over a border on their front lawn.

'Hope, hi! How's your mum?' She twists round, welcoming her with a kind smile.

'She's okay, thanks. Off visiting Dad today. She took Lily with her. Rose, like me, still refuses to see him.' She tries not to stare at her house beyond the prickly hedge. It's always strange to think of a new family, mum, dad, three children, in there. As if it's happening all over again somehow.

Going on inside, she finds Tom poring over a list of names on the kitchen table.

He bolts up as he spies her, grabbing her to him. Planting his lips on hers. She laughs into his mouth. It's as if he hasn't seen her in weeks. When it was only yesterday.

Him

He wasn't going to show her, but he can't hide it now. 'Ethan brought it over. His team have added more names to their Cloud 9 surveillance.'

He watches her eyes widen as she glances down the list.

'Will it never end?' she says with a long sigh, absently twisting her fingers through his hair. 'My post from yesterday got more trolls than ever. Maybe I should stop writing it.'

He rubs her arm and tries to keep from saying, *I wish you would*. 'How was Mikey this morning?' he sniffs.

'Fine,' she says distractedly, her eyes still focusing on the names. 'Some funding's slowly trickling back in. But it's not enough.'

'Unhappiness is still not a priority,' Tom says, grimacing. 'Shall I get us some Cokes for the treehouse? Unless it's too cold for you?'

'Never,' she says.

Her

It's where she's happiest. Sitting up here with Tom. Above the rest of the world. Beside one another on the treehouse platform, shoulder to shoulder, fingers laced together. Faces close, still a little bronzed from memories of a hot summer. Their legs swing off the ledge, occasionally knocking into one another.

Him

'Do you ever wish I'd never started all of this? That you were still taking *Leata*?'

Her

She shoulders him. 'As if.' Only fleetingly she thinks: she'd still have her old life; she'd still think her dad was the best, not the worst. 'The truth is all that matters isn't it? Even if it makes people miserable?'

Him

'I thought you wrote on your blog today that 'happiness is the sum of the lies you accept and the truths you reject'?

Her

'You liar – you do read it!'

Him

'Just so I can see how *super, super* excited you are about Christmas already.'

Her

She nudges him hard. 'Oi. People still need my brand of enthusiasm. Life *can* be exciting you know, Mr Harbinger.' Hope laughs as he makes pokes at her. Leaning her head into his chest, she glances briefly between the gaps in the trees at next door, then blinks away again. No – she mustn't think about how her old house makes her feel. Tom would suggest they didn't meet here any more if he knew. And she doesn't want that either. So she'll keep it to herself.

Him

He leans his face down towards the top of Hope's head, kissing her hair softly. 'Pavlin's suggesting we road trip next summer to visit Hari at his swanky California Apple job.'

Hope laughs. 'How come he became some internet sensation when we still get bad-mouthed?'

'It's his god-like appearance, you said.' He waits for her to deny it, flicking her when she fake swoons.

Her

'I'm just counting the days till we get to go to university together.' She looks up at him. 'Have you got your UCAS form yet?'

He doesn't answer, instead he says, 'I'm counting the days to the new *Star Wars* film.'

Him

'I'll get the form,' he says, as Hope glowers at him. He drifts his gaze away so she can't glance the lie in his eyes.

Hope settles back against his chest. He lifts and examines their weaved fingers. His are pale against hers, still coloured from summer.

Gazing beyond, onto the ground below, it's never hard to imagine his dad down there, messing about, smoking his spliffs and cursing inappropriately.

He lifts Hope's hair and kisses her neck; her skin is warm. He can feel the beat of her pulse. Her hand grips his tighter, like she knows what's on his mind. Like she knows too, that if they don't hold on, they're in danger of falling off.

Her

Keeping some things back, but telling Tom the truths she tells no one else . . . maybe it's the only way to be with the people you love.

Him

He buries his face further into the warmth of her neck. He wishes he could pause time on moments like this. 'You make me happy,' he says suddenly, realising that's the only truth he needs right now.

Her

Hope twists round to kiss him hard on the lips. 'Life will be okay, as long as we stick together.'

Him

He thinks of his dad below again. 'Life's short.'

Her

Hope reaches up, removing Tom's glasses so she can see his eyes. 'So – enjoy it.'

Acknowledgements

A huge thank you goes to my editor, Naomi Colthurst, for prodding and poking me to think bigger. Also to Georgia Murray and Sarah Odedina, and all at Hot Key Books.

Thank you Jet Purdie and Levente Szabó for yet another head-spin of a beautiful book cover, and to Kirsty Mclachlan for such incredible support and advice. Plus I'm indebted to the Arts Council England, for the funding enabling me to write full time. I can't describe what that means without writing another novel.

I want to thank all my family and friends for their support and love, but special mentions go to: Tom Jordan, not only for lending me his name, but for his inspiring teen spirit; my parents for essential childcare needs; the Newhall clan, for fervent flag-waving. For valuable insight and reading duties: Christina, Harprit, Sally, Lucie, Jo, Rosie, Chloe, Lucy. To all those who travelled from afar to support me last year – it meant so much. To the book world, big and small: my writers' group, book club, local library, bookshops, and the book blogging community, for all your support and enthusiasm. Oh, and a cheer for babies born (Benji, Caitlin, Eadie) and weddings wed (Camilla and Kevin).

Most importantly, thank you to Duncan for keeping the home fires burning and providing the neat and order so I am free to create the chaos. And a huge kiss-smack of appreciation to Laurie and Mae – for always making me laugh uncontrollably, whatever the weather.

And last of all, thank you to Julian House in Bath, most especially Donna and Jamie, for giving up your time to talk to me and for opening my eyes to the amazing work you do for the homeless. The world needs more people like you.

Alex Campbell

Alex Campbell announced she was going to be a writer at eight years old. But no one took much notice. After a nomadic education daydreaming in back rows across Luton, Chester, London, Sheffield and Middlesbrough – and one English degree later – Alex moved into the world of PR and copywriting. Here she worked on getting other people noticed instead.

Alex now lives near Bath with one husband, two children and a fat smile on her face – that her eight-year-old self's ambition has finally been realised. When she's not gazing dreamily out of windows, Alex can usually be found, notebook at the ready, in dark art-house cinemas, propping up coffee bars, or worse. Follow Alex on Twitter: @ACampbellWrites

Thank you for choosing a Hot Key book.

If you want to know more about our authors and what we publish, you can find us online.

You can start at our website

www.hotkeybooks.com

And you can also find us on:

We hope to see you soon!